MOTHER OF THE WOLVES

MOTHER OF THE WOLVES

Daniela Parker

Plum Rose Publishing LLC• Florida, USA

© 2020 by Daniela Parker
ISBN 978-0-9884154-2-3

MOTHER OF THE WOLVES

A print Book from
Plum Rose Publishing LLC

Cover Art by K Sierras

All Rights Reserved.

No part of this book may be reproduced or transmitted in any form or by any means, electronic or mechanical, including photocopying, recording, or by any information storage and retrieval system without the written permission of the author, except where permitted by law.

Printed in the United States of America.

For my children
You are the loves of my life.
I hope this book teaches you to care for the world
you inherited,
So it may be a blessing to all.

Thank you Mom and Dad.
You are always right behind me,
Standing in shadows so I can catch light,
Encouraging me to never stop daring to dream.

Thank you my love and dearest friend, Ken,
You are my partner in life,
And the wind beneath my wings.

Thank you God,
Who always keeps me focused.
I am relentlessly striving to be better,
Shining brightly in the radiance of Your love.

MOTHER OF THE WOLVES

Part One

Unlikely Heroes

Under Her Breath

Two doors linger at the precipice of a great destiny.
One leads to a steep fall.
One leads to flight.

I stood at the doorway and for an uncertain moment, thought I might turn away. One may not know the hour of their death, but they can choose when to start living. Maybe we don't know how to live, but only how to survive. I knew surviving and living are something all together different, and wondered which I was choosing as I gripped the long handle with both hands and leaned myself back to pry the heavy glass entrance ajar.

Ice cold air stung my cheeks as it expelled from the building and dissipated into the summer heat behind me. I caught my foot in the space between the door and the doorframe and pulled my body into the lobby, letting it slam back into place with a heavy thud.

The lobby secretary was a delicate boned teenager, sitting crosslegged in a knee-high pleated skirt and short sleeved white v-neck. She blew a purple bubble that grew as big as an orange before popping against her bored face. Then, licked it up placidly with one hand propped beneath her chin and began chewing again. The soft hand holding up her lazy head was covered in brass bracelets from wrist to elbow. With her right hand, she lackadaisically pressed the buttons on the keyboard of her white laptop and instantly, a long sheet of paper began printing.

The crowd of people seated in the waiting room inched forward nervously. Most were reading magazines on eReaders or doodling on electronic crossword puzzles, but it was only because this felt more familiar than sitting empty handed while the reality of the situation pressed adamantly upon their minds. And it didn't matter much as they listened to the horrifying shrieking of ink lasers moving back and forth on crisp paper. Even as they played the latest video games muted in their hands their eyes stole anxious glances up at her and at each other. Who would it be this time? Was it someone's mother, father? Would someone lose their son?

I took a deep breath, whisked my long brown hair away from my shoulders, and began the slow dreadful walk up to the glossy white desk surrounding her like a round spaceship. The paper that had printed detached automatically and fell onto the desk. She caught me straining to see the words and before I could read anything, turned it upside down with a snap into a wire letter tray. Then, looked at me squarely and half annoyed.

"May I help you?" she forced a smile.

"Yes," I cleared my throat. "I'm here for my annual check up."

"Fill this out and have a seat."

She handed me a tablet.

Heads shot up from the waiting room towards me. I could feel their spying eyes burning into my back, but when I swept myself around to look at them, they turned back to their fake reading. There were only a few seats left. One beside a lady crocheting a long green scarf that dribbled down her fat leg. Her arms covered both armrests and her body obstructed both seats beside her. And then there was one vacant seat beside a man dressed in stained blue jeans and a blue collared work shirt with

3

the name BILL printed on a patch above his left breast pocket. I could smell the stench of his sweaty body wafting from him through the other half of the lobby and decided to squeeze into the seat next to the lady. But it wasn't just because of his odor, but mainly because I didn't care for men or their proximity.

"Sorry," I said as she shifted her weight away from me and continued crocheting, needle swirling in effortless circles.

She smiled, round dimpled cheeks blushing.

"We're all here for the same reason, dear. Good luck to you."

I had known nothing else in my lifetime. They had already trained the dogs when I was born. But my parents said they had lived in a world without fear of GC/MS which stands for gas-chromatography/mass-spectrometry analysis. People used to go to the doctor and come home with a diagnosis, and then they would return to get medication. And if they had cancer, they would get things like chemotherapy. About fifty years back, there was a huge medical break though. Scientists learned how to detect cancer by using a breathalyzer that measured aldehydes, hydrocarbons, alcohols, ketones, esters, nitriles, aromatic compounds, and things like that. It was going to save lives by giving early detection, or so they thought.

An old black man sitting to my right leaned his gangly body against me.

"You're young," he whispered.

His breath was hot on my ear.

"If the dogs come, run. If they come for me, I'm done for. But you, you have young legs."

His voice was deep and raspy. I knew he was serious, even as he chuckled a bit and gave up a mucousy cough. But there were only rumors of those who had escaped. My hands began trembling. I took left hand in right and held them tightly against my lap. The cold of the room made my shaking worse and so my teeth chattered a little as I bent my head towards him to respond.

His skin was like old black leather, dry and white in the creases of the wrinkles. A man that old was a rare sight and I hadn't seen one personally in months. His black face was spotted with dark freckles and blotches where the sun had burned into him over the years. And loose skin created deep folds of puffy circles under his eyes.

"How did you survive for so long?" I whispered.

"God blessed me with a healthy body and a lively spirit. But it won't be long before I go to my creator. You got to run, though. Understand?"

My parents told me the classes had been separating for a long time. The rich had slowly gained too much control. Poor people were always too busy finding sustenance to care what anyone did or what the politics of the country were. And the middle class? The middle class had been caught up in the American Dream, which only turned out to be an illusion invented to distract them while the one percent did the real trick of taking over the country. As the middle class struggled to obtain the most attractive body and to wear the most fashionable clothes or buy the biggest house and the newest car, they took up loans in everything without realizing they never really owned anything. Most had more than six hundred thousand dollars debt including college loans and property.

I guess no matter what you have, you at some point get unhappy. And the elite became greedier with each passing year. Government politicians pushed for huge taxes to be placed on the middle class that excluded the wealthy, and bankruptcy laws were tightened so no one could get out of their debt unless they paid it off. The bank owners and CEOs of large companies had grown so rich and powerful that they essentially owned the middle class. And the middle class found they were merely slaves, worse off than the poor by far and more hungry than those in third world countries. They didn't qualify for basic government help like Medicare, Food Stamps, or even WIC. They could only do what the banks told them to do and try to pay off their debt before it defaulted in exchange for food and shelter. Many began working twelve hours a day just to keep their jobs. Some, who were more courageous, worked up to twenty hours, hoping to stow away enough money to pay off more than the huge interest fees. But thousands soon fell sick from malnutrition.

By this time, the one percent were into everything. They even controlled voting and the supreme court with their money. When the middle class couldn't afford their own medical insurance, the President was finally able to pass socialized medical insurance so people wouldn't die in masses on the streets. But the rich wouldn't have it.

That's when they started using the dogs. Someone high up had their monetary interest in the access Medicare. They enforced a new law to be able to euthanize all cancer patients in order to cut government healthcare costs. Hailed as population control and propagandized as the next evolutionary step for humanity, it became a modern Holocaust that no one could do anything about. The poor had no human rights or public voice and all that mattered for the big companies was the bottom profit line.

After the law was passed, the government trained German Shepherds to do the same job as the GC-MS machines. When the dogs found too many volatile organic compounds under the breath of a patient, they would be dragged down the hall. No one ever returned. In ten years, all of Eurasia had joined in the same practice as the U.S. and the population was cut back by thirty percent around the globe, the extra money from their therapies and basic life necessities going directly back into the pockets of the filthy rich.

The secretary tapped on her microphone, sending a high-pitched noise through the speakers wired to the ceiling corners of the waiting room.

"In five minutes the test will be conducted. At that time, those of you who are not selected are free to leave. Please return all tablets now."

Her monotone voice sounded deeper over the speakers. I imagined her thirty years older, but she probably wouldn't make it that long the rate things were going. I turned towards my tablet.

"Don't fill out your name," the man whispered, placing his long wrinkled fingers over my wrist.

The lady beside me glared at him.

"You'll get her killed," she said, angrily.

"If she has cancer, they'll try to find her. This will give her time."

My eyes hovered over the blank where NAME was written underneath a long white box. My heart was racing. Maybe I would have typed my name there and shrugged him off as just a nice old man, but I hadn't been feeling right, so I quickly made up an alias and fake address and then filled out the bubbles of my past medical history like normal.

When I finished, I looked him in the eyes for some kind of reassurance. He seemed like a sincere man. Cataracts had put a foggy layer of film over his deep brown pupils. But deeper than that seemed a history filled with grief. His eyes conveyed an intense pain to me and in one heartfelt look, told me I should take a chance.

"Return everything now," her voice demanded over the microphone.

I stood up with tablet in hand. Maybe she wouldn't read it. Maybe she would let me go because she might be in my place at some point.

"Are you done?" she asked.

"Yes," I said, handing it to her.

She took it in her hands.

The phone rang and she thrust the tablet aside.

"Hello?" she said, giving me a cold look to return to my seat.

I breathed a sigh of relief and sat back on the cold black plastic waiting room seats. I could hear the dogs behind the door leading to the hospital's hallways growing louder. Their leashes were jangling and we could hear the indisputable sound of muffled boots marching towards us.

Both the lady and the old man took my arms tightly.

"Dear God, please help us, dear God, please..." pleaded a woman as she fell to her knees on the floor.

People gasped in fear and someone dropped their tablet on the cold marble of the waiting room, startling the rest of us so we all flinched and jerked backwards. The door opened suddenly and a group of three large leashed German Shepherds entered. Their handler was wearing green army canvas pants and a bullet proof vest and had a gun strapped to his waist. Two other soldiers dressed in the same United States army uniform were following directly behind him with long rifles. The dogs began to sniff.

One, good.

Two...good, three...

Bark, bark and a scream.

The crowd gasped in horror and lurched back. Someone had cancer.

A man sprung up, but the two other soldiers caught both his arms before he could fight. He screamed and implored them, but was dragged away mechanically.

Then, the dogs returned intensely to their work.

Four, good.

Five, good....

"Stay with me," the man said.

The dogs were close now. I could see their sleek muscles flexing under their long coats. They would have been beautiful dogs, with their pointed ears and healthy brown and black fur, but they looked terrible and menacing in this occupation. They sniffed the woman who was praying on the floor. She was clean.

Then, one of the Shepherds shifted his attention towards me. I stared back into his dark eyes and already knew he could smell me as he pierced into me with that focused look. My heart pounded hard. I was sure at any moment my chest would rip open from fear. And was sure the dog could hear the blood pulsing through my veins. He was merely waiting for the moment to declare me to his handler.

"Uh, ma'am," said the secretary. "I am not finding your name in the system."

The secretary had walked up to me and was standing in front of me now with the tablet in her hand.

I stammered for a response.

They were sniffing the old man. He was good but he still gripped my arm tightly. The dog's snouts came up to my face.

They gave up a long ear piercing howl. The old man shot up with me.

The two soldiers who were standing in the back rushed forward.

"Which one was it?"

"It was me," said the old man, shoving me away.

This was my chance. I'd either die now or make a run for it. And suddenly, my will to live overcame anything else in my being. It squashed my fears and choked out logic.

I broke away from the crowd and thrust myself upon the door. The dogs growled and barked at me as soldiers lift rifles into the air. I pulled the metal handle of the door into my chest and felt the hot sunlight burst onto my breast as I ran out of the building. The old man had plunged himself in front of the dogs. Shots were fired and the door closed before I could look back.

I sprinted to the top of a hill just passed the parking lot and rolled my body into a storm gutter, tears streaming from my eyes. Breath wheezing as I cried, laying in the damp dirt. I could hear people shouting at the entrance and the dogs wailing. Then, two boots paused next to the opening of the drain.

I stopped breathing all at once. Pressed my body against the cold wet cement. Short waves of brown hair sprang from all directions as a man looked upside-down at me with beady hazel eyes and bushy brown eyebrows.

"Hurry," he said. "I can help you!"

Perplexed, I took his hand and he pulled me into a black van.

"Go, go, go!" he said before the door was shut, driver speeding down the street.

I huddled into a ball in the back of the empty van as the strange man stared at me on one bent knee.

"My name's Edward," he said, finally.

"Stephanie. Stephanie Elliot."

His lips were thin, and with the stubble on his face, looked to be in his mid thirties.

"Who..."

"Let's just say, we offer an alternative."

The Rose Garden

We were on the road for hours. Every so often the driver, a burly man in a navy blue shirt and jeans, stopped briefly for a snack and to use the restroom while he charged up the van. Then, we continued on. I didn't bother asking where we were going. I knew somehow I would be safe. And each time the van stopped, I'd grow fearful the government might find me, so I refused to get out, not even to use the restroom. I just hid in the back of the cold van.

The highway became wooded and bent around thick mountains. We must have been somewhere in Massachusetts. The van spiraled down a small road deep in the forest and dead ended at an estate enclosed by brick walls thickly overgrown with ivy.

The driver pressed a few buttons on the intercom.

"Yes?"

"We have a 2871," he said.

The steel gate slowly rolled open and we drove onto the large grounds. The driveway forked into a roundabout. There stood a tall statue of a woman whose hair was tied in a loose bun and whose delicate hand held a rose as she gazed pensively out at the rose bushes surrounding her stone body. Behind her lay a grand mansion. Two great oak doors with windows decorated in black iron were centered at the entrance. The building itself was a massive brick structure standing four stories high. The windows were framed in white wood and three triangular white peaks lined the roof. The middle section of the house held a beautiful white balcony at the very highest point. And on each wing were smaller balconies and windows that framed the center in perfect symmetry. The van pulled to a stop in front of the entrance and the driver hopped out and slid open the side door.

"Come on," he said, sternly.

We walked up to the door and the man who had rescued me struck the door knocker hard three times. Then suddenly, the heavy right side of the double doors swung open revealing a thin elderly man in a white hospital coat.

"Welcome," he smiled. "We are going to help you. Come in. Please don't be alarmed."

I stood in awe at the entrance. The mansion was really a hospital with patients bustling about. Some had shaven heads and some walked with oxygen tanks or were being wheeled by nurses. There were people playing pingpong in a room that would have been a den to the right and nurses dressed in light blue and white old fashioned style aprons and nurse caps walking gingerly through the foyer.

"My name is Dr. Levine," the man shook my hand. "When one escapes we try to be ready!"

He jerked his head backwards and laughed with his mouth opened wide.

"Come in!" he said again, ushering me into the den.

He sat me on a crimson leather sofa facing a lit fireplace, then stoked the fire a bit so it crackled and the orange flames swelled up.

"I thought this would be more comfortable."

"I'm sorry, but may I use the restroom?" I asked.

"Of course," he pointed to a small room with a dry chuckle. "Right there. Take your time."

The bathroom had twin marble sinks and towels trimmed in silk with an embroidered rose sewn into each of them at the center. I was spotting again. I wiped myself off and flushed the toilet and then washed my hands in the marble basin. There was a bouquet of flowers between both the sinks with paper towels sitting in a basket and soap and lotion bottles decorated with brass rose vines sitting next to the towels.

When I returned to the fire, Dr. Levine was sitting cross-legged on the sofa with his left arm hung over the back looking at me. His white hair was just long enough to start to poke straight up. He had a strong chin and a long defined nose and his eyes had huge bags under them, not from lack of sleep, but from years of age. His cheeks had fallen several centimeters below where they would have been in youth and sunk deep into his bones, giving his entire face a certain iciness of character as he sat waiting for me expressionlessly and half lit by the firelight.

"Did you know?" he asked.

"I knew something was wrong," I replied. "But now-a-days, you don't go to the doctor."

"I'm sorry," he lowered his head. "Come. Sit down."

He patted the seat next to him, smiling as I sat beside him.

"You may have figured out by now we are a hospital that helps treat patients with cancer. You will have state of the art care here. No one knows about this place. It's my home. It was my parents' and their parents' home. We are generations of doctors, surgeons, and so on. When things happened as they did, I converted this home into an underground hospital. We wait for people like you and try to catch them before the dogs get them."

"Are you going to test me now?"

He surveyed me up and down quietly, one eye lifted higher than the other in a scholarly manner. Then his face softened into another smile and crows feet appeared at the corners of each eye.

"We are going to feed you now and put you to bed," he chuckled. "You've had a long day. And tomorrow will be longer... Miss Bethany!"

A plump woman came quickly to his side.

"Take Miss Elliot to the cafeteria and then show her to her quarters, please."

"Yes, Dr. Levine."

"I haven't been hungry lately," I interjected.

"They never are," he smiled.

A sudden pain radiated in my head just above my eyes. I squinted, shielding my headache from the brightness of early morning. The long window in my room had filled with sunlight and the beams were dancing on the white sheets of my bed causing such a brilliance of light that I was roused from sleep. I saw a small french dresser sitting across from me. A huge bed frame with four wooden pegs at each corner towering high above me. There was a nightstand to my right with a blue Tiffany lamp sitting on it that matched the blue and white decor, and to the left, an upholstered chair with perfectly folded women's clothing set on top.

I moaned and sat up grasping at my forehead in agony. The pain was getting worse by the minute, and sitting up made my head feel like a bowl of water slushing pain around in a whirl. I urgently needed some CP. Reaching into my pants pocket, I pulled out a small black cardboard box. Empty. Panic suddenly overwhelmed me. It had been twelve hours at least and I would go into shock.

I grabbed at my head and curled into a fetal position throwing the covers over myself.

Someone came in, but I didn't look up to see who it was.

"We don't use CP here, ma'am. Let me give you something to help."

But before I could tell what she administered. Before I could even look up at her face. I went into a convulsion and blacked out. I felt like my brain was imploding and the crushing pressure gave way to brilliant light.

"Help me!" I screamed, grabbing at my head in horror.

My stomach was nauseated and my hands were clammy and trembling. I blacked out again and a series of horrible fever dreams ensued. And in them, men were surrounding me, laughing.

"Help me!"

I found myself lost in a labyrinth of mingling consciousnesses, stumbling from memory to memory like cobblestones. Caught in a morbid dream with the very real pain of my throbbing migraine gripping my soul and twisting and wrenching at every moment. Each time I gained consciousness, I swore I'd never take caffeine powder again. And when the dreams overtook me, I was drowned by an ocean of monsters deriding me as they stretched my body over a vast expanse of sea.

I struggled to yell, but the words didn't come out of my mouth, and so I dove deeper into the abyss of this dream and lingered there, floating in its deepest waters. The darkness was thick and peaceful and encompassed me like a warm embryonic fluid. My hair, soft and light fanning out like wispy peacock feathers. I stayed there for a moment, hovering in absolute isolation. Then was awakened, and the still water slushed around me, tiny air bubbles escaping from my mouth. Dream cycling again.

When I awoke, the same light was penetrating through the window and shining down on my bedspread, but my headache had subsided and now the peaceful song of a single bird was singing a celestial melody.

It must have been the following day. I sat up, remembering the clothes sitting at my bedside, and checked the size of the shoes sitting next to it on the floor. They were my size, and for a moment I felt uneasy with the fact they had clothing waiting for me that was exactly my fit. But those feelings quickly subsided as the desire to put on something fresh and clean took hold.

I tried on the black skirt and the blue blouse given to me and slipped on the new shoes. On the dresser was a beautiful mirror and a comb on a silver plate. I examined myself a bit and fixed my hair into a messy ponytail. Then ventured out of my room.

There was a long hallway with doors on either side. People were walking down the hall, so I figured if I followed them, I'd find breakfast somewhere along the way. We came to a huge dining room with a long table that must have seated about twenty people in very fine oak seats. A woman looked up at me from her chair and smiled gently.

"A new one!" she exclaimed.

She was a bit thin, had very short blonde hair, and wore a yellow sundress that brought out her pretty blue eyes. I hadn't brushed my teeth, so I smiled, but kept my lips shut as much as possible to hide my morning breath.

"Hi," I said, sitting next to her.

"Did you come in last night?"

"A few nights ago," I said, nervously picking up a fork and playing with it in my hand.

"That CP will kill you," she laughed. "But what can you do, working all the time?"

" Are there many runners?"

"Not that many," she replied. "But we get a few here and there."

She rest her hand on my shoulder. She was in her mid-thirties, but time had only increased her beauty.

"Don't worry," she said. "Dr. Levine is a kind man and will take care of you."

She studied me with an amicable smile, then added softly, "I have breast cancer."

I looked down at the plate and dropped my fork which clanked on the porcelain.

"I don't know what I have."

"They'll find out," she said, resting her hand lovingly on my shoulder.

A man rolled a cart with large white bowls of food into the room.

"That smells delicious!"

I hadn't smelled those scents since I was a child when my grandparents brought home bacon for a special surprise one Christmas.

Once global warming starting effecting the planet, we were only rationed a certain amount of meat per month. When the sea level finally rose one full meter, there were a lot of things people had to deal without. The ocean had become acidic, causing fishing to become almost obsolete. And drinking water had become scarce as rivers and lakes began drying up due to the higher temperatures. You could expect to pay about six dollars for an eighteen ounce bottle of water and forget drinking out of the tap, because they didn't purify tap water anymore. It was just too costly.

We all learned in biology about the food chain. Historically, no one ever thought those lessons mattered much. But then the coral reefs started dying away and many fish became extinct. The animals that regularly fished began dying off as well, but some of the larger birds and mammals flourished as they prayed on the weaker hungrier animals. Thousands of varieties of animals vanished when they couldn't adapt fast enough to the changing environment. But after years, the food chain rebalanced itself, for better and for worse.

With meat being so scarce, farming became more of a highly sought out job that provided resources for the elite rather than a blue collar job that provided a basic commodity for everyone. The farming market went up in value and poor farmers became rich overnight... If they knew enough science to keep their crops growing.

"Eggs and bacon," the lady said. "It's my favorite, too."

She put her fork down to shake my hand.

"By the way, I'm Alice."

"I'm Stephanie."

"Would you like eggs and bacon, ma'am?" the server asked.

"Yes, please!"

Just then, Edward, entered the room. He was clean shaven now and casually dressed. He noticed me as soon as he came through the doors and then found a seat at the very end of the table across from us.

"Does he have cancer?" I asked in a lowered tone, so he couldn't hear.

"Oh, him?" replied Alice. "No. That's Dr. Levine's son."

Suddenly, a young woman entered the room and began speaking with him. It seemed important, because he got up without eating and walked off.

After breakfast, Alice helped me find Dr. Levine's office. Alice and I had become friends from that first day. We didn't even want to part ways for my appointment, but the doctor insisted I be alone. And so, we waved goodbye and she closed the door, leaving me standing alone in the cold doctor's office with Dr. Levine.

"Please sit down," he said, motioning to the bed in the center of the room.

I tossed off my shoes and jumped up onto the white hospital bed, letting my bare feet dangle back and forth in the uneasy silence. Dr. Levine turned to the counter and sanitized his hands. The smell of the hand sanitizer filled the room with a strong lemony scent.

"How was your breakfast?" he asked, twisting and rubbing his long fingers together.

"Very good, thank you."

He turned to me and sat down in a chair next to the bed, placing his clean hands on his grey pant legs.

"Today is all about finding out what kind of cancer you have. Then, we will discuss your care plan."

His face sunk back into that melancholy look that was almost disheartening. But his eyes carried the liveliness of a small boy as they searched my face for answers. I worried he might find some secret inside my heart, so I turned away from him and looked submissively down at my dirty toes.

"I'm ready," I said.

This had been an amazing miracle for me. A second chance at life. It was as if the mansion was some wonderful dream come true. As if maybe I had really been dragged down the hall and this was a sort of life after death.

Dr. Levine got up and started towards a side door, then turned back to me and added, "Don't be alarmed, but we will be using a dog. His name is Dr. Marlow. He is the quickest way we have to tell where to start looking. Is it okay with you if I bring him in?"

He must have known from experience I'd have some PTSD associated with dogs. I really didn't want to see a dog, but I sighed and told him it was okay.

Dr. Levine opened the door facing an adjacent room and disappeared for a minute. I could hear him unlocking a kennel and the dog scurrying out. Then, he returned holding a black leather leash with Dr. Marlow trailing behind him. Dr. Marlow was an old German Shepherd. I could tell by the touch of white on his snout and paws. He sat beside Dr. Levine, panting.

"Okay, Dr. Marlow," he commanded. "Dig for cancer."

He let loose the dog and Dr. Marlow sauntered up to me while I jumped down from the bed and stood before him so he could smell me better. The dog sniffed around my body and then stood right in front of me burying his nose into my bladder. Then, he put his paw on my lower stomach and barked.

"Hmm. That could be a few things. Have you had any other symptoms?"

"My periods aren't regular. I spot a lot."

"Then it is most likely some sort of gynecological cancer."

He walked over to the phone and dialed.

"Miss Bethany... We need an ultrasound."

Then, he turned to me casually and said, "Strip off your clothing and put this on opening up in the back. Take off everything, even your underwear and bra. We'll conduct a pap smear and an ultrasound. I'll leave you for a few minutes."

I put on the gown and a few minutes later he entered with Miss Bethany who was wheeling in a huge ultrasound device. I laid myself back on the bed, then he put my feet in the stirrups and spread apart my knees. Dr. Levine put on his rubber gloves and felt around for my cervix with his cold fingers. I shifted uncomfortably, taking in a deep breath through my nose as I concentrated on the ceiling.

He took out a long metal tool and began pushing it up into my vagina.

"This will pinch just a bit. Sorry," he said, digging deeply.

I tried not to pay attention to the procedure. Tried not to notice him at all.

"Does this hurt?" he asked.

I looked back at him. It seemed that where a wrinkle disappeared one would appear in another spot. His lips pursed together as he felt around the inside of me with the cold metal tool. Then it clicked, scooping up a sample which he set aside on the counter. At once, he turned with his gloved hands to my abdominal area, pressing firmly on my right and left side with his other finger still stationed internally.

"Yes," I replied, uneasily.

Miss Bethany turned on the ultrasound machine.

"Now for the fun part," he said, grabbing something that looked like a microphone. "This is a transducer probe."

He squirted some gel on my bare stomach and pressed the probe firmly on my skin. Miss Bethany pushed some buttons on the machine and a 3-D hologram appeared above me.

"This is your uterus."

He glided the probe to my right and a fallopian tube appeared with an ovary. It looked exactly like it was really standing in front of us. A grotesque white veiny thing that looked to me like an alien rather than an organ.

"Here is your right ovary. As you can see, there are two cysts growing on this one. And now let's check the left..."

Another image of my left ovary appeared.

"This looks like the cancer, but we will biopsy all of the cysts. Do you see this cyst?"

He pointed with his other hand to the hologram, showing me a huge cyst that was grown into my ovary.

"We may have to remove this left ovary... Bethany, two Endometrial Cysts on the right ovary and a Pathological Cyst on the left. Please conduct general blood tests and a CA-125. We will schedule surgery as soon as possible."

"Yes, Dr. Levine," Miss Bethany said as she methodically began getting the needles ready for my bloodwork.

"Have lunch and dinner and enjoy. Tomorrow you will not eat all day as we have to prep your bowels for the surgery. We will do the surgery Thursday morning. Don't worry. This is pretty standard. I'll see you soon."

Dr. Levine left and Miss Bethany sat me up for my bloodwork. She took a few vials of blood. She was an inherently quiet woman. I tried to start some light conversation with her.

"It must be wonderful working in a place like this!"

She looked up at me but did not smile or say anything in response. Then went back to the vials, writing on little white stickers she placed on each one. Her dyed dark brown hair was swept up in a bun, and during the morning her hair pins had loosened, causing the bangs to fall a little more loosely around her face. She was a plump woman. Her breasts were large masses that sat on a round stomach. She was a woman with some heftiness in the arm as well. She looked like she could have played sports as a young girl, but the muscle had turned into fat over the years making her arms look like two strong branches growing out of an apple.

Miss Bethany was a woman not to be messed with. Her years had given her such maturity and discipline that her presence in the room carried the weightiness of a barge. Somewhere inside her there must have been a tale of suffering and perhaps passion which ended tragically, and that is why I guessed she did not speak a word to me. Over the years, her lack of laughter had caused her skin to dry and crack around the mouth. Her lips had tightened and shriveled and her cheeks lost their rosy hue. I felt for her. For all flowers blossom too soon and wilt too fast, and the prettiest ones are plucked and always die the fastest.

"You are free to roam the premises. Lunch is served at 12:30," she said, dispassionately.

"Oh, okay," I said as she stood up with the vials and began rolling the huge cart back out of the room.

Once I put my clothes back on, I searched everywhere for Alice, but couldn't find her anywhere. Soon, I found myself outside on the patio where, to my amazement, lay before me a huge garden of roses of every different variety. The first of the roses was a bush of beautiful purple blossoms. I stopped to smell them as the sun lit up its large pedals, and buried my nose into one of the roses, taking in its soft fragrance with my entire being.

Then, I started walking through the garden, down paths that turned and winded around until I was lost in a sea of colors. The mansion was far off but could still be seen in the distance. And there were some trees scattered here and there with stone benches set under the shade of their majestic limbs. I sped up my pace, looking left and right. The walkway split like a maze and I forgot how to get back. I tried to peer over the large bushes but they were too tall. So, I walked a little more until I came to a ring of trees at the very center of the maze. There was a beautiful fountain and red rose bushes were climbing up its pedestal and enveloping a shallow bowl filled with koi.

Edward was sitting on one of the benches reading a book on his eReader with one shoe crossed over the other knee. He looked peaceful enough, and I didn't know if I should disturb him, but thought the greater social mistake would be to not say anything about my presence.

"Hello," I said, waving my hand up in the air.

"Oh, good afternoon," he said, putting aside his eReader.

"Sorry," I began walking towards him. "I found this garden and... got lost."

He laughed and his smile stretched from cheek to cheek and dimples appeared.

"That's okay. Have a seat, please."

I sat awkwardly beside him. He turned towards me just enough so we wouldn't be uncomfortable as we spoke together in such close proximity.

"Do you have family at home?" he asked.

"My mother passed away when I was a child and my father disappeared ten years ago."

"Anyone else? Children? Husband?"

"No," I said, nudging my body a little bit further from him. "You?"

"No. Only my father. Dr. Levine is my dad."

"You must feel very lucky. He does a lot for people."

"Yes, a lot."

He seemed disturbed by the conversation about his father, so I changed the subject.

"What are you reading?"

"It's a novel about an alien world. A science fiction."

"Oh."

Then *he* changed the subject.

"Do you like roses?"

"Yes," I smiled. "I love these! My favorites are the purple. They smell so good!"

We laughed.

"I like the ones with the peach and white on them," he said. "There are a lot of varieties."

He stood up, excitedly.

"This one here is a miniature rose. We planted it here so you can see the fountain easily."

He turned towards the wall of bushes behind us, surrounding the ring of trees.

"These are climbing roses. Beautiful, aren't they?"

"Yes," I replied, giggling at him.

I leaned back and my long hair flowed down to the bench.

"Anyway," he stood up tall, placing both hands on his hips, doing some sort of masculine strut. "Most people think of roses, like your standard hybrid tea. The ones you get in a bouquet or something."

"You really know your flowers," I giggled.

He looked at me for a moment, then caught himself from staring too long and hard and faced down towards his eReader on the bench.

"I can take you back if you want."

He took my hands as I stood up and suddenly we were facing each other awkwardly. I looked down, embarrassed. There was a spark between us, but I didn't intend to fall in love. I didn't look back into his eyes, but started walking away from him towards the fountain, skimming my hand across the surface of the cool fountain water, koi scurrying away.

He folded up his eReader and inserted it into his pants pocket. When I faced him again, his face had hardened. He started walking back through the garden as if I wasn't there. I followed behind him uncomfortably, wondering if I had offended him. When we reached the lawn, he gave me a nod and left.

Daniela Parker

A Dusty Transcendentalist

"Ugh! This is disgusting!" I said, raising a large bottle of bowel stimulating soda to my mouth.

My face cringed in expectation of the magnesium citrate.

"Just a little more!" Alice said, sitting on my bed.

"I'm just going to get it over with!"

I prepared myself for a huge gulp and began guzzling as much as I could before the urge to vomit overwhelmed me. Then I stopped abruptly, cupping my hand over my mouth as I dry heaved and Alice laughed at me.

"Were you scared?" I asked her.

"Yes! But the surgery feels quick, like a blink of the eye. It's all this stuff and then recovering," she replied. "I just can't wait to see my babies!"

"You're babies?"

"I have two, Sage is three-years-old and Michael is six. They're with my mom right now," she smiled.

"Wow! I bet you miss them."

"Every minute," she propped herself up on her elbow and curled her long slender legs up on their side. "Everyone says they grow up fast. But no one tells you that it's so gradual you're going to forget they're growing up. There was never an end day when they were babies. I just looked one day and they weren't. No more baby. They'll never be babies again. And then, no one told me they were going to stop being little tiny munchkins. Just one day, I turned around and they weren't tiny anymore. They were long gangly kids! Maybe when I get back, they'll be different. I hate missing it. There's just this intense pain in my heart that grows bigger every day I'm away!"

I sensed her mood had changed. She looked like she was forcing back tears, so I stood up and walked over to the bed, placing my hand on her shoulder. When she saw I had come to comfort her, tears spilled from her eyes and her nose turned red. She sniffled, laughing at herself.

"Alice, you'll see them again soon," I said, kneeling down beside the bed. "Don't worry. Anyway, I heard they never leave the house!"

She laughed.

"I heard that, too."

The next morning, I was directed into the surgery prep room and told to put on a cloth robe and lay myself on a cold electric bed to await surgery. Miss Bethany entered briefly to start an Iv for me and then left me alone once again. But before long, someone knocked lightly on the door.

"You can come in," I said.

A man entered dressed like a doctor. He was quite young for a doctor. About my age. He had just started balding, but his skin still had the soft youthful finish of someone in their twenties.

"Good morning. I will be your anesthesiologist," he said, flashing me a friendly smile. "I see you have your Iv started. That's good. I'm going to give you something that will put you into a deep sleep. You won't feel a thing. Is that okay?"

"Yes," I responded.

He took out a small clear bag filled with liquid and connected it to the tube of my Iv.

"I'm a little nervous," I said.

"Oh, don't be..."

I blinked my eyes and was suddenly in a different room and a dull achy pain throbbed in my abdominal area. I guessed that the surgery was over. It seemed like late afternoon as a cool breeze made the sheer white curtains in my room float like ghosts. I only had time to take in the fact I was in a different room than my usual before falling asleep.

When I woke up again, it was evening and a symphony of sound was being performed by the rhythmic hum of insects outside my window. I could feel the pang of hunger in my stomach, and the medication was wearing off, revealing a stinging sensation in my pelvic area that stabbed at my gut more than starvation. I searched the room, but couldn't make out any clear images yet, when I heard the soothing voice of a nurse at my bedside.

"Oh, hello," she said. "Sorry to wake you. I was just checking your bandages. I brought you some dinner."

"Hi."

I tried to lift my sore eyes open and her blurry image focused in and out.

"Is the surgery over?"

"Yes, everything went smoothly," she smiled. "You may have some soup for now. We'll see how you do with that. We had a problem with your Iv, so there'll be a small scar on your left arm. Don't worry about it."

I looked down at the white gauze wrapped around my forearm and tried to lift myself up.

"Careful," she said, placing some pillows behind my back. "You don't want to tear your stitches now."

"Yes," I said.

The soup smelt delicious. She laid a wooden tray over my lap that had homemade chicken soup, some apple juice, and a cherry jello sitting on it.

"Did Alice visit me yet?" I asked.

"Yes, but she's sleeping now. It's 11:30 at night, ma'am."

"Oh."

I didn't know that much time had passed.

"Just relax now. I'm sure she'll be by tomorrow."

She gave me a shy smile and then left.

The following night, they unhooked my catheter and encouraged me to walk. But sitting up with the nurse was such a feat that I really was not looking forward to my first real urination. Sure enough, after she left me my dinner, I had to use the restroom. Getting up was painful and the whole effort was excruciating and slow. The pee just trickled out in the bathroom, and as I walked backed to bed, blood started seeping through my bandages.

"Oh, no," I said to myself. "Hello?"

There was no one in ear shot. I tossed a look towards my bed and imagined the nice white sheets stained with blood, so decided to go looking for someone down the hall. I opened up the door to my room and hollered down the hallway.

"Hello? Is anybody there?"

The long hallway was empty. Red carpet trailed off some fifty feet before veering left and right. Several doors to rooms were closed and the occasional wooden lamp stand decorated the otherwise vacant corridor. A distant telephone ringing reverberated from one of the rooms. Assuming it was a room occupied by a nurse or some kind of night staff, I walked up to the door and knocked lightly.

"Hello?"

The door was partially open and when I knocked it swung ajar revealing a small office with a desk stacked with piles of papers, an old fashioned telephone, and a wooden pen holder. The walls were covered by shelves of old fashioned books. Paperback and hardcover books had gone completely out of circulation by the 2030s in efforts to stop deforestation and slow the effects of global warming. I wiped away the dust from the spines of some of them and began reading their titles one by one. There were hundreds of classic novels by some of the greatest writers in our history and books about philosophy and sociology. I picked one of the books up and opened it to the first page.

"Civil Disobedience. An essay by Henry David Thoreau."

Something jumped out at me. I leapt backwards, toppling over a stack of papers on the desk. It was a black cat who had been sleeping in the bookshelf and jumped down to rub itself against my leg.

I stuffed the book into my white robe pocket and pet the cat as it stretched out its long body on the desk.

"Hi," I greeted the cat, petting it under the ear and through its sleek black coat. "It's only you."

Sighing, I carefully knelt on the floor and began picking up the papers and re-stacking them on the desk. The oozing blood from my bandage had begun to seep into my shirt. I tried not to let any drip on the floor.

TREASURY DEPARTMENT. I noticed the words at the top right corner of one of the stapled bundles. It seemed an odd correspondence for someone working as a rebel against the government. I skimmed through the rest of the files quickly to see if there was any connection or explanation, but only found unrec-ognizable lists of numbers and figures printed on each paper.

Realizing I had stumbled onto something I probably shouldn't have, I put everything back as much as I could and quickly left the room. As soon as I closed the door behind me, the sound of heels materialized into Miss Bethany. She gasped at seeing me.

"Miss Bethany," I stammered. "My bandage had started bleeding."

Miss Bethany rushed towards me, taking my hand and turning me towards my room.

"Come, ma'am," she said, "I will change you. You *must* stay in your room."

She glanced at the door, as if for a moment wondering if I had been in the office. Then pushed me down the hall.

When Balloons Go Loose

The following day, Alice came to visit me. I felt more achy than even the day before, but I was much more alert and Alice's friendship uplifted my spirits quite a lot. I got to see my incision as well, which wasn't as big as the blood had first led me to believe it was. There were only three small incisions. Two near my pelvic bone where my underwear would hide the scar and one incision in the crease of my belly button. But the cuts were deep and they did have to remove one of my fallopian tubes and ovaries.

I enjoyed Alice's company all day, and our conversations were endless and happy as we talked about entire lifetimes of love, family, and adventure. Alice's family was from New York State and had migrated to Chicago for work where she was born. Alice hadn't seen much of her parents growing up. They both worked double shifts in the huge factories in Chicago. Her mother inspected the circuitry that went into large machines and her father worked in a metal factory near their house. Alice was raised by a Canadian nanny who lived with them. Her nanny taught her French along with her two birth children and raised her as if she was her own daughter.

Alice's father was one of the first to go, even before they had the dogs. She was only ten-years-old when he was taken away. When she turned sixteen, she met and fell in love with the man who would give her a wedding and two children before he died as well. She never loved another, but just busied herself with her kids over the next years. She said she knew if she didn't try to escape, her children would be without a mother or father, and that's what drove her to flee from the soldiers. I respected her even more for her resilience, and as she spoke, could imagine the characters in her life like they were friends and family I had always known.

We traced each others lives up to the present time and then laid on my large bed together staring up at the ceiling as if we had been sisters for many years. Once again, the afternoon breeze blew cool wind through the window, making the sheer curtains dance, and the sunlight flickered and sparkled as the tree limbs swayed.

When Alice left, I reached into my robe pocket and felt the book. I had forgotten I had put it in my pocket. I pulled it out and began reading Thoreau's essay, "Civil Disobedience." His ideas on government struck me as alarming and at the same time aroused some kind of hope inside my heart. Thoreau thought he could stand against an entire government and the smallest effort was not in vain. This was a new and inspiring idea for someone in my era. Even though he had written his words in the 1800s, when slavery was still being contemplated by educated men, I felt like he was speaking to me in my own time, because we ourselves were slaves to our flawed government. He wrote:

> After all, the practical reason why, when the power is once in the hands of the people, a majority are permitted, and for a long period continue, to rule is not because they are most likely to be in the right, nor because it seems fairest to the minority, but because they are physically the strongest.

How could I change my own circumstance when my vote didn't even count? How could one voice be heard over the screams of millions?

How does it become a man to behave toward this American government today? I answer, that he cannot without disgrace be associated with it. I cannot for an instant recognize that political organization as my government which is the slaves government also.

I felt a terrible guilt. I knew I was whom he had spoken of next. I carried my opinions quietly, but never stood up for the atrocities my government had committed because I was too concerned about my own life. And maybe at the moment I wasn't as affected as the person who sat next to me. It was easy casting a vote into a machine that shredded it into nothing and to walk away with a sense of American pride. Look at me, I voted. I did something for my country. Only knowing too well my vote was meaningless because the majority was taken up amongst the few with the majority of stock and because politics would always sway towards their whims.

I was a fool and even as I sat in bed, I was one of the lucky ones. But how could I go back to a complacent life, knowing I could have been killed by that very same government I called my own? Could I succumb to a dull life because it was shrouded by an illusion of safety? Thoreau thought by not paying taxes we could revolt against the wrongs of our government. I wasn't so sure one person would put any stop to the wheels of the great machine that was the United States by not paying taxes, but perhaps given the right circumstance, perhaps if one was lucky, they could make a difference somehow.

"They're giving me a new identity," Alice said during lunch.

"What about your children?"

"They can come, too. Even my mother."

Alice smiled brightly. Several months had passed and her blonde hair had grown long enough to fall behind her ears. She looked pretty today. She was already an attractive woman and even more radiant now that she was happy to go home. I was excited for her.

"When you get your new identity, come look for me. I'll keep in touch. I promise."

"I know you will," I said, clasping my hands over hers. "I can't wait to meet your children."

"How much longer do you have to stay, Stephanie?"

"I don't know," I said between bites of sandwich. "They'll recheck me for cancer again in a few months before sending me back if I'm healthy."

"Well, I leave in only a few days. So, promise to keep in touch! I love you so much."

We gave each other a big hug.

Seeing her depart from Dr. Levine's mansion was exciting, but I wondered if she had ever had the same apprehensions as myself. The patients at Dr. Levine's hospital were forbidden to share with anyone what had happened here. Even the slightest hint of our time here might endanger his whole operation. It would have to be a secret. And even if I tried to find this place later, I might not even be able to. Everything would just become like a dream to me eventually.

Of the people I knew here, Alice would be the first to return to her "real" life, but she was returning to her family, to the children she longed for every day. I had nothing to go back to. My transition would only be met by solitude and work. Although I was happy for my life and health, how could I be happy going back to two jobs, amounting to fourteen hours a day after this long break?

Alice's spirit was beautiful. It didn't matter to her what life situation was thrown her way as long as she was with her family. Her children's happiness had become part of the glow in her eyes. It was what gave her, her inner strength and kept her strong.

Her hands were smooth and glossy from the lotion she put on in the morning, and there was translucent pink tinted nail polish on her fingernails from when we stayed up late doing manicures a few nights back. As she spoke about her family, my eyes traced her from her hands up her slender arms. I noticed a scar like mine on her left forearm.

"Is that from your Iv?" I asked.

"Yeah, why?" she said, surprised.

"I have the same scar! Isn't that funny!"

We both giggled and examined one another's scars.

"Wow, that's quite a coincidence," she said.

We held hands and I glanced over at Edward who was still seated at the end of the table. As always, eating his lunch alone. He hadn't spoken to me or even looked in my direction since the surgery. I was pretty mad he had totally ignored me after our conversation in the garden. As a woman, I figured it was the pure asshole quality of men that made him so cold after such a lovely encounter. And every time I glanced at him or passed him in the hallway, I bubbled over more and more with a hot urge to smack him in the chest and demand to know what was with him.

Alice left and soon I found myself wandering aimlessly down hallways. The sun was still shining, but the September months had crept in and trees had turned brilliant colors. The air carried a cold crispness that made their leaves brittle before their time. As autumn took hold, I didn't feel like walking in the garden any longer.

I asked Miss Bethany if there was any place with an old fashioned library, hoping she would lead me back to the small office on her own accord, so I could honestly check out the books to read there. To my surprise, she led me to a real library. A large room with a dome ceiling filled with walls of books, and ladders that must have stood twenty feet high so you could reach even those on the very highest shelf. I found a new favorite place in the den beside the fire with books upon books, reading everything in their library I could. Wrapping a throw blanket around my shoulders and curling my toes in my snuggly slipper socks as I read.

On one particular night, I was walking back to my bedroom when I passed by Edward in the hallway. I hadn't seen him since Alice had been gone.

He glanced at me and then walked straight by without any greeting of any kind. I stopped, blanket still tossed loosely over my shoulders and hanging down to my ankles, and put both hands on my waist.

"Hold on, Edward!"

He faced me, shocked.

"Why have you been ignoring me? I demand to know!"

He grasped for words, but they weren't in his throat yet, so he walked towards me with outstretched hands instead.

"I.."

He took my hands.

"Can we go somewhere? Please?"

He put on his recycled plastic jacket, which was made to resemble the old leather jackets worn up until the 2050s. I could tell it was a fake. Not only because they were all fake now, but also because my Dad had one of the last remaining jackets. Then Edward, led me outside the house to the back porch lit up by large lamps that looked like lanterns. I wrapped myself tighter in my blanket and we sat on the cold bench together.

"Why have you not said a word to me until now? I find it very rude. I thought we were becoming friends," I started.

Edward took a deep breath and his breath made a cloud of moisture in front of him. He put both hands in his jacket pockets and thought about what he was going to say for a long time.

"I like you, Stephanie," he said, breaking the silence into a thousand pieces.

I smiled at him. If that was all...

"But, I can't like you."

"What?"

"You don't need to know anymore than that. I'm sorry. I just think it's better if we don't talk anymore."

We both turned our heads down to the ground by our feet. Both sad those flames, so ready to ignite, were already being smothered.

"Can't we even be friends?" I asked.

"No," he stood up. "I'm sorry."

He left me on the bench and now I didn't want to go back inside. I just sat there brooding, sure this was just another typical dead end relationship. Men hadn't treated me kindly in my lifetime. What was another stupid guy and a rejection anyway?

The next day, I noticed a young boy sitting at a small table in the foyer playing some sort of board game. He couldn't have been more than ten years old. His head was clean shaven.

Probably had been doing chemo. And he was wearing a navy blue knit beanie on his bald head.

"Hi," he said. "Wanna play chess?"

He pointed to the checkered board and smiled, pasty white skin accentuating his crooked yellow teeth as he smiled brightly.

"I don't know how," I answered.

"I can teach you."

He motioned for me to sit down and began setting up the board.

"It's pretty fun when you get to know the rules. Dr. Levine taught me."

He meticulously placed each wooden figure on its own square. The chess pieces were hand carved and were painted, one side black, the other white.

"These guys are pawns," he instructed. "They only move one forward, unless it's their first move, then they can skip one square. The object of the game is to take the king. This is the king. When you think you got the king, but he can move, you say, 'check.' If he can't move, you say, 'checkmate,' and the game is over."

He tilted his king towards me and then set it back on the square. After he told me about all the pieces, we played over and over again. Short games at first, because he always won. And then, as I got the hang of it, our games became longer, until we were saving our games overnight and returning to them the following day.

When I asked him how he could have escaped so young, he told me the reason was he was young and fast, so they couldn't catch him. Then, he found the mansion. Adam was very smart and we became good friends despite the gap in age. I'm sure he missed his family, and I think I reminded him of a mother even though I had no children. It was nice to talk to someone so young. His ideas were always fresh, but because he was mature for his age, he also had more perception about the world then he ought to have had as a ten-year-old.

Adam suffered from acute leukemia and it had been hard to fight. He had undergone stem cell transplants and multiple radiation therapy treatments, but the cancer only moved into his lymph nodes. That's why he said he had a hard time breathing, and sometimes I could hear him wheezing when he was concentrating on his chess game or walking with me down the corridor.

He had been the only child of very young parents. His mother had him when she was just fifteen. This generation often inherits the debt from their parents. It forces people to live their lives early I guess. The world makes it hard to live without accumulating debt anyway. Adam's parents didn't stand a chance in the system. They inherited seven hundred thousand dollars debt when his grandparents passed away and accumulated one hundred thousand off the bat in living expenses before Adam was even one. By the time his parents were nineteen years old, they were both working sixteen hour days in order to feed him.

"I can still hear my mom in my head. She said, 'Run, Adam!'" he recalled. "Then, I just ran as fast as I could. I can see her eyes now. She had blue eyes. She was so pretty. She was the prettiest mom ever."

"Don't worry, Adam," I reassured him. "You'll see her again."

Adam wheezed and fumbled for a chess piece uncomfortably. He took one of my pawns with his knight, but seemed to want to cry instead of gloat like normal.

"Listen," I said again. "You'll see her."

"Okay," he said. "I know."

We were silent for a few more turns.

"They're having a Fall Festival this Saturday. Will you go?"

"Sure," I said. "Look, I'm a little tired today. I'll see you later, okay?"

I tapped on Adam's door.

"Are you ready?"

"Yes!" he shouted, swinging his door open and running down the hallway without even looking at me. I followed him with the energy of a thirty-year-old, dragging my feet behind him, half sulking for being forced to socialize. But this is what Adam wanted, so I flashed a smile and continued to make my way outside.

When we arrived at the porch at the back of the house, the glass doors had been propped open, framing a picturesque late October afternoon. It was a breezy day and the trees were rattling and creaking. Red oak and maple leaves were falling everywhere, but the sun sat brightly in the sky, warming every-thing and shining brilliantly down upon autumn colors, making them translucent in the light.

Picnic tables had been placed in front of the rose garden and people were playing volleyball and BBQ-ing.

"I'm going to see what games they have," Adam said, taking my hand briefly before racing off into the sea of people.

The line was short for hotdogs and chicken at the BBQ, so I joined them.

"Which would you like, honey," said a hefty black man, waving a long metal spatula in the air.

"Two hotdogs, please."

"Here you go!"

He scooped up two hotdogs all at once and landed them on a plate for me. He was a cancer patient also. He flashed a huge white smile at me. Everyone here had a happy aura about them. It was like being instantly retired and striking it rich. Who besides myself, couldn't be happy?

"Thanks," I said to him, taking the plate from his hands.

"Isn't this weather nice?" he asked. "I've lived in New England all my life and it was always cold by October when I was a kid."

"Yes," I said. "It's beautiful."

At least we could take that positive from global warming: A few more summer days for New Englanders and Canadians.

Once I got my bun, a side of potato salad, and some cheese and mustard for the dogs, I wandered over towards the picnic tables and took a seat. After Alice had left, I hadn't made too many new friends. By now, everyone was familiar, but no one really paid attention to me.

Adam rushed over, wheezing, then took out his inhaler and took a puff on it.

"Will you do the gunny sack race with me? Please!"

"Uh, no!"

"Please!" he begged.

"No."

"Please!" he pleaded, louder.

"Why?" I asked, ripping my arm back from him as he tried to drag me away.

"Because it takes two people or I can't do it!"

I pitied him for a moment.

"I guess!" I said, smiling.

He dragged me away from my plate, taking me beyond the rose garden where a race track was set up using cones and orange ribbons. We stood at the starting line with a few other people. A nurse named Mrs. Wong was the person in charge of the gunny sack race. She had a wide face, and was thick boned and her wiry hair was swept up into a grey ponytail. She crumpled up a thin yellow rope tied to a metal whistle and then let it loose and swung it around in a circle in the air.

"Oh, good," she said. "More people. See if you can get Mr. Levine over there so we have an even number."

Someone ran up to him and after a few moments, Edward came towards the group. I tried not to look at him.

"Let's see," she said. "One, two, three. Now we have ten. So, we need group of two. Take this gunny sack. You and you. You and you…"

She didn't give anybody a choice and guess who I was teamed up with? None other than the elusive Edward Levine.

"Here you go," Mrs. Wong said, handing me a large gunny sack.

"Now everybody climb in. Use one foot like this. The other, like this. You walk to very end. First team to get to end wins a pumpkin pie. Other teams, you can get balloon. Okay?"

Everyone laughed. Most of us were adults. Adam was teamed up with a girl who was about fifteen and they were the only children.

"Okay, let's do this," Edward said, taking the gunny sack from me and slipping his right leg in.

I tried to get in without touching him, then lost my balance and instinctively grabbed onto his shoulder for support. We both smiled nervously. He opened the bag a little more and I stuck my left foot into it. Then, we hobbled to the starting line together, bumping hips and losing balance.

"This is going to be hard," I declared.

"Yes, it is!"

"Ready, set, go!" she yelled.

Mrs. Wong blew into her whistle and the five teams hobbled off. Some were already in the swing of things. Edward and I were one of the slowest.

"Look," he said. "Lock arms like those two!"

I put my left arm through his and held onto the gunny sack with my other hand. We sped up quite a bit, but there was already some distance between us and the three fastest teams. The track was on dirt and it winded downhill towards the creak. There were more and more trees and the ground beneath us was getting bumpy from the large shallow roots. We gained confidence and started to pick up more speed, laughing in nervous spurts of joy.

Suddenly, our feet tangled on the edge of a tree root as we took a turn and we both came tumbling down into the dirt on our knees and rolled down the hill towards the creek bed. My jeans tore and my right knee started oozing blood. I huddled up in a ball from the pain and whimpered a little.

"Oh," he said, crawling over to me. "Are you alright?"

"My leg!" I cried, then composed myself. "I'm okay."

He hovered over my face and brushed my long hair away from my wet cheek. I stopped and looked up at him, our bodies were only inches away from each other. His face was poised closed to mine. He could have kissed me.

"That's good," he said.

Then he looked at my knee.

"Come on, it's just a bad scrape. I'll get you fixed up. My dad's a doctor, remember?"

We sat up, brushing the dirt off our clothing, then limped without the sack on our feet to the finish line. My hurt foot was also sprained. Mrs. Wong saw our defeated faces and dirty clothes when we arrived.

"Awe, don't worry. You still get balloon."

She handed me a blue balloon and a green one to Edward, who gave his to me, saying I deserved both of them for getting wounded. Then we limped back to Dr. Levine's doctors office without saying a word. Both of us realizing we had crossed a boundary. Edward went to the cupboard and took out a package of bandaids and some alcohol wipes, then turned back towards me. I propped myself at the edge of the hospital bed and lifted up my knee to him, still holding my balloons in one hand. He didn't say anything, nor I. Then, he cleaned my wound and put a large bandaid on the cut.

"There you go. It's just a scrape, see?"

Edward looked at me, his hand still holding my leg. Another moment stood still like a ball tossed into the air, hovering for that one-second before gravity takes hold. Then, we toppled into each other's arms and my balloons went floating up to the ceiling. He took my face in his large hands and kissed me. First a peck and then couldn't stop himself. He slid his tongue into my mouth and there was a feeling like two souls locking together. He pressed me back onto the bed and my body heaved in ecstasy, breath quickening, skin tingling. He fished his hand between my legs and grabbed my thigh firmly, pressing it up towards him as I succumbed to him.

The Pawn

"Check."

Adam shoved his king back a square and I moved my white bishop forward so I could capture his king again on the white diagonals.

"Check."

"Not fair!"

He shoved his king into the corner of the board where I already had a knight waiting for him if he dared move into the adjacent squares.

I moved my rook, laughing triumphantly.

"Checkmate!"

"No!" he exclaimed, smashing the pieces with his hands.

He inhaled a giant wheezy breath and exclaimed, "Let's play again!"

"I'm sorry. I already played twice with you. I have to do a few things now."

"Do a few things?" he asked. "What kind of things do you have to do here?"

"Uh, I have a check up! With Dr. Levine."

"Oh, okay."

"I'll play with you tomorrow."

"Oh, okay."

"I'm sorry."

"Well," Adam said, setting up the pieces again. "I have a real check up. They're going to give me chemo again. The cancer isn't going away. It's spreading."

"I'm sorry for that. I'll come by your room tonight and check on you, okay?"

I pet him on his bald head and kissed him between the eyes, then put on my coat and vanished into the garden. The flowers had all withered away, leaving stubby rose bushes that looked rather dry and dead. I walked briskly through the paths that winded through the rose garden and sat on the cold stone bench next to the fountain.

The gardeners had brought in the koi for the winter. I reached into my jacket pocket and put my gloves and hat on. It was probably 45 degrees today. Too cold for me, since I was from New Florida.

"Boo!" Edward said, hugging me from behind.

"Eddie!"

We embraced cheerfully, and he gave me a dozen warm kisses on the neck.

"Oo, stay close to me. I'm so cold."

"I don't ever plan to let you go," he said, wrapping himself around me and straddling the bench.

"What about when I leave?"

He let out a sigh.

"I'm still thinking about that one."

"Come with me!"

"It's a little more complicated."

"Just tell your father."

"I can't. We have to keep this a secret. At least for now. Trust me. When the time comes, he'll know for sure."

I smiled, snuggling my hands into his warm jacket lining, then tucked my gloved fingers into the back of his jeans for extra warmth. When you are in love, you can meet anywhere. It doesn't matter the cold or the discomfort of the place. Once we did it in the back of the van. Another time we spent hours in one of the broom closets.

"Wanna go for a walk?" he asked.

"Sure."

I took his hand and we walked into the forest of trees lining the creak that flowed deep into the acres of property surrounding the mansion. The trees were almost bare, but it still looked like lollipop land or rather a Dr. Seuss book to me, with tufts of red, orange, and yellows on wispy treetops.

We found a nice spot next to the babbling brook and spent hours kissing and giggling like new lovers do. I felt like I had to be close to him. Like the only right place for him to be was inside of me. He laid his jacket down on the dirt next to the creek and we made love. Then we lay in each others arms and a deer sauntered over the hillside to sip from the ice cold brook.

"Hey! Look at the deer!"

"That's awesome," exclaimed Edward, lifting his head up and propping himself on his elbow. The deer leapt away and Edward turned again towards me, brushing my long brown hair out of my face with his right hand.

"What do you do for a living out there?" he said, gazing into my eyes.

I suddenly remembered we didn't know very much at all about each other.

"I'm a teacher," I laughed.

"You're a teacher?"

"Yes."

His face lit up.

"What grade do you teach?"

"I have a credential in elementary school education. I teach second grade," I said, proudly. "That's why I never had any kids. I have thirty new ones every year!"

He laid next to me, squeezing me tightly.

"And, I never found the right guy," I added. "I mean, no one nice or anything. Or right, I mean. Not that you aren't nice or right. Just that I didn't find anybody before you."

He laughed again at my awkwardness.

"It's alright," he said. "I feel the same way."

"You do?"

"I didn't think I'd ever find someone that I'd... Well, want to, maybe spend the rest of my life with."

"Wow..."

That was a little fast for me.

"I mean... I don't know how far this will go, but I like where it's going. I just didn't expect it."

"I have trouble with commitment."

He kissed me on the lips.

"Don't worry. I'm not asking you to marry me or anything."

"Okay, good."

"Well, yet," he added with a nudge.

We got back just before dinner was served. I didn't see Adam in the dining room, so I climbed the stairs to his quarters to check in on him. When I got to his room, I found him throwing up in the bathroom.

"I don't feel good," he said after he vomited.

"Did they give you chemo today?"

"Yes, but something's wrong."

I helped him into bed and found a bowl for him to throw up in, setting it beside his nightstand. But, when I went to cover him up, I noticed his arms were heavily bruised.

"Is this from the Leukemia?"

He mumbled an affirmation and then turned on his side with a moan, taking my hand as firmly as he could.

"Stay here," I told him. "I'm going to get Dr. Levine."

When I arrived with Dr. Levine and Miss Bethany, he looked even worse than when I had left him. Miss Bethany and Dr. Levine rushed to his side as he weaved in and out of consciousness.

"It must be a recurrence," Dr. Levine said, placing a plastic clip over Adam's pointer finger to instantly read his vitals.

"What does that mean?"

"His cancer is not in remission anymore."

It was a partially rhetorical question, but somehow as the only adult figure who cared for him in this place, I naturally assumed a maternal role. And as a mother figure, it was hard for me to wrap my mind around the idea that he was not getting any better.

Dr. Levine checked Adam's pupils, but gave no hint of his findings. His lips pursed together tightly and the wrinkles of his face swallowed the edges of his mouth up like wet tar oozing slowly down the sides of his cheeks.

Adam put his head into the toilet bowl and vomited again. His vomiting was uncontrollable and he lost his ability to breathe. He started panicking and crying between heaving. I couldn't stand to see him that way. I touched him on his back to try and comfort him, but it was no use. He had vomited so hard blood came out and mixed with his stomach acid in the bowl.

I gave Adam a fresh towel and he wiped away some of the vomit trickling down his chin, staring at the blood in horror.

"He's reacting to the treatment, but let's check his blood count."

"Yes, Dr. Levine," said Miss Bethany, cooly.

"I'll stay with him," I said. "I'm right here, Adam."

Dr. Levine cast a quick look of disgust before he stretched his wrinkled face into a forced smile.

Did he know about me and his son?

"He's lucky to have you," he said, gathering his things into his hands before he left.

I waited at Adam's bedside all night. I sat with him while he threw up in the toilet and pet his forehead gently while he slept. He searched for my hand to hold when he had the strength, and I made sure I kept his hand in mine as he tossed and turned uncomfortably in his sleep.

The next morning, Miss Bethany softly nudged me awake.

"We have the test results," she said as I sat up in the chair I had pulled up to the bed. "He has an extraordinary amount of white blood cells, Stephanie."

"What does that mean?"

Miss Bethany got down on her knees now and almost whispered it in my ear.

"We'll try everything we can to get him through this, but he may not make it this time."

I sat there, staring at her in a state of shock. Even though my whole body was frozen, tears were still draining from my eyes.

"What will you try?" I cried.

"He's already undergoing the chemotherapy treatment. We could try CAR-T-Cell therapy, but at his age the side effects could cause severe organ damage and would not be recommended. His immune system is already down. We can assist him as he needs and try to make him comfortable. I'm sorry. I just wanted you to know. Since you are close to the boy."

I dried my eyes, but the tears were flowing uncontrollably.

"Thank you."

Just then, Adam started mumbling in his sleep. I sprung to his side and held his hand firmly in mine.

"I'm here, Adam."

Miss Bethany watched us for a few moments somberly and then left.

I didn't eat. I kept remembering how he had wanted me to play another chess game with him. I thought about setting up the chess pieces right then, but I knew it might be too late. I had to wait now and see if he'd make it.

Sometimes Edward would visit for a time, but he had little to say, except that he was here for me and I should eat something or get some rest. After a few days, the nurses seemed more concerned with my health than Adam's. They begged me to eat and to go to my room and get some sleep. He'd be okay for that long. But I didn't want to miss it if he awakened. If there was a moment when he felt better, I wanted to be there as he opened his eyes.

But after three days, they insisted I eat a good meal and go to my own bed. And exhausted, I succumbed to them, falling asleep in my quarters for a good twelve hours. When I woke up, I rushed back to Adam's room. He was still sleeping, but seemed more tranquil than before.

Suddenly, he lift his eyes open and smiled when he saw me.

"Am I still alive?" he laughed, weakly.

"Yes, you are!" I said, smiling back at him.

His usual spirit was fighting to emerge in the manner it had always done, but his movements were tremendously slow.

That usual bright spirit was deflected by the pale blue of his clammy skin. And his youthful vigor was like two candles flickering from light brown eyes smothered by puffy swollen lids.

I gave him a hug and he tried to sit up, so I put some more pillows behind his back.

"Can I get you anything? Want something to eat? Wanna play a game of chess?"

"All of the above," he said, laughing.

For a moment his face was flushed with pink at the cheeks, then his pigment turned back to that pale blue.

"Okay," I said. "Let me get someone."

I ran out to the foyer and grabbed the chessboard, hollering out to Miss Bethany as she walked by in the distance.

"Adam's awake! Adam's awake!"

"Good," she said, chuckling happily. "I'll tell Dr. Levine to look in on him."

When I arrived back upstairs, I tapped on the door a few times and let myself back in.

"Adam! I got the chessboard and Dr. Levine is on his way. I'm so excited!"

Adam was wrapped up in the covers.

"Adam?" I whispered, peeling away the sheets.

The Fish Tank

"Stephanie."

"Go away."

I had brought my chair to the window of my room and was looking out towards the front of the estate, staring endlessly at the statue of the woman. Vines had crawled up her leg and tangled around one of her arms. Her face was discolored from years of rain and snow and a faint crack had emerged, extending from her left cheek down her breast. It was funny how the emotion on her face seemed to change from day to day. And as the heavy sky pressed down on her body this morning, her thin lips grimaced and her eyes were crying.

"We're going to be holding the funeral soon," Eddie said, gently. "Come on and get dressed."

"Go away."

I began crying.

Edward opened up my closet and fished out the black dress the maids had left for me and some glossy black flats. Then, he laid them on the bed and knelt beside me, giving me a hug.

"You were a good friend to him," he said, quietly. "He'd want you to be there."

Leaves were rolling and scattering across the driveway as the wind sighed like a huge monster exhaling in his sleep. It reminded me of Adam's asthma and made me want to stay close to the window and listen so I'd never forget the sound of his wheezing. Maybe I could even hear him speaking to me if I listened closely enough to the wind. But he was gone and I could hear nothing but the low whispers of autumn.

"Okay," I sighed, lifting up my arms.

He pulled off my shirt and put my dress on over my head. Then, I laid down on the bed so he could take off my pants while I stared remorsefully up at the ceiling. He kissed me and laid his body on me and then rest his head next to mine, empathetically.

"I love you," he said. "I'm so sorry this happened."

I didn't say anything. I just cried silently.

He began to leave.

"Eddie," I stopped him. "I can't do this alone. Please stay with me."

My eyes were all red and puffy from crying. He stopped by the door and looked at me, contemplating the severity of our being seen together. Then, let go of the door handle.

"Okay," he said, taking my hand.

He led me outside to the side of the house and down a thin path where there was a small cemetery scattered across a shallow valley. The weather was heavy and grey that day, like those days when it should probably rain, but doesn't. It was a day when the weather just sits there, sulking and cold, clouds rumbling through the sky with no light breaking through.

Dr. Levine and a group of people were already standing around Adam's grave site with the pastor. As we approached, I could feel Dr. Levine's anger growing.

We stepped into place as the pastor began to read an excerpt from the bible. I wasn't listening to most of his sermon. I just gazed out onto the valley of tombstones and green grass and imagined Adam looking down on us, all dressed in black with our black jackets on. I wondered if Adam was really here with us or if there was absolutely nothing when he died. No consciousness of any kind. No heaven or hell.

"Stephanie," said the pastor. "Would you like to say anything?"

I turned towards the small wooden coffin.

"I didn't know him for long, but he was like a ray of light... If you knew him, you would know he was so smart."

My tears interrupted my voice for a moment, but I still tried to smile.

"He was very sick, but still he was happy all the time. I guess he teaches us all how we should live life. He had a great attitude and I will always love and remember…him."

I couldn't go on, so the others began sharing their stories. And when the ceremony was over, I grabbed Edward's hand and he led me back to my room. Then, Edward brought me up some food and I spent the rest of the day sitting at the chair beside the window.

The following morning after breakfast, I returned again to the same place beside my bedroom window. The statue stood in the front like always, but this time I noticed somebody coming up the driveway in a black SUV. I sat there spying with my head behind the curtain. Dr. Levine emerged with a large box in his hands and met with the driver of the car. He gave him the box and took an envelope from the driver. I wondered if those were the papers I had found in the office or maybe some other documents perhaps.

I hid my face behind the curtain and peered through the edge of the fabric, searching the vehicle for any evidence of treasury department on it. The driver looked like a businessman, but that wasn't enough. There must have been something more. Some other clue.

Dr. Levine went back inside and the car rounded the statue and began its slow descent out the driveway. Then, I caught a glimpse of the license plate. It was government issued.

I recoiled in shock, like a lover who had caught their significant other cheating. How was Dr. Levine doing business with the government? I slid on my shoes and ran down the hall to find Edward, but he was nowhere in the East wing or the foyer. The dining hall was empty and so was the library and his room. The only other place I could think he'd be was the West wing, and that was forbidden. It was Dr. Levine's private quarters and all the patients left it alone out of respect.

Normally I would have never gone there, but considering what I had just seen and my relationship with Edward, I decided to defy the unspoken rules of the hospital and creep up the stairwell, slowly tiptoeing down the long red hall. In the distance, I began to make out the muffled sound of voices arguing. It sounded very much like Dr. Levine and Edward, so I continued making my way closer.

The sounds were coming from the door at the end of the hallway. There was an armoire and a plant about ten feet off from the door on the right, so I hid between the two, incase they were to leave the room suddenly.

"Why? Why did you get involved?" said the stifled voice of Dr. Levine.

"Maybe I love her."

"You love a dead woman!"

The voice was muted, but the sound was clear enough. I backed up into the plant, stupefied, and the long dusty leaves enveloped my body.

"We don't have to do this!" he pleaded.

Then, the voices trailed away.

I turned around as they continued their argument and ran down the hallway back to my room. I was horrified. I had to leave, yet had no place to go. And I didn't know what I would even take, since nothing was really mine. I paced the room like a frightened animal, all the scenarios playing themselves out in my head all at once. I imagined running down that driveway and them killing me on the spot. I imagined them killing me in my sleep. What did he mean by dead woman? Would they let me leave if I asked them to go? I knew I needed more information, but who could I trust to help?

I wiped the tears from my eyes and fixed my clothes and hair in the mirror. I had been in a fish tank this entire time. They had made everything look like it was the ocean, but we were really living behind glass.

That night I lay awake in my bed listening to every sound. The clock's rhythmic ticking beat a chilling solo in the dark. And the old house creaked and braced itself against the roaring wind, rattling through the windows.

Suddenly, there was a light knocking on my door.

I shot up, frightened.

"Stephanie."

I opened the door and Edward came rushing in with a suitcase.

"We have to go now. I know where to go. Pack your bags."

He threw open the suitcase on the bed and started stuffing my clothes into it in a jumbled pile.

"Wait a minute!" I said, pulling him away from the suitcase. "I know what you're doing. Why should I trust you!"

"Please, Stephanie. I'm the only one you *can* trust."

"I heard you today, Eddie."

"What do you mean?"

"I heard you fighting with your dad. I know you plan to kill me. When were you going to do it?"

Edward collapsed onto the bed. I thought I had won the argument. I was sure I had exposed him and all the evil at the mansion.

He stared across the room remorsefully.

"We already did."

I stood in front of him, puzzled.

"What do you mean?" I asked, my voice cracking.

"When they operated on you they inserted something into your left arm that gives off ionizing radiation poisoning. It makes you get cancer and anyone else who is around you."

I looked in horror at the scar on my arm.

"How?" I said in disbelief.

"As the device releases a certain amount of radiation, it removes a part of the epigenetic markers in the DNA. After exposure, the body tries to repair itself, but the human system is imperfect and up to 25% of the repaired DNA strands are incorrectly repaired. Normally, when acute radiation syndrome occurs, the cells die and cancer doesn't persist. But with a lighter dosage of radiation, the cells are able to become stable and reproduce. These 25% may reproduce cancerous cells. No one can tell the difference in cancers caused by ionizing radiation and naturally occurring cancers because the damaged cells are random. This whole thing is a set up. It's like your chess games. If you survive the hospital, you must be smart or quick and deserve to live longer. But they can't let you win. They will play until checkmate, Stephanie."

"Get it out of me!" I screamed.

I went into hysterics. Shaking uncontrollably. Ready to pass out from the thought of having a death sentence stuck in my arm.

"How dare you!" I said, hitting him in the chest with both fists.

"Look! Stephanie," he said, holding me in his strong embrace. "I've been around you this entire time. I've risked getting cancer for you. It's because I love you. Please come with me. Please trust me. We'll go somewhere and they'll really help you. There's another place. A group of people who have resisted."

I searched his eyes for a glimmer of the love I thought we'd shared. He kept his gaze on me and I knew he was sincere. And if I was wrong, then I might rather be dead, because I knew I loved him too much already.

"Okay, Eddie. Just get it out of me." I said, collapsing into his arms.

We packed my stuff, snuck outside with our luggage, and climb into his bronco. When we reached the gate, Edward hit the intercom button for the gate to open and the camera spun towards us.

"I'm taking her out. She got her new identity."

"Why so late?" asked the voice over the intercom.

"She's going to Oregon. Long drive."

"Roger that."

The gate opened and we drove into the thick night. As the mansion and everyone in it faded into the distance, I felt for the first time like we were creating our own path. The future was unknown, but I knew even if for a moment, a life lived free is better than a life shackled by its misconceptions. The world marched in unison to a series of routines and traditions. It was choice without choice. Wakefulness without consciousness. As we took our first step away from the orderly shuffle of the world, suddenly out of the black night, I began to see the faint edges of life's infinite possibilities.

Helga

The windshield wipers swung rhythmically back and forth, wiping tiny snowflakes off the glass which collected in small piles at the base of the hood. I lay my head against Eddie's shoulder, staring out at the flurry. In the headlights, we could see the snow drifting in every direction. Some nocturnal eyes caught the light, but before I could tell Eddie it scurried back into the forest.

"Where are we going?"

"New York state. Up by Lake Erie."

"How do you know where they are?"

"They've been keeping in touch with me since I was a kid. I've never enjoyed my father's line of work per se. I've been looking for a way out. Just never had the chance. Never had the guts to go, I guess."

I snuggled my face into his jacket and wrapped my arms around his thick arm. Then jolted up as I remembered.

"Where's Alice?"

"Why?"

"We have to go to her. We have to tell her!" I said, urgently.

"We don't have much time, Stephanie. Remember, you have a time bomb in your arm."

"Where is she? She has children. Please! We have to help her."

"Okay, okay," he said, stopping the car along the side of the road.

He made an illegal u-turn on the vacant highway.

"She's in Cape Cod."

The sky turned a brilliant orange as the sun rose over the Atlantic. Long blades of grass along the beach were poking up from the soft light powdering of snow. The ocean lapped quietly on the shoreline of the peninsula. Not one bird could be seen on the lonely beach.

Eddie told me Alice owned a shop in downtown Cape Cod and lived above a small gift shop on the main street. Nothing was open when we arrived but a little twenty-four hour diner. We stepped in for some breakfast to pass the time before walking over to her place. Going out to restaurants was a luxury I had never been accustomed to and I felt a little uncomfortable on Eddie's arm as we took our seats in the empty diner. But he was quite used to the decadence of the elite. He took his menu and asked for two plates of pancakes without hesitation while I gasped at the price of a triple stack.

"Her new name is Helga," he explained.

"Helga?"

"We were thinking tall, beautiful blonde from Germany."

"Okay," I said. "I see now."

The ground was covered with a thin layer of salt, so our boots made little slushy footprints as we walked along the brick sidewalk up to her place. The buildings downtown were mostly grey and wooden with white trim and looked like they were spray-painted white with a soft dusting of snow. Many were re-done after the Tipping Point to rest on a slab of cement which lifted it high enough to protect the interior from flooding during frequent storms.

It was 9:30 in the morning when we arrived at the little shop and it didn't open till ten, but I knocked loudly at the door anyway.

"We're not open yet!"

Alice sauntered up to the glass drowsily and slightly slumped, saw me, and sprung to life.

"Stephanie!" she shouted, excitedly.

"Helga!" I said with a wink.

We embraced wholeheartedly.

"Oh my gosh! It's so wonderful seeing you again. Come up and meet my family!"

She took me by the hand to a small set of stairs beside the cash register counter. We climbed the stairs to the house on the second floor. Her children were sitting on the couch watching television.

"This is Sage, Michael, and my mother, Ellen," she said.

Ellen dried off her hands in the kitchen and came towards us.

"Mom, this is Stephanie and Edward Levine, Dr. Levine's son."

She shook my hand.

"Sorry for the wet hands. Nice to meet you," she said, kindly.

"I've heard a lot of good things about you," I said, smiling.

"And likewise," she said, drying her hands a little more on her thighs. "You two became good friends. I'm glad she had someone to keep her company. And I'm glad to have my little girl back."

Ellen's hair was in a bob cut like her mother's. They looked very similar, but Ellen was just about twenty years older, had a few more laugh lines than Alice, and her sleek physique had become a bit bonier in the hips and shoulders with age.

"That's what we've come to talk about," I said.

"What's going on?" Alice asked. She gave her kids a piercing look. "Go make your beds!"

The children leapt off the couch, but by the sound of it, were running off to play in their room rather than do chores.

"Please have a seat!" she said.

"Alice."

I stared into her eyes.

"I don't know how to say this."

"What's wrong, Stephanie?"

"Remember the scars we had? That they were the same and we thought it was a coincidence?"

"Yes," she said, nervously.

"Well..."

I looked up at Edward for help. The words seemed too crazy to say out loud.

"Dr. Levine put something inside your body that leaks a certain kind of radiation poisoning. It gives you and anyone else around you cancer."

"What?" Alice exclaimed, eyes watering. "No, I can't believe it."

I held her slender fingers in mine.

"Please believe us. It's absolutely true."

"But you still have yours?" she asked, looking at my arm.

"We are headed to a place. A place that can help us. I want you to come with us. Bring your entire family. They're going to fix us. You'll be safe there."

Alice jerked her hands away from me and stood up, pacing the room. Ellen stood beside her, stunned.

"No, Dr. Levine cured my cancer. I have a new life now and we can all be together. I like this place, this job. We're at peace here."

She backed herself up against the door and opened it up for us.

"I need you to go."

Edward and I looked at each other. Then Edward took out his tablet and typed something quickly.

"I sent you the directions just now, Alice. If you change your mind, meet us."

We both got up and nodded to Ellen awkwardly.

"It was nice meeting you, Ellen," I said, politely.

"I'm sorry, Stephanie," Alice said as we left.

When we got outside, Edward kicked a trash can with his boot.

"Damn it!"

"If she doesn't change her mind, she'll die, right?"

"That's right," he turned to me. "And her entire family with her. And all her friends. But there's nothing we can do. Let's get you taken care of."

We drove down the road and parked in a vacant beach parking lot. Eddie reached into the glovebox and took out a knife and a black case.

"Uh, what's that for?"

"I forgot that radiation device has a tracking device in it. We can't risk showing them our position. I'll have to cut it out now. It's going to be ugly, but it has to be done."

I backed myself into the corner of the seat against the door.

"I don't think I can," I said, staring at the long blade of the knife.

"Come on. Let's do it on the beach."

He opened his door and hopped out.

"Don't want to get these nice seats stained," he joked.

"Right."

I followed him onto the beach where the waves were just missing our shoes and then lapping back. He took out his lighter and began heating up the blade.

"What are you doing?"

"Sanitizing the blade."

Then he opened up the black case. It was a portable surgical kit.

"Never leave home without it," he said, sarcastically. "At least when your dad's a doctor."

I let out an anxious laugh and turned my head away, making a small squeal.

"I haven't even cut you yet."

"I'm getting ready."

"Okay, put your arm out."

"I'm going to be sick."

"Just keep breathing."

"I'm going to faint!"

"You'll be fine."

He placed the sharp tip of the blade to my skin where the scar was.

"Look out at the ocean. Don't look at it."

"Okay," I whined in anticipation.

I felt him begin to make an incision deep into my arm. There was a sharp pain and a stinging sensation as he cut through my nerves.

"Almost done."

I hadn't stopped whining.

"I'm going to faint! I'm going to faint! Hurry!"

He pulled out a long wire with a small object at the end that felt like it was embedded in my bone and showed it to me. It was very small and thin and looked like a robot bug. Then, he tossed it as far out into the ocean as he could.

"Okay. That part's over, but we're not done yet."

He took out a pre-threaded needle and thread from his kit which was enclosed in a small plastic bag and began to sew up the incision.

"There will be a scar, but it's better than being dead."

"I guess," I said, finally breathing.

Blood had dripped down into the moist sand and collected into a puddle. Then the frothy waves rushed up and washed it out to sea. Now there was no evidence at all of Edward's surgery on the shore. We sat for a few moments on the sand looking out onto the vast ocean as I nursed my stinging wound. Then, we took a deep breath and started our long journey together.

"What's wrong?"

"I'm getting a lot of phone calls from Dad."

"Take your phone out."

He pulled his phone out of his earlobe. It was a little black thing that hooked on the ear and had a small speaker which inserted itself automatically into the ear canal when there was a call. He took it out and tossed it into the center console.

"Are we going to charge up?" I asked as we passed a charging station, noticing he was almost out of batteries.

"We're almost there now," he said, taking a left hand turn away from the station.

We had been driving for more than six hours. He drove the car off road onto a little dirt path surrounded by long grass and bare wispy trees. The sun was low on the horizon at this point of late afternoon, creating long shadows across the snowy brush.

Eddie drove slowly. Tires crushing newly fallen snow along the unattended path. Then he came to a dead end next to a small frozen waterfall and stopped suddenly.

"What are you doing?"

"We're here."

He got out of the car and walked up to a large stone situated between white shards of ice. Felt his hand around the stone, then reached inside a long crack in the rock. Suddenly, the ground opened up like a garage door from the ground, snow and all, revealing an underground tunnel. Eddie got back into the drivers seat and drove the car into the tunnel. A bunch of cars were already parked. He parked in an empty parking spot and hooked the car up to a charger in the stall.

"This is great!" he gasped. "The garage is completely run on solar electricity."

I got out of the car and looked around at all the cars that were already parked. What kind of place was this? There were even tanks and army vehicles here.

"Grab all your stuff. We still have quite a hike."

Eddie popped the trunk and took out both our suitcases. Then, put on a large black backpack. I had nothing else to bring with me. So, I just put on my jacket and followed him out the garage.

We hiked for several more miles, until we were deep in the forest. My legs were achy as we trekked on and on in the brisk cold. We seemed to be going where no tourist went, to an isolated part of the reserve. I caught a glimpse of a few deer and some small animal tracks scattered along the white fields, but other than that, we were completely isolated.

The sun was setting when we arrived at the compound. Eddie found two large boulders and then paced himself so he was six steps from each and began digging.

As he wiped away the snow and dirt, he unveiled a circular metal door with a small handle on it and gave it a hard knock.

"I forgot my phone in the car or I'd just call them."

He knocked again and waited kneeling in the snow. A few moments later the door swung open. My eyes widened when he appeared from the ground. The same old man who had saved me before popped up from the hatch like a groundhog.

The Compound

"I guess I have a lot of explaining to do now," he chuckled. "Come in!"

"Want some hot cocoa?" he said, leading us down a metal hall and into the main part of the compound.

Several other people were seated.

"Sure," Eddie said.

"This is DJ," he pointed to a young Indian man.

He was very thin and his ears seemed too big for his head.

"And Alexis."

"Hello," she said.

She was in her early twenties. A redhead with long wavy hair bound up in a thick braid. She looked pretty muscular. They all seemed rather malnourished and really fit.

"Hi," said a dark skinned man, the healthiest looking of them all. "I'm John."

"Nice to meet you," I said, shaking his hand.

"And this is Smith," said the old man.

"Okay," I said. "Now I'm on name overload."

We laughed.

"That's okay. He's the last of them. And there is me of course. My name is Reggie Codwell."

"You saved me!" I exclaimed.

"We tried, but Edward got you first."

He looked at Eddie, who was holding my hand.

"I guess he came over to the light side, by the looks of it."

"Yes, sir. If you'll still have me."

"Stephanie," Reggie started, leading me to an old sofa. "We've been keeping tabs on you for awhile now. See, I knew your father. He was a good man. And even before that, I was good friends with your mother."

"My mother's dead," I said, surprised.

"They both are now, God rest their souls. Your mother escaped the dogs. She came to live with us for a long time. We wanted to change things, but we could never find a way. Then your dad came looking for her one day. He just wouldn't give up looking. So, she brought him into our community about 2060. You were only fifteen. You were just a child then, but they couldn't give away our cover by having too many family members disappearing at once. It was so dangerous. It's one thing to lose a crazy old man, another to lose a family off the grid. We found this machine. They went in and well, we lost your mother that night. When your dad passed ten years later, he made me promise to look after you. I don't know if you knew it, but I've always been there with you. Sometimes I'd walk my dogs real close to you, when you'd be walking along on the street, so they could give you a good sniff. You know, to make sure you were okay. Well, one day you came up positive and I knew I'd have to be there at your next exam to make sure you got away. It wasn't easy saving a seat for you, but no one refuses a big old geezer like me. When I say that seat's taken, it's taken!" he chuckled. "We were going to get you after your new identity. But look now! You've come to us!"

"Wow!" I said, trying to absorb everything he had said. It was all too confusing to me. "I had no idea."

"You look like your mama. Tan and beautiful. You're her spitting image. It's even hard to look at you. How'd you end up with this guy?" he joked.

Eddie and I looked at each other, shyly.

DJ brought us two mugs of hot cocoa and broke the awkward silence.

"Thanks," I said, taking one of the cups and blowing on it as the steam drifted up.

"I'm going to let Alexis show you around. Put them up in her parent's old room. I think that'll do nicely."

Alexis stood up and motioned for us to come with her.

"This compound was made in the 1950s by the military and used all the way up to the early 2000s. Then, it was forgotten about, like many other things," she said as we walked with her down a labyrinth of narrow hallways.

"It goes on for three acres underground. It was meant to protect the President and his government officials during a nuclear attack. There was never a World War III. No need for these self-efficient metal boxes until we came along."

She led us into a huge greenhouse that must have gone on for an acre or more.

"Wow!" I gasped.

"This is where we get all our food. We have livestock, vegetables, fruit bearing trees and bushes. They did a bunch of stuff in the military to prepare for long term space travel. We didn't do that either. But we got this!"

We were laughing now. It seemed this group benefited a lot from failed government spending.

"And through this room is where we train."

We went through a door that opened up to a full sized gym that had free weights, weight machines, ellipticals, treadmills, and even a pool and a huge rope tied to the ceiling. Eddie punched one of the punching bags sitting near the door.

"Ever play any boxing matches?" he asked.

"Sometimes," Alexis said. "John likes to play, but no one wants to get their ass kicked by him."

I already sized Alexis up as being much more masculine in nature than your average woman, and I wondered if we could ever be friends, or if there was too much of a difference in personality between us.

We wound through some hallways which felt like the hallways of a huge barge. A single person could barely fit through. She showed us where everybody slept and then to our room.

"I'm assuming you'll want to sleep together?"

I blushed.

"This is your room. You can leave your stuff here and I'll take you back to Reggie."

The room was larger than the others she showed us, but was still only about ten by ten with an old full sized bed in the corner and a desk. The rest of the room was quite bare. I opened up the desk drawer.

"Oh," she added. "Those are your parent's things. We don't get a lot of new blood around here. We just left their things when they died. You can have them if you want."

"Thank you," I said, stopping tears from flowing down my cheeks.

I picked up a picture of my mom and dad together. It had been taken after they disappeared. Mom was much older than I had remembered her. She was still beautiful with salt and pepper hair flowing down passed her shoulders and a huge smile. Her arm was wrapped around Dad, and he also had a tranquil smile on his face. They both looked so happy. But, even though Reggie had explained it, I still couldn't understand why they hadn't come back for me. I was heartbroken.

Alexis led us back to Reggie. We finished up our hot chocolate and he told us a few more stories about my parents which brought back my own memories of them. Then, we ended our reminiscing and went to bed.

"What are you thinking about?"

"I just keep thinking about Alice," I said the next day, on the couch in the community area.

"She'll be okay," Eddie said, petting me on the back. "I gave her my phone number and all the directions she needs. If she changes her mind, she'll be able to find us."

"Your phone is in the car!" I pressed my hand into his knee. "Maybe we should go get it."

"It's cold out there!" he complained.

"We should at least have your phone. Come on!"

I stood up and started pulling on his arm, but his body was too heavy to move.

"Okay," he said, getting up. "Nothing like a four mile hike in the middle of the morning to get us up!"

"There you go," I laughed.

"Take Smith with you," Reggie interjected from across the room. "Just incase you get in trouble."

I actually felt good about walking, but had to stretch my scarf up over my face because the wind was so cold it stung my cheeks. Eddie teased me for wanting to get the phone for a good thirty minutes as I shivered and griped about how freezing it was. Smith didn't look out of breath or cold. The only thing that gave away he was standing in twenty degree weather was his red nose.

"I feel like my hands are going to freeze off!" I said, sinking my gloved hands deep into my jacket pockets.

"You wanted to get the phone, remember?"

"This way," Smith directed.

Smith was thirty something and was built like a weight lifter with a huge chest and massive upper arm strength. His neck was covered by a grey scarf, but the night before, I had been examining his thick neck muscles from a distance and wondering what exercise could possibly create muscles that big. He looked like people I had only seen before in movies.

We continued until we were walking parallel to the frozen river. Smith led us through the rocky valley that cradled the stream for several miles. Then we climbed up the steep creek bed again and came upon the garage from the top.

"Duck down!"

We shrunk down in the bushes and Smith peeked over the ledge where the waterfall sprayed over the edge and had frozen into a large icy glob.

"There's somebody down there," he whispered.

"It might be Alice and her family. Are there two women and some children?"

He nudged himself a bit further over the ledge to see.

"A woman," he announced.

"It's okay," said Eddie. "I gave them the directions here."

"You gave them directions? This is supposed to be top secret!"

I rushed over some fallen branches and slid down the hill shouting, "Alice!"

"Stephanie!" Alice yelled, waving her arms high in the air.

We embraced. Then, I pet Sage's head in her carseat from the open window of the car.

"What kind of directions are these? 'Rock is secret entrance.' Do you know how many rocks there are in a forest?" Alice criticized.

"Do you still have it in your arm?" he asked.

"No," she said, lifting up her sleeve to show the bandage. "Mom took it out in the kitchen before we came. I had to see if it was really in there anyway. And once we found it... Well, there was no other place for us to go other than here."

"I guess we are still twins," I said, showing her my bandage with a sad smile.

Smith opened the door to the garage.

"Park your car in here," he directed Alice.

"How does this work?" I asked.

"It's a metal underground garage camouflaged in fake dirt and rocks," Smith said.

I examined the dirt at the entrance. It seemed like a real landscape even after touching it.

Alice parked her car and we got Eddie's phone and a few more things from the trunk. Then, the kids toppled out along with Ellen and preceded to race around the car, clomping in the snow like tiny marshmallow monsters. Thick snow jackets and pink gloves on Sage, and forest green gloves and jacket on Michael, with scarves circled twice around their tiny heads and snow hats covering most of their face so that their eyes and a nose were their only visible features.

"It's nice to see you again," I said to Ellen.

"Thank you," she said. "Thank you for thinking of my daughter. Of all of us."

"You'll probably want to take all your things. It's a long hike," said Eddie.

"We have a lot of stuff. The kids wanted to bring their toys."

"I can help, ma'am," said Smith, taking some of her heaviest luggage out of the open trunk.

"We all can," I said. "We're just glad you're here."

When we returned to the compound, I collapsed on the sofa in agony. My legs felt like they were mushy sacks of jello.

"My muscles are actually in pain. Not sore. They hurt," Alice said.

"I know how you feel," I said. "Imagine walking that three times in the span of twenty-four hours."

We both moaned a sigh of empathy for each other.

Suddenly, Reggie came in. Alice and her family had already met the others. The kids had tossed off their snow gear, had taken out their toys, and were playing quietly on the carpet beside the couch.

"I'm sorry," Reggie said. "I was in the garden. Who do we have here?"

We stood up.

"This is my good friend, Alice. She also had a device in her arm. So, we asked her to come here so she could be safe with her family. I hope you don't mind."

"Device you say?" he said concerned as he knelt next to the kids. "It's been a long time since we've had children here. Of course you're welcome. Maybe you'll put a little zest back in our lives. These guys get a little too military for my taste."

He stood up, facing Ellen.

"And who is this gorgeous woman?"

"This is my mother, Ellen," Alice replied.

"How long were you all living together with the device in her arm?"

"About four months, sir," she replied.

"So, you have abnormal cells in your body. Everyone will need to come with me. I think it's best to put all of you through the body scanner. It will find all the abnormal cells and repair them."

"That would be a cure for cancer," Edward laughed, sarcastically.

"They've had a cure for cancer for about twenty years," Reggie answered. "The elite have been using it on a hush hush basis. No rich man wants their precious wife or daughter to go to the dogs now."

"Of course," I said.

"That's messed up," Edward exclaimed.

"There's about five of these machines scattered across the world. We stole this one right before your mom passed away, Stephanie. We were going to use it for good for the people, but realized too fast, they were a lot stronger than us. If we're going to win for any length of time, we gotta get some more people together. An army. And make them strong."

He led us through the garden. We passed Dj watering vegetables and made our way to the garden edge where we passed through a large threshold with rooms numbered one through twenty-five. Twenty-three was the room number we wanted. It was a small space with a white pod in the center and a computer console. I peered through the pod window. There was a chair with arm straps and what looked like a head brace. Two metal gun looking things were pointed towards the chair.

"Looks like fun," Alice said.

"Looks like a torture chamber," Edward added.

"Funny you'd say that. It uses laser technology to find abnormal cells and then kills the anomalous cells. I guess the idea is a bit torturous. But it's better than being dead, right?"

He let out a deep chuckle which caused him to cough a little.

"That seems to be the theme of the week," I concluded.

"It uses the same idea as a computer virus scanner," Alexis explained, taking a seat behind the computer desk. "It scans your entire system and then takes out all abnormalities one by one."

"Who wants to go first?" asked Reggie.

"Oh, I have to go first!" Edward said, jumping into the seat.

Reggie strapped him in and closed the heavy pod door.

"Now, it's important not to move. That's why we strap you down."

"I'm ready," he said from the pod.

Alexis turned on the machine and suddenly there was a hissing of air as the air inside the pod stabilized. Then, a long purple laser began scanning him from his head down, riding over him with a purple light like a barcode scanner at a supermarket. I peeked over Alexis' shoulder and began reading the display number as it counted abnormal cells.

"Is that right?" I asked.

"About two hundred," she said. "Not bad."

Suddenly the purple light beam changed. Just as a car wash switches from water spray to soapsuds, the beam turned off and a new laser appeared over his body. This time, the two gun looking machines sent a thin red light stream into his arm. Then, into his chest, shooting at him like staccato notes jumping out from a Mozart piece.

"There are close to fifty-trillion cells in the human body," Reggie explained.

"Does that hurt?" asked Ellen.

"Not much," said Reggie. "The lasers are so targeted and the cells so minute it feels just like a tickle."

Suddenly, the machine paused and the lasers took their places once again in a resting position. The pod door opened with a hiss.

"Who wants to go next?"

I went and had close to three thousand abnormal cells. Alice had about five thousand. Ellen was similar to Eddie in his count, but had the least amount out of all of us. And the kids cried and refused until Reggie finally bribed them with more hot chocolate.

"Tomorrow, we'll begin the training," Reggie said as we walked back.

"Training for what?"

"Training to go up against the system," he said. "We will train you how to survive the dogs, how to be as fit as soldiers, and how to grow your own food and be self-sufficient. Everyone has a place here in the compound. Everyone's job is important. And when the time comes, we will rise against them. Why us? Because we are the only one's left who understand what's really going on and can fix this God damned world. So, goodnight. Get a good sleep. Tomorrow we'll begin the work."

The Work

The community area reminded me of your typical bachelor pad. The black leather sofa and grey carpet were very old and tarnished and the walls were mostly bare, but for a few posters, namely one of Marilyn Monroe in her famous white dress and another of a Ronald Reagan re-tinted in red, white, and blue with the word HERO at the bottom which was beginning to tear at the upper right corner.

The next room was the kitchen, a massive place like a restaurant. The compound had a dining hall, but no one used it because it was built to seat five hundred soldiers and family members and felt too large and vacant. Everyone would rather bring their food in from the kitchen and eat on the sofa, so the sofa was littered with crumbs of food wedged in between stained cushions.

"Good morning y'all," Reggie said as we finished our breakfast. "Before we begin, I'd like to know if you have any talents or trades that may benefit us as a group."

"I've done some carpentry," Eddie said.

"Good," Reggie said. "And we can use your medical expertise."

"I don't really do that anymore."

Reggie looked sternly at Eddie.

"When the time comes," Reggie said as if they had held the conversation many times, and with one look, said it all over again.

And with some assurance that things would never change, they both left it as it was. But Reggie's years had taught him the only certainty in life is uncertainty, and he knew when the time came Eddie would use his medical training. Such was life.

"I can sew and crochet," said Ellen. "And I used to do inspection."

"Very good."

"What about you?" he asked me.

"Uh.. I'm a teacher. I guess I'm good with kids."

"That may be useful considering we have some kids right here," he smiled, kindly. "What else? Think of everything."

"My son, Michael, plays the piano," Alice said, laughing.

"A musician! And you?"

"I'm not talented. I'm just a computer nerd," she said.

"We need computer nerds, too," he chuckled. "And what does little Sage do?"

"She's just cute!" said her mother.

"Good enough," said Reggie. "She can keep me smiling on a bad day. We need that, too."

We all laughed, feeling a little lighter about what was to come, but he hadn't finished.

"You will eventually use your talents to help in the compound, but first you need to know how to survive. You will all learn how to grow and prepare your own food. And then we will start your physical and mental training. We typically physically train two to three hours a day. We grow food when we want to eat. Who here is hungry?"

Everyone confirmed they liked to eat.

"Now I'm hungry all the time. So, I grow food all the time. We grow our vegetables and fruit and raise and butcher our own meat. Let's start in the garden."

"What about the kids?" Alice asked.

"The kids will learn right along with you. Alice, what would happen if the army came in here and killed every single one of us? Now imagine your kids were hiding somewhere the whole time. Wouldn't you think they should know how to survive?"

"Yes, sir."

"Now you see the severity of the situation. Don't depend on your brother to do things when he may not be there the next day. Let's move out to the garden."

The garden sprawled out for most of the three acres underground. It was truly a site to see as we were some three stories under the surface of the earth in a huge manmade dome and not even the trees touched the top of the ceiling.

"This ceiling is equipped with special metal halide lights that mimic the sun's natural rays. There are actually two rooms here. One room creates a chaparral biome, similar to the weather you would have seen in sunny California. And because we all love bananas and coffee, one room represents a tropical rainforest biome. Actually, just a side note: President Dwight loved coffee so much, he had this biome put in especially for him. If you get cold, you can go hang out in there. But watch out! The ceiling does make rain, so don't get caught in a storm!"

"How did you get this place?" Eddie asked.

"It was a combination of luck and a lot of hard work. Smith's dad was one of the guys who originally worked in this underground facility. He was a key guy in their high security operations with a top security clearance and all that. They only had a handful of guys working here to keep up the facility and after a hundred years, well, this place had become a file in someone's office. It was just a figure in our national budget," Reggie paused for a moment as he remembered.

"The recent Presidents didn't really care about it and had barely even heard it mentioned in conversation. That was the luck. The hard part was removing all evidence of operation Underground Biome from government documents and computers. That took a few of my best guys and the lives of two of my dear friends. The other workers were won over, because if they didn't join our side, we said we'd kill 'em. Yes, we used to have more people with us, but slowly, everyone has been taken out. It's risky bringing in new players. If they aren't the right people, our whole operation could be completely lost."

"I'm sure other people would want to join you," I said.

"You are indeed like your mother, an optimist."

"Most of the middle class is a paycheck away from starvation and a doctor's appointment away from the gas chamber anyway," Ellen said.

"Yes, ma'am, but the government would pay to have information on our whereabouts, and starving people have a hard time seeing a line between good and evil."

While we were talking, we had strolled over to the vegetable garden. It was only a fraction of the land in the biome, but still quite large for the five of them. Dj was already there, watering squash.

"Dj handles this garden mostly, and I like to help when I can. It soothes my old soul."

"I like to water the old fashioned way. I don't trust those timed systems. You get the best plants by giving them your love and care," Dj said.

"And that's why Dj is in charge of the garden," Reggie said, smiling. "Dj, tell us what you do here."

"Well, we have all sorts of vegetables. There's three sections of land we plant seasonally. So, we eat a ton of squash and apples in the fall, etc. We alternate the plots so the soil stays rich. We also use manure from the livestock to fertilize it. So don't eat the dirt, kids! There's not too much to it. Just need a lot of patience. When the vegetables are ready, we pick them. We have to plan ahead so that the next batch will be ready. Think of it like a squirrel saving nuts away before the winter. You have to start the seeds for the next season at the right time, so you can have fresh food all year round. There are also some fruit trees in the back. See them? We can pick fruit all year round. The trees make a ton of fruit. Apples are in season right now."

"What ya' doing today, Dj?" Reggie asked.

"I'm planting herbs. We got some basil, chives, oregano, and garlic!"

"Well, you got some helpers today."

"Great!"

The planting went quickly and was really fun, and the kids enjoyed playing in the dirt and putting little seeds in pots. We learned how to tell which seed was which and a little more about what vegetables were planted during the winter months. The biome did have a regulated change of seasons, but it was milder than the outdoors and this ceiling used an older technology than the tropical biome and didn't rain.

After lunch, we walked over to the livestock. It was quite a ways off, but there was actually a farm. There were pigs, cows, chickens, turkeys, and goats. Smith's job was to take care of the farm animals. He showed the kids the chicken coup and let them collect some eggs for our breakfast the next morning. We were then shown the butcher house, but there was no need to butcher an animal. I guess the meat lasts for some time, depending on how large the animal is and they had just slaughtered a pig a few days before we came. It had already been cleaned, cut up, and frozen for the weeks ahead.

After we helped take care of the animals, it was time for dinner. John was the lead cook at the compound. He showed us the huge fridge, freezer, and stoves. By then, the kids lost interest and ran into the community area to play. All of us girls followed them out, but Eddie stayed behind to help cook. Our first day was very full and I was beginning to see how time consuming this lifestyle could be. Yet, there was still something very basic and peaceful about the place, and I knew it wouldn't take long before I would call the compound home.

The next day, Alice told the kids to lay their toys out in the corner of the gym, so Sage ran to an open spot, blonde pig-tails bouncing up and down, and laid a blanket out over the hard gym floor. Then she tossed off her pink backpack and emptied out all its contents at once in a big pile of miscellaneous trinkets. Michael followed her, a bit more methodically, kneeling beside her blanket with straight dirty blonde hair. He took out his plastic toy action heroes one by one and lined them up against the pink cotton blanket edge.

"Alright, ladies," said Smith. "Today, I'm going to lead you in some exercises. Some of you may think you're strong. Some of you may think you are in shape. But I can tell you right now that you are all weak, fat, slow, and obnoxious slobs. By the time we're done with you, you will hurt so bad, that you won't be able to think straight. This isn't some housewife aerobics class. I'm going to turn you into warriors. Ruthless killing machines. Today, we're going to break down your marshmallow and chicken wire bodies and build them back up with bullets, brass, balls, and all kinds of kick assery. And when you start to put the pieces back together, you won't even recognize you were the weaklings you are today."

Michael hit Sage with her doll and she let out a wail.

"Michael!" Alice scolded, then turned to Smith. "I'm sorry. Somebody's got to watch the kids. I'm going to have to sit this one out."

Alice began walking towards her children, but John stepped in with a friendly smile.

"I'll watch them," he said as he leapt over to them, slid down on his knees, and began playing. The kids seemed content enough. I looked towards Alice to see what she would say and she was smiling.

"Thank you," she said.

"I used to have younger siblings at home. I'll watch them anytime. We workout all the time anyway. Don't worry, I'll catch up later."

"Well, thanks," Alice said again.

"Fall in!" Smith hollered.

We all spread out into our places.

"The bend and reach!"

"Huh?" I said.

"The bend and reach!" Smith said, a little louder.

"He wants you to repeat it!" John yelled from the corner.

"The bend and reach!" we replied.

" In cadence!" he hollered.

"Huh?" I asked.

"In cadence!" Alice and Eddie yelled.

They had already gotten the hang of it, but Ellen and I were still standing in a daze.

" Exercise! 1,2,3-1! 1,2,3-2! 1,2,3-3! 1,2,3-4! 1,2,3-5! 1,2,3-halt!"

We all stopped.

"Position of attention. Move! The next exercise will be the side straddle hop."

"Huh?" I said.

Alice laughed at me.

"A jumping jack!" John yelled again. "Christ, man, they're not soldiers! Speak English!"

"Side straddle hop!" Smith repeated, yelling it so loud the veins in his red neck showed.

After we were done 'warming up,' John put us on the treadmills. I began running at my own pace which I thought was very reasonable for a beginner. Who knows how long this crazy gym guy would have us running for anyway? But then he came along and turned my display level up from 3 to 3.5.

"I can't do that," I told him.

"You are an athlete! You are strong! It's all in your mind. Say it!"

Smith was yelling the words so loud he was almost vomiting them out of his mouth with spit and all.

"I am an athlete. I am strong. I am an athlete..."

Then, he walked off and did the same thing to the others, turning up their dials.

I am fat, I thought. Wow. I really did need to change my thinking. All I could think about was, *I am fat. I am slow.* I guess that's what I accepted was true about myself. Of course, I really wasn't fat, but I was no model. Just a delicate boned latin American woman. Even though people told me I was beautiful, who ever believes what people say about you unless it's something negative? When it came down to it, I figured maybe I could use a little of what Smith was saying. So I kept telling myself in my head 'I am strong and I am an athlete,' even against the other thoughts that tried so hard to intrude in my mind.

Sage had walked up to Alice's treadmill and was moaning.

"Mommy, I want to go home," she whined, swinging her doll into the air like she was about to hit the treadmill with her.

"Let Mommy exercise," she told Sage between heavy breaths.

John walked up and took her little hand in his.

"Is it okay if I take the kids to the garden, Mommy?" he asked.

"Yes," she giggled, eyes sparkling like Christmas tree lights.

I gave Alice a look, but she hadn't noticed. *Did she like John?*

Smith had us run for a whole hour, and when he yelled halt we tumbled off our machines like we had no bones. But we weren't done yet.

"Take a break. Get some water, but keep moving," Smith said. "Now, you will begin your training."

"I thought that was our training," Ellen said, panting.

"That was exercise," he said. "Now we will train you how to fight."

My head spun. I thought I was going to either faint or throw up. I sat down defiantly with my legs crisscrossed.

"I didn't tell you to sit down, did I?" Smith said.

"I quit."

"Okay, you quit and when someone comes in here and tries to kill Sage and Michael or your precious friends, who is going to protect them? Quitting gets people killed! Get up loser!"

I began to cry. I was utterly exhausted and now embarrassed. I didn't want to be any hero. I was just a girl. You know, the one who gets protected. I hadn't signed up for this, but I couldn't let anyone down, so I gathered up my strength and stood, one tired leg at a time.

"That's better," Smith said, arrogantly.

Alexis had joined him. She was putting on a black body suit.

"First thing we will teach you is self defense…"

The Run

Several feet of densely packed snow still blanketed the ground in these late days of March. That wasn't as much snow as they used to have around this time of year. I had heard stories of up to six feet in these parts. For us, several feet was a lot. It seemed the seasons had shifted over the years. Spring was a colder season than novelists generations back had written about. Winter didn't seem to really start until late January or reach its peak until February. So, the cold was still nipping at our bones.

Normally, we woke up early, ate a good breakfast, worked out, and trained for several hours. Then ate lunch, worked in the garden, enjoyed a little personal time, and did some directed work. After that, we ate dinner, had some more personal time, and went to sleep, only to begin our routine again the following day.

I was the children's school teacher. Sage learned her ABCs and did cute little craft projects with colors, shapes, and tracing. Michael spent the better part of his time learning math and writing. The children's very favorite subject was science. We'd go to the kitchen and make strange concoctions we named "poison" and "gooey goo" and watch how different kinds of liquids, solids, and gases interacted in chemical reactions. They were fascinated with these experiments and spent hours afterwards imagining they were scientists.

"3,2,1 blast off!" Michael yelled, flying by me. "Shooo!"

He was running down the hallway with the rocket he made in class the day before. Alice was walking behind him, holding Sage by her petite hand.

"Are you ready to workout today?" she asked.

"Nope, but after I have some coffee I will be."

"Me, too," she said, laughing.

Eddie made a kitchen table for the community area. It was a big enhancement for life at the compound, at least for us girls. I sat down in the newly assembled oak chairs, but before Alice could sit next to me, Eddie came crashing down into the chair beside me, giving me a sloppy kiss on the cheek.

"Just wait till you taste breakfast this morning," he said. "We made eggs Benedict!"

"Yummy," Alice said, steering her children into their chairs.

" Good morning," Ellen said, putting some placemats on the table.

"That looks so nice," I complimented. "By the way, I love the blanket you made me and Eddie. Thank you."

"It's fun," she said. "It's no problem."

Reggie brought out two hot plates of food for the kids.

"Rule number one in the morning is always feed the kids first," he said, placing the plates in front of Michael and Sage.

"I heard you can run a ten minute mile now," Reggie told me.

"Yes, sir, finally!" I said. "Smith told me I have to get eight minutes by the time snow lets up."

"I have a surprise for you," he said.

After breakfast, we met like always in the gym, but when the warmup was done, Reggie came in wheeling a large luggage bag behind him.

"Today, we're gonna train a bit differently," Smith said. "Now that we finally got our slowest runner up to speed."

Smith tossed a quick sarcastic wink at me and smiled.

"You will continue your tactical training in the field."

He motioned to Reggie and Reggie unzipped the luggage and took out something that looked like robot shoes. They were made of some sort of metal I had never seen before. A bit heavy looking, with dials and lights on their sides and slits on the soles where small plates of metal overlapped each other.

"What's your shoe size, Ellen?" Reggie asked.

"Ten."

Reggie punched in a number on the dial of one of the pairs of boots and the surface of the boots re-calibrated to her size.

"Put those on," he said, giving Ellen the boots. "Next, Alice."

"Same," she said.

"Like mother, like daughter," Reggie said, changing the size on the next pair of boots and handing them to Alice.

"Eddie," he said. "What size?"

"Mens twelve, sir."

"And what are you, dear?" he asked me.

"Seven," I replied.

"Here you go."

He handed me a pair of boots and I realized they were actually very light, weighing even less than a typical hiking boot. Smith and him put their boots on as well.

"This is where you power on the boot," Smith said, showing us a small button on the inner side. "The display in front allows you to change the size. It will remember everything you program into it and learn your terrain. The soles are equipped with sensors that allow you to run in the snow, ice, and even over water, although it takes some practice."

Reggie and Smith both chuckled to themselves.

"These boots were part of the space exploration program. They were built to allow people to walk on alien terrain. It's part of a full body suit that allows us to walk on gaseous planets, ice planets, you name it," Reggie said. "They're a little tricky at first, but once you get used to them, they'll perform faster and better than any shoe you've ever owned."

"You will also wear these headsets," Smith said, handing each of us what looked like a cell phone ear piece.

"And it's cold out there, so you'll need these," Reggie added, taking out a pile of thin grey jackets. "These jackets regulate your body to exactly 98.6. If you get into any trouble now, we'll all be nearby to help. So, let's get started."

I strapped my feet into the boots and we all tried walking in them. They were a little awkward for a few steps and then the soles adjusted to the ground and felt normal.

When we got outside, the cold air stung my cheeks, but my body still felt nice and warm from the jacket. I brought my scarf up over my mouth as far as I could and pulled down my hat over my ears.

Reggie laughed at me.

"You won't stay cold! Everyone follow Smith," he directed. "We'll run a total of six miles."

"Double time!" Smith shouted, running off.

Eddie and Reggie were right behind him. Alice was next, with her mom running behind her. I don't know why I was always the slowest, but my boots didn't seem to work for me either. I started off a couple of feet and then fell over.

"Hey guys!" I hollered from a pile of snow.

"What's-ss-wrong, babe-sss," Eddie said over my headphone set.

"I just fell on my butt," I explained. "And I can barely hear you! There's a lot of static. Can you hear me?"

"Yeah...hear-ssss."

"Uh," I said. "I can't hear you guys."

"Come...back?" Reggie said.

"She's fine," Alexis said, jogging passed me.

I picked myself up from the snow, gave Alexis a resentful look, and began jogging again slowly as she disappeared into the forest.

"Babe---ssss. Coming?" Eddie said.

"I can't hear you," I said, annoyed. "I'm coming. I can see your tracks in the snow."

I started running towards them. The wind was like a sheet of cold water pouring over my body, but after a few minutes, I started feeling warm enough to take off my gloves. So, I pulled them off and stuffed them into my jacket pocket.

I could no longer hear anybody ahead of me without my headset. There was an eerie quiet in the forest with only the clomping of boots crushing packed snow. The wind sang through the branches of bare maple trees which rattled and bent under each crescendo. And the sound of a flock of birds was growing louder from behind. I searched the sky for them as the honking intensified, imagining dozens of birds swarming over me, but couldn't see a thing. They must have flown off somewhere behind the tree line because the sound eventually faded.

The boot prints of the others trailed through a meadow and wound towards a steep mountain. The snow was lighter here and the prints disappeared in the grass and rocks. I stopped at the edge of the mountainside and searched for a clue to where they went.

"Uh, guys?"

"sss-k?"

"Did you go up the mountain?"

"sss- around the-sss," Eddie said.

"Oh my gosh, I cannot hear you!" I said, angrily. "There's too much static."

"sss- hill!" he said, shouting.

I figured he was telling me to run up the mountain. I took a few steps. My boots tried to re-calibrate as they changed from snow to rocky terrain and I slipped, tumbling down the steep part of the slope, rolling first on my left hip and then toppling over my shoulders and sliding about twenty feet down on my butt. I lay in pain in the snow looking up at the trees. Then mustered a little energy to sit up and examine my scraped hands and aching body, cursing everyone in my mind.

"sss."

"I'm okay!" I yelled, angrily.

I had fallen into a dense thicket. In the quiet shadows, I could see a white rabbit scurrying away, leaving a trail of little footprints behind him.

There was a large metal cage half buried in snow.

"Aren't we supposed to be alone out here?"

There was nothing on the other end of my headphones but static. The forest was silent and cold.

I limped up to the cage. The meat inside was swarming with insects. I found a stick laying on the ground and poked at the cage with it, activating the door so it slammed shut with a thud. The noise surprised me and I fell back into the deep snow again.

The wind was rustling the tops of the trees, but I was protected in the valley from its cold bite. The shade of the hillside and forest made everything dark even though it was midday.

I sat in the snow, this time not even trying to get up, hugging my legs. I was achy from my fall and pretty much had lost all contact with everyone. I knew it was time for me to give up finishing the run and return to the compound.

Then suddenly, I heard a strange noise.

I crawled out of the hole of snow I was sitting in and followed the high pitch sounds around the bend of the mountainside. On my feet, I didn't sink down into the snow at all, but I knew without the boots it would have been difficult to walk. I followed the sound until I couldn't walk any farther, then stared awhile at the snowy wall. The sound seemed to be coming from within the mountain. It was whining, like a strange animal was stuck inside the rocks. I slowly uncovered the snow and as it fell away, a small cave was revealed with an opening about two feet high.

"Hello?"

Without the snow, the muffled sounds were clear for a moment. Then, there was silence.

I backed up and peered into the cave opening from the distance. I could make out what looked like a large mound of fur, but it was very dark and I couldn't be sure what kind of animal was hidden there. The fur was so close to the opening I could have reached my arm into the hole of the cave and grabbed up the fluffy mound, but the sunlight only lit the first several inches of the mouth of the cave. The rest was shrouded in deep black shadow. I didn't dare reach my hand in, for fear the mysterious animal would bite me. So, I sat at the cave opening instead and waited.

Time went by and still I sat. It began crying again inside the cave.

"Ten white horses, Ten white horses, Gallop 'cross the green,

As the sunset kisses them, Lovely and serene."

It was a song I taught in elementary school.

"One went free, they didn't see, he followed honey bee,

Running so fast that he tired and sat beside a stream."

Something stumbled out...

"Hi there."

A second emerged behind the first. They looked famished. Their fuzzy grey coats were all they had clinging to their bony bodies. One came right up to me, wagging his tail. I picked it up. It was male.

"Hello."

The other blue-eyed pup came up to my lap and stood on my thigh. They were both trying to come as close to me as they could, tails wagging, voices giving off little whimpers.

"And you're a girl," I said, petting her as she nuzzled her nose into my leg. "A boy and a girl."

I peered into the cave for others, but the fur inside looked lifeless.

"Are your brothers and sisters dead?" I said, holding the boy pup up close to my face. They were both so little and fluffy, but as I dug my fingers into their coats, I could feel their ribcage and knew they were starving. I wondered if the mother had gotten caught in a trap or something. Little fleas were nesting in their fur. I had to get them home, so I could clean them up and nurse them back to health. They wouldn't survive here another day on their own.

Milk

"Look what I found! Look what I found!" I said, carrying the puppies into the living room.

"Uh," Alexis said as they turned towards me. "Those are wolves."

Everyone gathered around.

"What do you mean?" I asked.

"You've found wolf pups," Reggie said, petting them.

"How do you know they're wolves?"

"There ain't any dogs around these parts," Reggie, chuckled. "See their coats? Those are grey wolves. They've been in this part of the state now for about fifty years."

"Oh my gosh! They're so cute!" Ellen said, taking one of them into her arms.

"Please, don't make me take them back!" I begged. "Their mom was dead. These are the only survivors of their entire litter!"

Reggie frowned at me for a moment. Then his old mouth opened into a smile, black freckles speckling his cheeks like stars.

"Ask Smith for some goat milk," he said, finally. "You can nurse them back to health, but chances are, they'll be wild. Wolves don't make good pets."

"You'll have to release them when they get older," Alexis said, smugly.

"Okay," I said, gripping the male wolf pup in my arms.

I took off my boots and brought the wolves to the stable where Smith was busy feeding the pigs. His hair was still wet from having taken a shower, which made me stand there for a moment to try and calculate when he must have gotten back to have had the time to shower and change, and then come here and start working. I decided he had to have sprinted the entire run. By the looks of his arm muscles as he poured the slop into the pig corral, I was sure he had been abducted by aliens as a child who enhanced his body. Because no human being could really have muscles that large without being genetically mutated.

"Enjoy your run?" he asked.

"Found something," I said, showing him the two pups.

"Look at those two," he said, petting them behind their ears. "They're both pretty famished. Did Reggie send you here?"

Smith led me into the barn, carrying the two empty pails back with him.

"About how old do you think they are?" I asked as he searched the dark cupboards along the barn wall.

Smith pulled out a few glass bottles, set them on the counter, and then ran his finger over the gums of the male pup.

"Less than three weeks," he said. "Don't even have teeth yet."

Turning back to the cabinet, he took out some plastic nipples and laid them beside the bottles.

"These should do," he said, screwing the nipples on both the bottles for me.

"Feed them every three hours, and they'll probably need some extra fluids because they went so long without their moth-er's milk."

He handed me a plastic jug of clear liquid.

"This is for the dehydration."

Then, he took out an empty plastic jug and led me out to the goats where he sat down on a wooden stool and started milking one of the females. He collected quite a bit of milk into the jug and handed it to me.

"Keep this refrigerated until you need it. Then, warm it up and give them about 1/4 ounce for every pound or just look to see if their tummies are round and not hard after feeding."

"1/4 ounce," I repeated.

"For every pound."

"1/4 ounce for every pound," I confirmed.

I had put the jugs down beside me and been sitting with the pups in a blanket on my lap, but when I went to get up, I realized I had too many things to carry.

"I'll help you," Smith said.

"Thank you."

I had only seen the rough and tough side of Smith, but I detected something different from him in this setting.

"You like animals?"

"Yeah," he said. "My dad taught me all this stuff. Taught me how to hunt. And taught me how to care for animals, too."

He looked at the wolves and smiled.

"Are you going to keep them?" he asked.

"I don't think so. They're going to get big, aren't they?"

"Yep," he said, petting them. "I'll help you with them. They need an alpha. Just remember to be assertive from the beginning. This one will probably get bigger than you. One hundred fifty pounds maybe. They can socialize with the other dogs and I'll help you show them who's boss."

I stood up with them in my arms.

"Well, thanks," I said. "Like I said, I don't know if I'll be keeping them. Probably just raise them until they can go off on their own and then return them to the wild."

"What are their names?"

I looked down at their grey coats and the mask like colorings on their faces. Suddenly, a name came to me.

"I think this one will be Sasha," I replied.

Then, as I looked into the male pup's blue eyes and thought of the perfect name for him.

"I'll name this one, Adam."

"Your turn," I mumbled as the alarm sounded.

"They're your wolves," Eddie grumbled from his side.

"Please!" I begged, fatigued.

"I'm pretty sure it was my turn at two this morning," he said, a little more awake.

"Fine!" I shouted, lifting my body up from bed.

It had been a week already and the cuteness of nursing two pups back to health had worn off, leaving us utterly exhausted. Adam and Sasha were getting better everyday, but still slept quite a lot and had more weight to put on before they'd be considered a healthy weight for their age.

I made the bottles and took the pups in my arms under the covers of the bed.

"It's like having babies," I said, smiling.

"You're the proud mother of baby wolves!" Eddie mumbled under a mound of covers.

"Don't you feel like this is what it would be like if we had babies?"

"It's too early to start that conversation. I'm going back to bed."

"I'm just saying I'm starting to like them. Look at their cute little faces. They need a mommy."

"Oh no!" Eddie rolled away from the wall and looked at me. "You can't possibly take care of wolves. Don't even think about it."

"Smith said he'd help me."

"You have to release them back to the wild. That's where they belong. I love you. One day, we'll have babies. I promise! These aren't our babies. Now, I'm going to bed!"

"Okay," I said as he turned back towards the wall.

The pups finished their bottles quickly and fell asleep in my arms. Then, I put the empty bottles on the nightstand and fell asleep myself.

The next day, Reggie called us into a meeting.

"You're probably wondering why I called this meeting," he said. "I've noticed everyone seems to have a different opinion about what should be done with these wolves."

I had left the pups in a box in my room. Now my cheeks burned red with embarrassment for having caused such a problem at the compound. Eddie took my hand supportively.

"It *is* possible to raise wolves, but most of the time a wolf cannot be taken from the wild and become domesticated. The only thing working for these two are that they are so young. That increases their chance of being able to stay with us. That said, I think I should make a decision. And after hearing both points of view, I've decided the pups will get raised until they can return to the wild and be on their own. Normally, a wolf will leave their pack at ten months to find their own, so you have until then, Stephanie."

I sighed. He wasn't being mean, just realistic, and I knew that.

"Smith and Alexis will help you, Stephanie. You can't cuddle them so much. They need to learn how to be wolves. Start spending time with our dogs. Leave them with the dogs during the day. You can keep them with you at night until they're weaned."

"Alright."

"Sorry, Steph," he said. "It's for the best, kiddo."

Everyone left, but I stood back with Eddie and Alice.

"It *is* for the best," Eddie said, rubbing my back.

"But they're so cute," I whined, sadly.

"But they will only be like that for a few months," Alice said. "Then, they'll be large wolves. Reggie is being stern, but he's right."

"You could have helped me, Eddie. You could have said something."

I was starting to cry. I looked down at the ground, so I wouldn't show them my tears.

"Adam's going to grow as big as me. How can you handle that? You'll get yourself eaten!" Eddie said, his voice deepening.

He was genuinely worried about my wellbeing. But he had never yelled at me so furiously before, and the surprise of his loud voice made tears well up at the corners of my eyes.

"Hold up!" Alice said, raising her hand in the air. "I know what this is. You two haven't had any rest for a week now. It's time for a date night!"

"Date night?" I asked.

"When my kids were babies, it was the same thing in our house. You just get so tired and there's no break. It can take a toll on any relationship. Even you two lovebirds. I'll take Adam and Sasha tonight. The kids will have fun with them and you two can do whatever you want."

"Okay," I said, smiling.

Eddie took my hand in his.

"It's been awhile since we just fooled around," he flirted.

"Now you're talking," Alice said, putting her arms on both our backs, steering us towards our room. "Now, go!"

"Come in."

The door opened.

"Hope I didn't disturb you," Reggie said as he entered my room.

"Nope," I said, running my hand through Sasha's coat. "I was just spending time with the wolves."

"They're getting bigger everyday."

He picked up Adam and looked him up and down.

"Are they on solids yet?"

"Just started to mix a little raw meat into their diet."

Reggie set Adam on the floor and walked over to the desk.

"What brings you here?"

"Just checking up on a friend," he said, gazing at the picture of my parents clipped to the wall above the desk. "You kept the pictures, I see. I haven't been in this room since your father passed."

"I like to look at them. I never really knew her."

We both took in the silence for a moment, then Adam started begging to go on the bed, so I picked him up and kissed him on the face, inhaling the milky aroma of his breath.

"It doesn't look like you're following my directions with those pups," he said, his deep bass voice growling disapprovingly.

"I'm sorry," I said. "I love them. I can't leave them with the other dogs."

"That's okay," he turned from the picture towards me. "Your mother never listened to me either."

"What happened to her?"

"Like I said before, we were going after something. We were trying to find a very important man."

"Who?"

"His name is Mr. Henry A. Bernstein. He is the great great great grandchild of Dr. Phillip Bernstein and *he* created the Key to the World."

"The Key to the World?" I laughed.

"Ever wonder where they store all the data on everybody? How does the world keep track of rich men, poor men, dead men, and the living?"

"I guess."

"Back a long time ago, people in America used paper documentation. Well, someone'd have a fire and they'd lose everything. Their only birth certificate maybe. Folk didn't know where they came from, or how old someone was sometimes. Then, computers came along. We stored identity information on them. This is common sense history stuff."

"Okay," I said, urging him to make his point.

"But what about billions of people? What about the debt of countries? There had to be a supercomputer that links to the others. A main control center that keeps all those files organized and legitimate."

Reggie sat down in the chair by the desk and the chair creaked under his weight. He put his hand over one knee and rocked himself a bit before continuing.

"This man's ancestors invented the first computer that kept all the information on finance for everyone in the country. It's linked globally to the entire world and contains all the money information for everything and everyone... In the world."

"I thought the credit bureaus did that?"

"Now, the government knows man is corrupt. Why, he's corrupt himself. There has to be something to check the legitimacy of those agencies. Think about it. They can write off someone's debt in a second or give someone debt. Agencies have to be controlled. So, the government is the true and highest control. We see the credit agencies. That's the public face. But the government holds the real records."

His voice grew softer as he leaned forward.

"One computer controls our entire system."

"Wow," I sighed. "Ever find it?"

"We found the man who built that computer, Dr. Bernstein. And in the process, well, your mother died."

"How?" I asked.

"The dogs found her. Then..."

We both sat again in silence. Both angry. Both remorseful.

I sat up.

"I'll find the computer," I said.

"You could lose your life."

Part Two:
Key to the World

The Key to the World

"What do we need this computer for again?" Eddie asked.

"When the government was first erected, the founders intended for us to change the constitution every few years to reflect our changing society. It has never actually been revised, only amended. Now, we live in an America that has severe separation of class and a check and balance system that no longer works," Alexis said. "We believe there is a computer that holds and manages all the financial information for the entire world. A supercomputer."

"Sometimes you gotta put a dog to sleep," Reggie said. "We're going to reset the system."

"If you have no wealthy or poor. If everyone is the same, there will be a fresh start," I explained to Eddie.

"You do know there are only nine of us, excluding the children," Eddie said. "That computer, if there is one, will be protected."

"Listen," Reggie said. "This job isn't for the meek hearted. You'll be using a gun and fighting a war."

"Sometimes it's just what you have to do," Smith added. "My father gave his life. Your parents did too, Stephanie. We all may die, but we'll be dying for our country. To put an end to some of the corruption."

"So, what do we have to do?" I asked.

"Train hard. All of you are going to have to step it up. And in the meantime, we'll get the whereabouts of Henry Bernstein and pay him a visit. If he helps us, we will know the security systems, as well as the location and other pertinent information."

"You suck at shooting a weapon," Eddie teased me.

"You suck at martial arts," I said, taunting him back.

"We all suck," Ellen said. "I'm a sixty-year-old woman. What can I do, but get us killed?"

"You'd be surprised," Reggie said. "Rely on your strengths and work as a team."

"Dismissed!" Smith shouted.

"Fuck," Alexis mumbled under her breath.

"We're all going to die," Alice told her as they walked out the living room together.

"Henry A. Bernstein lives in New York City. He is twenty-eight-years-old and is currently single," Alice read.

"How'd you find that out?" I asked.

"I'm from a family of computer nerds and Reggie's been showing me their system. It's not too hard to get someone's address if you have their name."

"So that's easy," Eddie said. "We just go there."

"Now hold up," Reggie said. "We have some enemies. There will be federal agents looking for all of us and keeping a close eye on him."

"Is he part of the elite?" Ellen asked.

"No," Reggie answered. "His dad was a gambler. Gambled away their inheritance. This guy lives like you and me. But he's got his grandpappy's brains. What little we know about him is he's a child prodigy who got in trouble for hacking Google. Changed their homepage as a joke once when he was just twelve-years-old. Now they got agents on him 24/7."

"Okay," Smith said. "So, it sounds like we could use him."

"What's our inventory like in the armory room?" Reggie asked Smith.

"It's pretty full. Alexis and I bought some more ammunition on the black market after our last incident."

Adam and Sasha were racing around the living room in circles around the kids.

"Don't pull their tails!" Alice said to the children as they tried to jump on the pups and force them down by grabbing onto their long fluffy tails.

"It's all been replenished," Alexis added. "We've been using some to train, that's all."

"Get some more guns," Reggie ordered. "Something small for the girls."

"I can handle my weapon," Alexis said, offended.

"You're not a girl!" Smith said. "They are. Girly girls."

Alexis whisked her long red braid back behind her shoulders, and reminded us she was in fact still a girl.

"Thanks," I said, tossing her a sympathetic look. "And yes, I'll take a pistol. I can't shoot a rifle worth anything."

"We all know that," Eddie laughed.

"Hey," Alice said. "Be nice to my friend!"

"How many do you want to take to New York, Reggie?" Alexis asked, steering us back to the important things.

"Ellen can stay with the kids. Smith and DJ will stay here and keep up the compound. I definitely want my computer experts, Alexis and Alice, with us. Eddie and Stephanie stay together as a team. John and I will come for backup."

"When?" I asked.

"Have that address?" Reggie asked Alice.

"Yes, sir."

"Then, we'll go as soon as we get the guns."

"Alexis and I will get them tonight," Smith said.

"Okay, then."

Alice looked down at her children. I knew what she was thinking already. As everyone went back to their own activities, I walked up to her and gave her a hug. Then, I put my arm around her shoulder.

"It'll be alright."

"Do you think it's really going to be dangerous?" she asked.

"They know what they're doing, but I'm not a soldier. I'm just an elementary school teacher. We'll stay as hidden as we can and we can use our guns in self-defense."

"Okay," she said, smiling again.

"Hey!" John said, coming up behind us. "Don't worry ladies. I'll be there right with you."

"Thanks, John," Alice said.

"We go out all the time. You just got to know how to blend in and get in and out of places without them seeing you or following you."

"How do you do that?"

"Okay," he said, raising his hands at chest level. "Here's how it is. If you live normally, you lock up your house, go to work, come home. Do you look around you?"

"No! I never do," I replied.

"Do you check to see what cars are in the neighborhood? Do you look behind you to see if someone was following you?"

"No," Alice said.

"Now we're playing the game. They try to find us and we stay hidden. It's like cat and mouse. If you get too relaxed, you'll pop up on their radar and they'll find you. If you are cautious, then they won't. Just like that."

We laughed.

"Thanks, John!" Alice said, a little more relieved.

"Anytime."

Alice knelt down beside her kids and started picking up their toys off the floor. John's gaze lingered on her figure for a moment before turning away.

"Come here," I said, gathering Adam and Sasha up off the living room carpet. They were getting little sharp teeth now and as soon as I picked them up, the cubs started gnawing on my hands.

"Oh, no you don't!" Smith yelled, looking at my hands. "You're hands are all chewed up."

"They're teething now," I explained. "I try not to let them."

"Listen."

He took them from me and held them so they wouldn't chew his fingers. Then, he sat down on the sofa with me.

"You can never let them think it's okay to chew on you. Give them a toy. Always redirect their attention to a toy. Be firm. Do you have a toy?"

I grabbed one of their toys from beside the couch and handed it to him.

"Like this," he said, giving them the toy.

He put his hand in front of Sasha and she nibbled on it.

"No!" he said firmly and gave her the toy, which she immediately started gnawing on.

"Can you train them how to protect us?" I asked.

"I'll teach you how to train them. Remember you are the alpha. When you stare them in the eyes, never look away first. When you play with them, always be on top. Keep your voice

116

deep and strong when you speak to them. You must always do this."

The river was awaking from its slumber, babbling and trickling with freshly melted snow. Light stretched over the white ice with a dazzling brightness, reflecting a warm blinding light into my face as I walked. The air was still cold, but had lost its stinging edge. I was getting the hang of my boots now and the jacket really helped, but it was warming up enough I could go without any scarf or hat.

"Look!" Alice said. "There are buds on the trees!"

"Finally," I moaned. "I'm so ready for spring."

I looked up at the maples and saw the bare branches growing little grey bulbs.

"Everybody stop," Smith said, suddenly.

"A footprint," John whispered.

"Someone's been tracking us."

"I saw a cage the other day," I said. "An animal trap in the snow."

"Why didn't you tell us?"

"I forgot," I said, dumbly.

I recalled when I told them, that they hadn't been able to hear me over the headset and struck my forehead with my palm in frustration with myself.

"Damn," Alexis said. "Those are pretty fresh. What should we do?"

"Let's keep going," Reggie said. "We have to get to the car."

"But we've left tracks," John interjected.

"Retrace our steps and wash the tracks clean. The sky looks pretty clear. There won't be any new snow today, so we need to cover where we've been."

John walked off, smearing our tracks away as he went.

"The rest of you, stay quiet in case he's close."

We all walked more slowly. No one spoke a word. We separated and covered our tracks as best we could as we went, but the snow didn't make it easy. And what snow had melted, left a thick sticky mud. I felt so bad for not telling anyone about the trap. I had been so busy with the pups I hadn't remembered. And after what John told us the night before, I knew these mistakes could get us killed.

We finally made it to the garage, but still waited for a long while before we opened the secret hatch, making sure no one was around. Then, all we could do was wait for John to come back. I was terrified. I hadn't realized the cage might have been from someone living out here, waiting for us to come out of the compound. Everyone was nervous about John separating from us. We couldn't be sure if it would be him emerging from the snow or the tracker in his place.

John didn't come for a long time. After we put our things in the trunk, we sat in the seats listening to the quiet sounds of the garage and staring at the red dashboard lights glowing in the dark. Melted snow was leaking through the cracks of the old cement and dribbling down to the ground, making puddles along the edge of the walls. We could hear the high pitched rhythmic sound of droplets splashing into little pools echoing in the dark.

Still, no one spoke. Not to lift the tension. No one dared give away our position. To turn on a light, even briefly, or the radio, might give away our location. Eddie just sat beside me with his hand holding mine, the sweat between our palms communicating all our unspoken anxieties.

The silence was broken by a rat scurrying across the floor. It rattled something in the dark and what sounded like a tire hubcap toppled over and rolled onto the ground. Eddie and I tightened our sweaty grip as we waited for John's return. Our breath amplified by the thick silence.

Suddenly the door opened and the light from outside poured in. Reggie was the first to turn around and see him. My heart stopped.

New York

I squinted at the bright light, hand on my gun, until I was sure the man emerging was John.

"I took the tracks far away from the entrance of the compound and put some fake deer tracks over ours," John said as he climbed into the minivan.

"How'd you do that?" asked Eddie.

"With this!" he started unfolding a pen sized wand with a fake deer footprint attached to one end. "It stretches up to six feet, so you can get those prints way out away from you. DJ made it."

"Cool."

Reggie pressed the garage door opener button. Then, we slowly made our way out of the wilderness reserve towards New York City. New York: The epicenter of capitalism in America. Where the New York stock exchange bustled as busily as its people, and where lights glowed brighter than stars. It was dark when we passed into the great city. White lights shimmered on skyscrapers like sparkling crystals growing on massive slates of concrete.

Water had seeped into the subway system permanently during the mid 2040s, so the New York subways had been rebuilt as city trains floating as high as the buildings. Metal water barriers standing three feet tall were assembled to dispel water from the large roots of these giant buildings. New York had become a walled city. A city standing against nature itself. Its monument, the Statue of Liberty, knee deep in water, stretching her old candle high above the waves in defiance of the raging sea.

Walls on the eastern coast were erected ten feet tall in order to shield the metropolis from large waves. But still, severe storms rolled across the sky and waves rising twenty feet above sea level often crashed over the barriers causing flooding along the streets.

Small boats lined Street Level instead of cars and Street Level became a barren refuge for the outcast and impoverished. Its lowest citizens, who had only a blanket and the clothing on their backs to protect them from the harsh rain and flooding, often drowned during the night and were left nameless and forgotten to bloat and rot in the salty water.

Level One was a highway system of bridges spanning across New York City where many of the lower and middle class rented apartments and stores. All of the buildings were renovated with doors on this level, and to most people, this was New York.

The highway led us straight to Level One where we wound through the tall walls of skyscrapers in a labyrinth of steal and brick. We finally came to an old apartment complex in the downtown area and Reggie parked the car in a small garage.

"Is this his house?" I asked.

"No," Reggie replied as he took the keys out of the ignition. "This is a dear old friend of mine's apartment. He won't be there. Works at night. He let us use the place."

The walls on the inside of the building needed painting. Huge sections of hallway were stripping and bubbling from water damage. We passed a small elevator with Victorian style brass doors that looked rather like a cage enclosing the elevator shaft.

"Should we take the elevator?" Eddie asked.

"No," Reggie replied. "It's better to take the stairs. That old elevator is from the 1900s. It's a death trap."

"Only take that elevator if you want to dive straight down to Street Level," Alexis joked. "Smash!"

"That elevator probably'd get stuck before it would work," John interjected.

We began our long walk up four flights of stairs winding up the building like an old snake. Reggie took out his keys and unlocked the door. The place was as small as small could be, kitchen sitting immediately off to the right, nothing more than a sink, fridge, and small cabinet. And the living room space was only a hallway stretching about five feet by five with a small metal card table for a kitchen table set against one wall. Two doors were at the end of the tiny space. One was slightly opened, some cracked bathroom tile showing, revealing it to be the bathroom. Reggie opened up the bedroom door and we all laid our things out on the floor, some of us sitting on the twin sized bed, whose old black comforter was left partially unmade. We looked around the room, quietly disgusted by our surroundings.

"Yep," Reggie said. "It isn't much, but no one will bother us here tonight. And in the morning, we'll do what we need to do and hopefully be home by tomorrow evening."

There was a faint hint of mildew wafting in from the water damaged walls a few floors down. With the window open it was bearable, but then the cold started seeping in, chilling through to our bones. Some of us found a corner to huddle into and rest. Nobody fought for the bed at first out of respect for the ones who wouldn't be able to fit, but a group of us eventually shared the bed after trying other parts of the uncomfortable room, sitting upright and curling our bodies tightly around each other so we wouldn't fall off. It's safe to say most of us stayed up the entire night. John being the only one to get a decent nights sleep, snoring loudly in the corner.

After a long sleepless night, the sun finally began rising above the city, but the tall walls of skyscrapers cast shadows over the streets, coloring even the pedestrians a melancholy grey. We made some breakfast and Reggie left his friend a note and some money for the convenience of his place and his food.

As we were getting ready to leave, we heard a siren wailing outside. John pushed open the curtain a little and looked out the window.

"We'd better go now," he said, observing two police cars parking outside the complex.

"It's for someone else, right?" Alice asked.

"That's right," Reggie said. "But, walk carefully and slowly."

We went outside the hallway. A few tenants had begun lining up in front of their doors.

"Darn," Reggie said. "They're doing a scan."

"What's that for?"

"In these parts, they conduct regular scans to make sure nobody's wanted."

"We better go," John recommended. "We're all wanted for conspiring against the government and if we're caught it's the death penalty."

A few police officers were coming up the stairwell. One brought his black scanner out of his holster to begin scanning the retina of each of the tenants on the first floor.

"Move to the roof," Alexis ordered.

We started climbing the stairs when an officer caught sight of us from the stairwell.

"Hey! Line up!"

We didn't comply.

"Stop right there!" he yelled, motioning for the other officers to back him up.

We ran up the stairs to the roof, but the door to the roof was locked with an old metal combination lock, forcing us back down to the eighth floor. The police were still climbing the stairwell at the seventh, so we dodged into the eighth floor hallway, pressing passed tenants, standing in a daze by their doors.

We were trapped. I could hear the police nearing. Black shoes scuttling up the stairwell to our inevitable encounter.

"Either out the window or the elevator," John said.

"Let's take our chances," Reggie yelled, opening up the brass door of the elevator shaft.

We climbed in and closed the door just as the police officers caught up to us. The elevator creaked and sighed under our weight. Our bodies filled the small elevator way beyond capacity. One of the officers tried to pry open the elevator door, but Reggie pressed the button and the door locked and began rolling slowly downward.

"Follow them down!" the officer shouted to his three partners.

The elevator paused for a moment near the fifth floor. Time stood perfectly still for us as we listened to the sound of one of the thick wires unraveling. Then suddenly, we dropped several feet as the first wire ripped apart with a sharp pop.

We all cried out. Then waited as the old elevator creaked and dangled in the air on its last ancient wire.

"Grab onto something," Reggie commanded.

The wire unwound a bit under the tension, lowering us down a little farther.

We braced each other and in that moment as we fell, time hovered around us like a mystical fog. On some other plane, gravity was taking hold, slamming us down into street level with its fierce fist. It was over in a single moment, but my mind clearly recorded every nanosecond of our limbs flying into the air. Hands grasping for someone to hold onto or for something to stop our inexorable end.

The elevator struck something hard along the wall and tilted, sliding down the elevator shaft on one top corner and one bottom edge. It made a horrible screeching sound as metal scraped against metal. Sparks flying, exuding a foul burnt odor. We slowed somewhat and, for a second, all found some relief. But then the elevator groaned and rumbled as it swayed again under our weight and we splashed to the bottom of the building, hitting the top of the elevator ceiling in a jumble of body parts. Rolling around, bones breaking, muscles tearing, and then coming crashing down to the floor again. The elevator slowly floated down into the water, hitting Street Level with a loud deep thud.

"Wanna go after them?" one officer's distant voice asked.

"Naw," the other laughed. "They're already dead."

We all laid in a pile as the elevator filled with water.

I barely moved. I was afraid to try.

Then, someone moaned in pain.

"We gotta get out," I said, pulling my aching limbs from the water as the floor flooded.

"I think I broke my leg," Reggie announced.

"I definitely broke my arm," said Eddie.

"Alice!" John exclaimed, holding her limp body up from the water.

I rushed towards her lifeless body, my heart breaking into a thousand pieces as I held her limp hand. Her lips were tinted blue. Then suddenly, they trembled as she sparked back to consciousness and began to move her bloody head and flutter her heavy eyes open.

"Thank God!" John said, hugging her.

"Everyone else, alright?" Reggie asked.

"I might have broken a finger and tweaked my neck," said Alexis. "But I'm fine."

"I'm fine," I replied.

I helped Reggie stand up on his good leg and those that could, tried to pry the doors open.

"It's stuck!" John said.

Then, we heard laughter coming from outside.

"Sir," Eddie said. "Can you help us?"

The man cackled.

"And what are you going to give me?" he bartered.

"One hundred dollars," Reggie offered.

"I would have stole that from you after you were dead anyway."

There was silence on the other side and some slushing of feet in the water.

"What else?"

"We'll give you a gun."

There was no sound of rejection or affirmation from him. We all sat in our old metal prison, nursing each other's wounds. Eddie looked over Alice tentatively for signs of concussion. After a few minutes there was another sound at the door. The man had returned and was prying the door open with a crowbar.

"Thank you!"

Street Level was very dark because the sky was covered by the streets on Level One. I could barely make out the man's features when he finally tore open the doors, but saw he was unshaven and his long hair was matted under his felt hat. He was a young man, of about twenty-years-old and as skinny as a skeleton, riding in a row boat wearing jeans, a thick torn jacket, and some heavy tan work boots.

"Where's my gun?" he grumbled.

"There you go, sir," Reggie said, handing him one hundred dollars and his gun which he quickly hid deep in his inside coat pocket.

We all waded out into the icy water. I was more afraid to be out of the elevator than stuck inside. There was hardly a person around, but those who were, were covered up in cardboard, laying in what used to be windowsills and porches of apartments from long ago. Their faces were old before their time, with cheeks so sunken in from starvation they looked like their skin had been pasted to their skull with a cheap glue stick.

A woman wrapped in a dirty wool blanket sat on a porch in a cardboard box. Long oily hair fell passed her shoulders in front of her. She was staring vacantly out at the river covering the old streets of New York. Her brown eyes appeared so sunken in their sockets they didn't seem to fit her face any longer. There seemed to be no life at all in her, but I couldn't help but think in an alternate reality I may have found myself in her situation and still felt empathy for her. What kind of harsh life had put her here? Was she born into this despondent circumstance? Or did a series of horrible events lead her to this hopeless conclusion?

She turned her cold eyes towards me and I grabbed onto Eddie's good arm nervously as her deathly gaze followed me.

"How do we get out of here?" Alexis said, holding her broken hand.

"We'll have to climb an old stairwell," Reggie said. "Used to have them as fire escapes. Look for one on the sides of the buildings."

We walked a ways, then Alice screamed and buried her face into John's jacket.

"Oh my gosh!" I said, dry heaving.

A dead body floating along the street in the water had drifted near us. It looked like it had been dead for sometime, because from what little I saw before I turned away, I couldn't tell the features any longer.

"Look, there!" John said, suddenly pointing to an iron stairwell.

We helped Reggie climb up and once we were on Level One, hobbled back to the car again.

"Let's get to this guy's house," Eddie said. "Then, I'll take a look at all of you."

"When the time comes," Reggie reminded him with a quiet smile.

Alice drove this time, and when we arrived at his apartment, we parked the car along the street and piled out together.

Reggie took another look at his tablet to confirm the address one more time, then pressed a button on the intercom of the apartment. It looked like this neighborhood was a little more middle class. The apartments were well taken care of with refurbished roots that kept the foundation of the buildings dry and mold free. And there were small bushes in pots lining each building for aesthetics.

"Yes?" said a voice over the intercom.

"My name is Reggie. May we come up?"

"Are you a cop?"

"No, sir. Just an old man and his friends. Please, if we could talk to you. It's important."

"Everything is important, but nothing is important at all."

"Sometimes a person can make a difference."

"There is nothing unique about a difference. A tapestry is woven from many different spools of yarn, but it is still only a tapestry."

"We have to try."

"Why should I care?"

"It's what makes us human," Reggie said, releasing the button finally.

We turned towards each other, confused. It didn't look like Mr. Bernstein would answer the door at all. But then the intercom came on again.

"That's right," he said as the door beeped. "A few of us are still human."

John caught the door as it unlocked. We limped up to Mr. Bernstein's apartment and knocked gently. A young man opened the door, tiny lips pursed between a long nose and sharp jawbone. He examined us, then his high cheek bones spread into a smile and his eyes twinkled with an amicable glow.

"You look like shit."

Potato Chips

"You know you guys shouldn't come here. I already got heat," Henry said as he opened the door and we hobbled in passed him.

"We just fell in an elevator," I explained.

"You need a doctor."

"I am one," Eddie said. "May I use your couch?"

"Sure."

Eddie brought Reggie over to sit on the couch and motioned Alexis over to sit beside him. Then he stood straight up, feeling his right arm with his left hand.

"I think I found out what's wrong with me," he said. "John, can you help me?"

John stepped towards him.

"On the count of three push my arm upward into the socket as hard as you can."

John took hold of his arm.

"1,2…3!"

They both let out a loud moan as they popped his arm back in the socket. Eddie writhed in pain for a moment. Henry was standing ready with a glass of red wine.

"Wine, huh?" he said as he took the glass and drank it down.

"It's the only alcohol I like."

"No worries. It's my favorite," Eddie said, then sat the empty wine glass on the coffee table and turned to Reggie and Alexis.

"I'm going to need you to drop your pants, Reggie. You aren't shy now are you?"

"Yes, I am!"

Henry interrupted.

"You can use my bedroom."

"Okay," he replied, helping Reggie up. "I'm going to need an old mop or broom. I'm going to need something to wrap it, like an old shirt or some gauze. And I'll need some alcohol or antiseptic."

"Okay," Henry said, running for a mop standing in the kitchen beside the fridge.

We overheard a lot of muffled conversation followed by low moans of pain from Reggie. When finally, Reggie came out of the room, he was splinted up in a makeshift splint with a broken mop handle strapped to his leg.

"That's some break," he said. "But I have so much adrenaline running through me right now I can't even feel it."

"You will," said Eddie.

"Are you okay?" asked Alexis.

"It's a fracture. But when we get back, we can fix it. Eddie got me covered for now. Thanks, Eddie."

"No problem," he said. "Okay, Alexis. You're next. Let me look at your finger."

"I think it feels better," she said, hiding her finger in her lap.

"Let me see."

Eddie brought her hurt finger up to his face and examined the bloated and bruised looking appendage. He felt around the bone and she squirmed in pain.

"Definitely broken," he said. "Henry, do you have a tongue depressor or something about that size?"

Henry went to the kitchen and fumbled through his cabinet drawers while Eddie cleaned the rest of Alexis' wounds.

"Will this work?" he asked, holding up a plastic knife that seemed to be the only thing left over from a Chinese takeout napkin packet.

"That will be fine."

Eddie rinsed her hand and then splinted up her left ring finger.

"This doesn't take the pain away, but it won't get any worse until we get home. What about you?" Eddie turned to me. "Are you sure you are alright?"

"Yes," I said. "I'm starting to feel a little achy, but I'm fine. How's Alice?"

Alice put her hand on my shoulder.

"I'm fine," she replied. "Eddie told me to not let myself fall asleep for awhile and tell him if I feel nauseous, dizzy, forgetful, or tired. So far, I don't feel any of that."

Alice had a bruise on her forehead but the skin wasn't cut deeply.

"Well, now that you've used my house for your personal hospital, wanna tell me what you're here for?"

Reggie looked at him with his old earnest eyes.

"We're looking for the Key to the World."

"Many fools look for the Key to the World," he scoffed. "Its secrets have been passed down to me, through my father and his father before him. But I've never found anyone that might be trusted to do right by it. How do I know our minds are in alliance?"

"We don't need riches. We need a new beginning. A world where the rich man has no power over the poor."

"Reset the game board, huh?" he leaned forward, intrigued.

"A reset of the entire world."

"I would have done it myself, but I like living. You got the balls for it?"

"We're willing to die," John said.

"But only one will be able to go," he said.

"Can't we go as a team?" Eddie asked.

"Only one can get in and survive," he said. "Look, we've said too much already. I've taken all the bugs out of this apartment, but people are still watching through the windows. Take me to your place. I'll give you the Key to the World if you promise to do what you say."

"If you come, you will be part of our team," Reggie said. "You won't be able to ever go back."

"A life lived under surveillance versus a new start and a little adventure," he said sarcastically. "I think I'll take the latter."

We arrived at the wilderness reserve, but instead of driving onto the hidden path, John drove passed it and stopped the car along the road.

"What's wrong?"

"I saw boot prints near the entrance."

"Go to the warehouse and park there for now," Reggie instructed.

"Awe, it's already getting dark," Alice complained. "I was hoping to see my babies tonight!"

"We'll be there in the morning," Reggie said. "We can't take any more chances."

We drove down the long forested road to a small vacant warehouse that could be seen from the highway. It looked like an old abandoned factory, windows broken and boarded up. Concrete walls cracked and crumbled from decades of neglect.

John drove behind the warehouse to the back entrance where trucks once pulled up to drop off deliveries. He stopped there, got out, and lift up the metal door to the factory. Then got back into the car and drove inside, parking in the cold building along aisles of dusty metal shelves.

We all got out, led by the sunset shining into the open garage. Reggie hobbled to the worktable and lit some candles. He set them around the room and Alexis took out a flashlight from the car glovebox.

Henry jumped out of the car and began exploring the warehouse.

"An old toy factory!" he said, happily.

He plucked an old dusty doll from one of the empty shelves with his long slender fingers and examined the cobwebs in her hair.

"Luckily, I always bring a few blankets in the trunk," John said, pulling them out and passing them around.

"I left some food and supplies in the office from last time," Reggie said, seating himself on the cold cement floor as John tossed him a blanket. "Take Eddie and go get them, will you?"

"Yes, sir," said John, taking the flashlight from his hands.

I laid the other blanket out for the rest of us to sit on and Reggie did the same with his.

"Get ready to be in the dark," Alexis said, reaching up for the factory door handle. Then she slid the metal door down to the ground.

"It's kind of eery in here," Alice said as we listened to the wind whistling through broken glass windows.

"And cold," I added.

Even with our fancy jackets on, I could feel the chill on my hands and face.

"It's only for tonight," Reggie said. "You don't need a blanket under you. Put it around your shoulders and cover up."

I gathered up our blanket and wrapped it around Alice and my body, nuzzling into each other for warmth.

"Body heat," I sighed.

The boys came back with a box of supplies.

"Thanks for keeping her warm," Eddie said. "Now give me back my girl."

We laughed.

"You'll have to share tonight," I teased. "That's why I have two arms!"

"There wasn't much in there," John said, tossing the box down in front of us. "A lot of bags of chips."

"Chips for dinner!" Alexis exclaimed. "My favorite."

"So," Reggie started. "Mr. Bernstein. Tell us about the Key to the World."

Henry slinked over to us and slouched down, his skinny knees protruding from his body like spider legs as he balanced himself on the balls of his feet.

"I guess this place is safe as any," he said. "As you know, my great, great, great grandfather built a supercomputer for the United States. It stores everything on it. Census information, financial information, you name it. Do you guys know anything about computers?"

"I don't," I blurted.

"We have all types of backgrounds," Reggie disclosed. "But Alexis and Alice are great with technology."

"Okay," he said. "So, you have one central server. It's a main computer hub. And it speaks to all these other computers that are part of a server farm. Those computers go out to the others. Follow me?"

He jumped up, like a spider leaping into the air. His face flashing in the candlelight like a madman as he tried to contain all the information he had and translate it for us into laymen's terms.

"Well, my Great Great GG was a pretty smart guy. He decided the government was pretty much corrupt and based on his findings on the nature of man, the direction we were going politically in the early 2000s..."

He waved his hands up in the air as he spoke, pacing back and forth. He was so excited about what he was saying he'd drop a few words here and there, making it hard to follow him.

"He put a safety on this unstoppable computer system and didn't tell anyone about it. It's a way to wipe the system if the government gets out of hand. Like now, us being in a second freaking Holocaust."

"So, how do we stop it?" Reggie asked.

We leaned towards him, searching for his form in the darkness as he paced in and out of the light.

"It's hidden, but hidden in plain sight. The main server is in a room. But the walls are also part of the wiring. You got to climb up into the ceiling. There's a place. A different room. No one knows about this. It looks like nothing. No reason to even look up there. You can't break into the system from anywhere else. It's secure and even I can't get into that. But up in this little space is a key hole and another computer display. It's a way in."

We all smiled.

"What do you do once you're in there?" Eddie asked.

"You take this key. I have it. You unlock the system. Once you're in, you can delete the entire operating system software with a virus. It'll disable the security software, access the hard drives, the servers, and all the connected computer networks, and like dominoes, everything will be wiped clean across the globe."

"A new beginning," Alexis said.

"But what is a new beginning?" Henry said. "You'll have to have a damn good plan. Once there is no information on anyone, there will be total chaos. That's why no one has ever tried. It's foolish."

"It will be one problem solved," I said. "If we are all equal, then Americans won't be enslaved by the rich man any longer."

"There will always be a rich man," Henry said.

"We'll have no identity, so no one will be able to separate themselves and be better than the other," Alexis said.

"It's better than we have now," John said.

"Someone will have to show the world the cure for cancer. Someone will have to rewrite the constitution," Eddie said.

"It's clear there will be a lot of work to do," Reggie said. "But this is our best chance to change anything. As long as the rich hold the cards, nothing will change. And they hold the cards with their wealth."

"King of the mountain, Reggie," Henry said. "King of the mountain. But I'll give you the key anyway. What the hell."

"I'll go," said John.

"No," Henry interrupted. "The space is small. Whoever goes will have to fit in an opening like a square about two feet wide. And it's high. You'll have to climb up into the ceiling about as high as your average ceiling."

We all looked around. Everyone's eyes fell on me.

"She should do it," he said as he gave me a hard look.

I blushed.

"Oh, I don't know," I said, shaking my head no.

"Of course we'll all be there helping you get into the building in our own way. It will take a team to break into the facility, but only one will get in. And the guards will be following close behind. Any other person will just get themselves killed. They won't be able to hide. No, she should do it."

The way he spoke those words was almost perverse, making me recoil instinctively.

"You can do it, Stephanie," Eddie repeated. "We'll all be there for you."

"You'll have to train harder," Reggie said. "You'll need upper arm strength."

"I'll do what I have to do."

We all grew quiet after that. I, sitting in the dark next to Eddie, listening to the sound of plastic chip bags being torn open and the crunching noise of chips crumbling against hungry teeth. Then suddenly the chips were all eaten and the candles were left to flicker and dim in the cold April night as we fell asleep.

Bodies were flying slow motion in every direction as we fell. Limbs severing and necks breaking against walls which enclosed us like a coffin. And as the elevator crashed down to the ground, my body broke apart into a million pieces, sprawling and spiraling into a new dimension. This time my hands were tied behind my back, and I found myself sitting in a wooden chair with eyes squeezed so tightly shut blood seeped from the edges rather than tears.

A group of boys poked at me, laughing and skipping around the chair.

"Stop it!" I cried. "Let me go!"

But their jabs grew closer and their taunts, louder.

"She thinks she's better than us," one boy said to the others.

"She's not better now," jeered another.

My body trembled and they laughed at my trembling, tossing their heads back as they reveled in my frailty.

"Please," I begged.

"We'll see who's better now," said the leader as he reached for the button of his jeans.

The Love Triangle

"Stephanie," Reggie said, shaking me. "Stephanie."

My eyes opened and I found myself back in the warehouse where everyone was sleeping soundly. Reggie's face was lit up by the very last candle to remain flickering. Burnt down till it was just a flame in a metal holder surrounded by a shallow pool of melted wax.

"You were having a nightmare."

I sat up, wiping the sweat away from my face.

"Wanna talk about it," he asked, gently.

I looked at him quietly, unsure if I should tell him or if I should avoid the subject like I always did. But after the whole incident with the police chasing us, I found I needed a friend.

"When I was sixteen there was this guy. We were competing in our class for this science fair. The winner was going to get a scholarship to college. It was a pretty awesome chance for us..."

I paused, letting myself fade back into that time again.

"Well, he told me not to win. He said if I did, he'd teach me a lesson. His mother was very sick and like everyone, we were all in debt and desperately needing a way out. But I had this great idea. I made a little robot that babysat children. It made sure they didn't fall or go down stairwells and kept them safe when the parents were busy. I wasn't sure if it would win the fair, but it did. Well, after the fair, I was walking out to my car when his friends and him surrounded me. They tied me up in the back of their truck and dragged me down to the basement of his house. Then, raped me. The whole bunch of them took turns."

I wiped away the tears from my eyes.

"Now you know," I said. "You know too much about me."

I tried to hide the tears behind a few forced giggles.

"I'm sorry that happened to you, Stephanie."

"Well," I said. "I never went to college on the scholarship. Thought it would remind me too much of being raped. So, I became a teacher instead."

"I know you're confiding in me," he said. "I'm glad to be a good friend to you. Just so you don't feel so exposed, I'll tell you a little secret about me."

"Okay," I sniffled, listening.

The candle began to vanish and then flickered up again.

"Eddie's mom and I were in love."

"No way!" I gasped.

"Yes, we were. Her name was Monica and she was the love of my life. But Dr. Levine was also in love with her."

"What happened?" I asked.

"We had a very wonderful romance. Had been together for several years, but while she was attending the University, she met Steven. That's his first name, Steven Levine. And he fell in love with her, also. He eventually asked her to marry him. Well, at the time we thought by marrying him, she could find the cure for cancer. We were both young radicals back then. So, she went ahead and did that. But he was a cruel man, and when he found out she was really in love with me, his jealousy consumed him. He took away her freedom, cutting her off from her University friends and her family. I didn't see her very much after that and he never told her where the devices were. Edward was born a few years later and I lost confidence we could ever be together. I always watched out for him though. He doesn't know I loved his mother. She passed away when he was still young."

"What did she die from?"

"A blood clot in her brain. It was very sudden."

"I'm sorry," I said, patting him on the back.

"You know that statue outside his mansion?"

"Yeah?"

"That's Monica," he said, smiling. "She was a beautiful woman. She took a piece of my heart with her when she passed."

The candle died away.

"I'm sorry," I said.

I took his hand and then a long yawn escaped my mouth. "Maybe we should get back to bed."

"Won't have too long to sleep. It's already about four. But rest anyway. I'm going to go looking for a coffee maker."

"Okay," I said, pulling the blanket back up over my body and nuzzling myself into Eddie's warm embrace.

Then, I closed my eyes.

We kept the car parked at the warehouse and walked back on foot in the morning.

"I can tell spring is coming," I said.

"Listen to those birds," Alice replied, happily.

"And I think the trees have grown even more buds!"

"Let's not talk," said Alexis. "That guy could be anywhere."

"Sorry," I apologized.

I was startled by the sound of a stick crackling, but it was just a family of deer grazing in the distance. We trekked through the snow dusted ground for many miles, following the long dirt road towards the garage, venturing deeper into the forgotten woods while John examined the ground for footprints as we went. The sun grew brighter and brighter in the sky, melting what was left of the snow into a slushy mess that trickled into the creek.

The creek was raging in some parts from the onslaught of melted snow, but still mounds of snowfall traced the river edge and spotted the dense forest. I held Reggie's hand at times to help him across the rocks and tricky puddles of water along our path. The others saw we were okay, so advanced a little farther than us, stopping every once in awhile to wait while we climbed up a hill before disappearing again over the top of the edge.

Reggie whispered to me as he took my hand.

"Look up dear," he said, taking my hand in his old weathered one, so I'd stop.

I looked up and before I could make out the shape, a huge bald eagle took off in the trees above us, stretching its massive wings above our heads in a majestic display. For a moment, its large wings spanned a good six feet wide above our heads. Then, the beautiful bird vanished beyond the mountaintops.

"Wow!" I gasped.

"Nature is truly amazing," he laughed.

For a brief time, we forgot we may have been followed. But we were instantly reminded by the sound of boots approaching from behind. I stopped in my tracks and ducked down, but Reggie didn't have time to hide. He twisted around taking out a gun from his side holster.

"Smith!" he shouted, lowering his weapon.

"I finally found you," he said, running up to us. "I got that guy over by the garage. He had found it alright. Tried to shoot me."

"Was he a fed?" Reggie asked, giving him a pat on the back as he greeted us.

"Most likely an independent contractor hired by the feds to follow us. That one got pretty close."

"Well, do us a favor and run up to the others. They're as scared as hell, you know."

"What happened to you?"

"That's a story we'll save for home. Go on now," Reggie said, waving him away.

When the others found out we were safe, they were so relieved they began running the rest of the way home. Smith came jogging back to us to grab the keys and then went off to retrieve the car. Reggie and I took our time with his broken leg. Sometimes we stopped along the river and just took in the wilderness and its creatures large and small. If we sat really still and watched the moist soil, we could make out very tiny blades of grass peaking above the ground.

"They all go too fast," I said. "They're missing this. It's beautiful here."

"That's what I like about you, Stephanie."

Reggie leaned back against a rock, dipping his fingertips in the cool river behind him.

"You have a pure heart. Keep looking to the simple things. There's always happiness in the simple things. Folk look too hard for the fancy things. But, fancy things make you broke and miserable."

"That's probably right," I smiled.

When we finally made it home, it was late afternoon and the sun was beginning to come full circle in the sky.

I helped Reggie into the compound and we joined the others who were relaxing in the living room. Sage and Michael ran up to me, giving Reggie and I a big hug. They had their toys out as always on the carpet. Mom was sitting close by, happy to be home with them.

"Home sweet home," Reggie said.

"And where are *my* babies?" I asked.

"I got them in with the other dogs," Smith said.

"I want to see them," I said, skipping happily off to meet them.

When I arrived on the farm, I walked out to where the cows were grazing and found the wolves sitting underneath an orange tree beside a female German Shepherd. They sprang up, barking, and ran to me excitedly.

"Adam! Sasha!" I shouted, kneeling down to them and giving them a huge hug as their tails wagged exuberantly. "You look like you've grown in only a couple days!"

They had already doubled the size they were when I had found them and were beginning to take on average puppy features, with oversized paws and little round stomachs. But they had grown even longer in their body in the days I had been away, and now their fluffy grey fur spread over their body in long strands.

"So," I said, looking over at the old German Shepherd. "You've been taking care of them?"

The dog panted under the tree tranquilly and then rest her head lackadaisically on her large black paws.

"Thank you, Abby."

I sat in the grass with them. Then, Eddie came up to me and sat beside us quietly.

"You'll have to train them while they're young."

"I know."

"I'll get some meat scraps from the slaughter house. Wait here a minute."

He came back with some scraps of cow guts and the dogs shot right up for them.

"Sit," he said, holding his hand up with palm to his chest.

"You use hand signals?"

"If you can't speak, you can still use your body to command them," he said.

He corrected them with a 'uh-uh' and showed them the treat again.

"Sit."

Adam sat and Eddie gave him the treat.

"Now you try," he said, giving me a scrap of meat as Adam popped up for it again.

"Sit," I said, giving him the same hand signal. "Uh,uh... Sit... Uh,uh. Sit."

Adam sat for me and I gave him a treat.

"Try it again."

"Sit," I said.

Adam sat right away, but Sasha trailed off. I gave a treat to Adam again and started following Sasha, shouting, "Sasha, sit!"

She turned back to me and like she was giving a human smile, took off at full speed as I raced after her.

"Don't chase her, she'll go further!" Eddie warned, but she was already far off, so I ran after her anyway. Adam jumped up next to me, trying to catch the long strand of cow gut flowing from my hands.

Sasha stopped at the entrance of the tropical biome, barking fervently. When, I caught up with her, I pushed the door lever, popping the metal door open. Then, Sasha trotted into the jungle ahead of me and disappeared into a conglomerate of over-grown tropical plant species.

"It's so beautiful," I gushed as a bunch of butterflies scattered above us in the humid air.

"Not as beautiful as you," he said, taking my hand and leading me to a bench in the midst of a dense forest of banana trees whose long green leaves sprawled up into the tall dome ceiling.

"Remind you of something?" he asked, sitting me down on a bench.

I smiled.

"Yes!"

He kissed me on the lips.

"Is a garden bench our place now?" I asked.

"My place is with you," he said, kissing me again. "I missed you. I've wanted to hold you and kiss you, but there was so much going on. I love you so much."

"I love you, too," I said, moving my face away from his kisses and looking towards the wolves. "We got to get Sasha. Who knows what kind of alligator or something they keep in here."

Eddie laughed.

"They don't have alligators in here. Let's make out," and brought me back towards him.

But Adam and Sasha found their way back to us and jumped on our legs like jealous children as we kissed. Eddie's strong hands groped me yearningly. Then suddenly, the man-made sky let down a shower of warm water, and we ran out of the biome in a fit of laughter.

A Year Later

"Go on Stephanie! You can do it!"

"Keep going! You're doing great!"

I let out a long high pitched moan, stretching my neck up from my shoulders as far as I could, arms shaking uncontrollably. My head was above the square opening and my eyes could see the wooden floor they had fashioned for me to practice, but I couldn't manage to get my arms up over the opening to heave the rest of my body up.

I jumped back down to the floor, defeated. Eddie knelt beside me.

"You'll get it, Stephanie," he said, kissing my cheek. "You're a lot better."

"She's not going to get it," Alexis said. "It's been a year. Send somebody else."

"Why don't you shut up, Alexis!" Alice defended.

"Hey!" I said, stopping them from arguing. "It's okay. Alexis is right. Maybe it's better to pick someone else. Alexis can do it."

Alexis jumped up on the chair and then leapt into the air, catching the opening with her fingers. She did a swift pull up, poking her head into the makeshift room. It looked as if she was going to get through, but she couldn't squeeze her hips passed the opening.

Alice laughed as she came tumbling down to the floor.

"Alexis has a big butt!" she teased.

"You try it!" she said, catching her breath.

Alice jumped up onto the chair and then caught the opening with her hands, but it was obvious she wouldn't fit. She pretended to lift herself up and then jumped down onto the floor again.

"My shoulders won't fit."

Alice and Sage opened up the door to the gym and ran towards their mom. Reggie strolled lackadaisically in behind them.

"I see you're all having fun with Eddie and my fake computer room. Did she get up there yet?"

"No," Eddie said. "Not yet."

"Let's see you try again," Reggie said, sitting on the floor.

Sage jumped into his lap, forcing a small whimper of pain out of Reggie as she pressed her little bony elbows and knees into his thigh. Then, he gave her a big hug and she collapsed comfortably in his arms.

I took a deep breath, examining the opening. I knew if I got my elbows up there, I could push the rest of my body up. The problem was my pull-up had to be brought in tight for me to fit, with elbows touching my sides as much as possible.

"Whoever thought of this anyway?" I said. "What a silly place to put a computer!"

I jumped onto the chair and leapt into the air.

"Come on!" I shouted at myself, pulling my body up as much as I could.

This time my fists came all the way to my chest. I could see the top of the wooden floor and that success was close.

"Yes! Stephanie, keep going!" they applauded.

I let out another loud moan, lifting up my right arm enough to press one elbow onto the wood floor panels. Hooked my body onto the floor and rest for a moment, legs dangling in the air.

"That's good," Reggie commended. "But in the mean-time, someone's going to come in and find you dangling from the ceiling. So, you're pretty much dead."

Everyone laughed.

"Hold on!" I said, tucking my knees into my stomach.

"You can't get up that way," Eddie said. "You won't fit. You have to go up straight."

"Okay," I said.

I pushed from my secured elbow and my body came up over the floor like a fish flopping out of the water. I lay my exhausted body on the wood, panting.

"Perfect," Reggie applauded. "Just need to do it faster and without getting too exhausted, cause you'll have lot's to do once you're up there. No time to rest now."

"I'm just going to stay up here," I said. "I'm not coming down. I'm too tired."

"Don't forget to run," Reggie said, following the children as they ran out of the gym ahead of him.

After a few minutes, I climbed down. Adam and Sasha sprang eagerly to my side, their long fluffy tails whipping behind them as I strapped on my boots. They had grown to their full size over the year, but hadn't gotten the thickness in their bodies of older wolves just yet. Sasha's coat was streaked with black, especially in the face, giving her a distinct mask around her amber eyes. The black vanished down her back, giving way to a thick mix of grey and black and then reappearing in her tail.

Adam was almost completely grey with only a touch of black on his backside and a small V on his chest. The lack of black in his coat made his nose appear longer and his body leaner than Sasha's, whose black streaks accentuated her fluffiness like a husky. Adam had grown into a handsome and dignified wolf. Reserved in nature. Always sticking by my side and watching my every move. He was quick to train and an easy and helpful companion.

Sasha, on the other hand, was endlessly unruly and playful, leading me to wonder if her puppy-like character would ever go away. She loved to chew on old tires. Any other toy wouldn't last very long and became a mess on the floor. But she never chewed on anything she wasn't supposed to. I figured her to be intelligent, but stubborn and resolved to test the limits whenever she could. The wolves complimented each other nicely, and one personality gave me a break from the other.

"Okay," I said to them, standing up. "Let's go, guys."

The entrance to the compound was a circular hole in the ground with a round metal hatch that opened up to a small space fitted with a ladder bolted to one side. The ladder extended down about twenty feet before opening up into the living room. This proved troublesome for the wolves once they started growing, so we fashioned a little elevator system for them out of a rope, a wooden crate, and a pulley. It was shaky enough to freak out any animal, but Sasha and Adam had grown up with the contraption and were used to it.

I opened up the hatch and climbed outside. There was nothing like the feeling of warmth radiating from the sky and shining down on my body after staying in the biome for weeks on end. No manmade thing could ever take the place of our real earth and our beautiful star, the sun. I closed my eyes and opened up my palms, taking in a deep welcoming breath. Warmth seeping into every pore of my skin.

The wolves hopped on the elevator after I got out, and one at a time, I pulled them up by turning the thick rope attached to the pulley. After they jumped out, I clasped the door tightly closed again, making sure the dirt and sticks camouflaging the entrance were still intact. Even spreading a little more foliage over the entrance myself to help cover up the hatch.

The reserve was in full bloom. For a few weeks before the trees got their leaves, all the blossoms opened at once, painting the forest beautiful pastels. Sometimes as I ran, the wind blew and the trees gave up their petals into the air, which floated mystically down around me.

I never put the wolves on a leash. I figured they were half wild no matter what, so if they wanted to go, then I wouldn't hold them like domesticated animals. And with that trust between us, their bond with me somehow deepened and they enjoyed running off into the forest, racing each other and tiring themselves out by playing in the meadow or running after some lone deer who would gallop away in horror. But after running freely, they always found themselves by my side again, trotting down the path with me as I ran. And as far as running partners went, I liked them best. After about four miles, I'd start to slow down considerably. Then Sasha would nudge me with her nose behind my knee, as if to say, "You can do it. And by the way, I'm not tired yet, so don't stop."

Eddie and Reggie felt safe with me running with the wolves, but still made me wear my ear piece so they could call in to check on me. I'd find myself miles out and get lost in the beautiful landscape, and after about six miles, the wolves and I would stop and sit somewhere together, just looking out at the untouched countryside, enjoying the complexities of nature and its beauty all around us.

Adam let out a happy howl when we finally collapsed on some rocks at the top of the hill.

"I know, Adam." I said. "It's awesome!"

A meadow of yellow flowers sprawled over the hillside from where we sat. At the meadow's edge began a dense forest of red maples whose blossoms painted the hard woods blood red. And a small pond in the distance reflected the tree's beautiful silhouettes back towards the sky. It was all devastatingly beautiful. Then, the tranquility of the forest was disturbed by the harsh sound of two rifle shots cutting through the woods.

The wolves gave off a low warning growl. Their fur spiked up on their backs as they stared across the meadow towards the intruders.

"Let's go see," I told them, standing up.

We crossed the meadow slowly. Knee deep in flowers. Straining to see beyond the thick forest. The wolves seemed to already sense them. They sunk into the flowers, stalking the intruders like they did a deer. We hiked into the forest of red maple trees whose scarlet blossoms enveloped the blue sky above us. Then, the muffled voices of two men laughing grew louder. Their voices were lost in the thick maze of tree trunks.

The wolves growled, low and resolute. Keeping their front legs low to the ground. Ready to leap at them at any moment. I stayed hidden behind the trees, feeling my side holster for my gun. Listening.

"What a shit face!" one of the men shouted, lifting a beer bottle to his lips.

He took a huge swig from the bottle, then wiped the dribbled alcohol from his long mustache and beard.

"Let's see *you* make that shot!" the other said.

"I'll bring back two deer when we're done," he said, tossing the empty bottle onto the ground and raising his rifle eye level.

The men were standing only a few hundred feet from us, so I began retreating slowly into the cover of the forest. But the wolves kept growling, and one of the men turned towards us.

I gave Sasha and Adam an irritated look and put my finger up to my lips, instantly quieting them. They came to my side like two wounded children. I motioned for them to sit next to me as I hid.

"Did you hear that?" he said, listening to the forest.

"Sounds like a wolf. Let's get out of here."

But the other man didn't back away. Instead, he inched towards the sound. He walked slowly towards us with his neck stretched out and ears turned towards the trees, searching for the sound of a wolf.

"I'm not afraid of any wolf," he said, pointing his long rifle towards us.

He was dangerously close to us now, and I feared he would see Adam and Sasha through the forest if he came any closer. I could have easily hid behind the tree trunks, but the wolves were clumsy and large and didn't understand the violence of mankind. So, I motioned for Sasha and Adam to follow and took off running.

"Look!" the man laughed. "It's a girl! Get 'er!"

They chased after us. I sprinted away as fast as I could. One of the men fired some shots into the air towards me, most likely just to scare. Then they both laughed, letting out a sharp exultant howl as the bullet shells came tumbling down in the dirt.

"Look at the wolves with her!" the other exclaimed. "Hundred bucks you can't get that wolf."

"You're on."

Beyond the Surface

The men started firing at Sasha. She ducked from the bullets as they grazed passed her shoulder and raced away into the forest, weeping. Cornered at the edge of the lake, I took a chance and ran onto the water. My boots sensed the water immediately and lift my body up over the surface, skimming across the top level of the water like ice skates. I ran as fast as I could, water splashing up around me, trying to get my balance over the boots. Then fell over, sinking down into the cold lake water.

The men hadn't expected me out in the middle of the lake. They wandered off, hollering drunken threats which became a faint mumble as they stumbled away. I stayed out on the water, catching my breath and searching the tree-line for Sasha and Adam as the sound of bullets whizzing through the air grew faint.

It was an awesome feeling to be able to walk on the lake. The boots floated me back up to the surface. Balancing was hard, since the surface was always changing. I lost my equilibrium and my body leaned too far in one direction, toppling me into the lake again. Then I lift myself up out of the freezing water, drenched from head to toe and practiced walking again. With some focus, I could control my balance and skate over the water like an ice skater. I tried running and then jumped up and landed back in the water with a splash. Never sinking passed my ankles before the boots carried me like two small boats up to the surface again.

Adam and Sasha came back and whimpered softly for me at the edge of the water.

"That was a close one," I said, when I arrived back with them, combing my fingers through their fur to check for bullet wounds. "Let's go home."

"You should have called for help," Dj said.

"Next time, I'm going with you!" Added Eddie.

They were all in an outrage over my encounter with the hunters.

"Smith," I said. "I need to teach them how to fight with me."

"They'll never be a match to a gun," he answered.

"But if I can command them. If I can communicate to them when it's okay to attack. Then, they could help me."

"There is no way in hell we are going to train half wild wolves to attack humans!" Alexis chimed in.

"What do you think, Reggie?" I asked, hoping for someone to take my side.

Reggie had been seated at the dining room table with the kids playing a game, but most positively listening to us argue. He inhaled a slow deliberate breath and then expelled it all out onto the table in front of him.

"I believe Stefanie and the wolves have come to us for a reason. They're not going to hurt us because we are a part of their pack. But they could protect us."

He swept his eyes to John and I, who impatiently awaited his decision. We knew it would be final no matter what.

"Train the wolves."

"Next time," Eddie came up to me and took my shoulders in both his hands. "I'm coming with you."

Eddie stormed off as the others started to argue about whether or not it was a good decision. But Reggie seemed untouched by the commotion and continued playing games with the kids as only someone many more years older might do. Then, Ellen walked up to him and they spoke together, laughing in inaudible voices.

I detected something romantic in their body language. It was in the subtle smiles she gave while blushing and in his old eyes, flickering with a certain twinkle that could be nothing else but love. And the love I could see growing between them was founded on a deep respect. It was as if the many years in their age had given them time to linger a little more on each feeling, enjoying the tiniest nuance of each look and the simplicity of every touch.

No one of course had caught onto their secret other than myself. And I didn't say anything either. Their attraction seemed like a fragile thing to me. Like a flower. Or even more delicate than that. Maybe the years had taught them love is often accompanied by pain. Or maybe the ghosts of their old lovers were still clinging to them from death. Reggie had told me about his long lost love on that dark night in the warehouse. It would take time for him to understand it was okay to love again, and I certainly didn't want to destroy their opportunity by exposing them.

"Tomorrow, bring the wolves to the ranch. Abby knows how to fight," Smith said. "She'll help them train."

I nodded to him my approval and we all finally dispersed to our rooms. Later that night, there was a knock on my door.

"Come in," I said.

Eddie and I were laying on the bed together. Adam was at the foot of our bed and Sasha lay on the floor next to us.

"Hi, Ellen."

"Hope I'm not disturbing you."

"No, that's okay. We're just hanging out. What's up?" Eddie said.

"Well, I've got a present for you, Stephanie."

I sat up excitedly.

"Oo! What is it?"

Ellen brought a black suit out of her big canvas bag.

"It's something for you to wear on your big day."

"That looks so cool!"

"You'll be like an awesome super hero," Eddie laughed.

"Super heroine," Ellen corrected.

"I made it from the old spacesuits they have here. Reggie showed me this room where they kept all their experimental stuff. It's the same place we got the boots. The material is weather proof, but not bullet proof. But it is fire proof and can measure up to extreme cold or heat. So, I put a bullet proof plate in the front. Sorry if it's a little sexy. That's the only part of the suit that doesn't move well, so I just shaped it around your main organs. It should be thin enough to help you get through the opening and sleek enough to not get caught on anything."

"This is so cool!" I said, feeling the material. "May I try it on?"

"Please," she said, handing it to me.

I ran into the bathroom and tossed off my clothing onto the floor. And then wiggled myself into the suit. Thank God it was stretchy material, because for a scary second, I thought I wouldn't be able to fit into it. But the suit actually slid right on me and zipped up in the back. The material almost felt like spandex or some exercise outfit. It was extremely comfortable and breathable.

I opened up the bathroom door and Ellen and Eddie looked at me happily, Adam and Sasha only sighing in boredom and adjusting themselves as they slept.

"You better watch out Stephanie," Eddie said. "Someone's going to think you have super powers or something!"

Ellen laughed.

"Well, with her boots, this uniform will give her super human powers."

I sat down on the bed and Eddie gave me a kiss on the cheek.

"What's wrong?" he asked.

"I don't know if I can do this," I said. "I'm not a superhero. I'm a human being. And I'm actually a very feminine girly girl. They should make someone like Alexis do this. I bet she could kill somebody and not even blink."

"I don't see a girly girl," Ellen said, brushing my long brown hair out of my face. "I see someone who is very strong-willed. Who can even command two huge beautiful creatures to do her bidding. You are a key person in our team. Our family. And we will all stand behind you, helping you."

"Sometimes a hero is only what people see when they get a glimpse of them in action," Eddie said. "But no one knows about all the people and events that happened before that one heroic moment. No hero starts out strong. They have others helping to build them up. All comic books heroes have a turning point."

"Some experiment gone wrong," I said, remembering Hulk and about every other comic book hero.

"But there's always Batman," he said.

"Yeah, Batman is like a regular person, just some vigilante," Ellen smiled.

"Okay," I said. "You want me to be Batman?"

"We want you to be you," Eddie replied. "We need you. The one percent are out of control. We have to take this step. If you don't do it, then who knows who could?"

I rested my head on Eddie's shoulder and Adam came to me and put his big paws on my lap.

"Down," I said, smiling through tears.

"Don't worry," Ellen said. "That material doesn't rip easily."

"I have something for you, too," Eddie said, digging into his back pocket.

"You do?" I asked, surprised.

He pulled out a small pocket knife and handed it to me.

"This is my lucky knife," he explained. "I've had it since I was a kid. Maybe it can give you some luck."

"Thanks," I said, hugging him.

Suddenly, there was another knock on the door. This time it was Alice.

"I'll let you two alone."

Ellen left the room and I went to the bathroom and quickly wiggled myself out of my suit.

"You look cute," Alice said.

"I'm sorry. So embarrassing!" I said through the door.

"I knew my mom was making it for you. You're going to need it. That space is too tight for a suit jacket and pants."

I emerged from the bathroom and sat down on the bed again.

"What's going on?"

"I wanted to ask your opinion on something."

"What? Anything."

"Well," Alice hesitated. "I'm starting to like John."

"Finally!"

"It's okay?"

"Why are you asking my permission? You two have liked each other since you met."

"Really? You noticed?"

Alice leaned her elbow on the bed and I tossed a look to Eddie who decided it was best to leave the room.

"I didn't know if it was okay with the kids and all, but I think I'm falling in love with him."

"Alice, you deserve to be happy no matter what. John is a very nice guy. He'll be a great partner to you and a good father figure for the kids. You have my blessing, but you don't need it."

"Thanks, Stephanie."

She leaned in to hug me.

"I guess I'm scared."

"I know," I said. "I'm scared, too."

Der Angriff

"Abby, heal," Smith commanded.

Abby had been sitting lackadaisically under her favorite shade tree when he gave her the command. Instantly, her ears perked up and she leapt to his side, tail wagging left and right. Every time he looked at her, she cowered submissively to the ground, but her demeanor was that of a puppy despite her age. And she knew it was playtime. There was an urgency in her to begin although she sat obediently at his side. It was as if she had played these games many times before and they brought back some youthful vigor to her old bones.

Smith and Eddie had set up a huge obstacle course for us. There was a wooden wall that looked like a backyard fence reaching at least five feet high, another long brick wall standing only several feet off the ground, and a bunch of hoops on stands lined up together in the distance that looked like something from a circus or a horse racing track.

"You will be the only alpha from now on. No one else will train them in this and they will belong to you forever. Are you ready for that?"

Smith was looking me squarely in the face. His dirty blonde hair had grown unusually long for him, coming slightly over his ears and falling in short bangs over his forehead, hiding the three creases that appeared above his brow when he became overly enthusiastic.

"Yes," I said.

"Then, follow me."

Smith hooked Abby up to a leash and began leading her through the obstacle course.

"Heal," I told the wolves, following Smith and Abby.

Abby jumped up on the long path and started balancing effortlessly beside her master.

"Up," I told Adam.

Adam looked at me confused for a moment and then carefully climbed onto the short fence and followed behind Abby.

"Up, Sasha."

Sasha sat beside the fence, panting obliviously.

"Sasha, up," I said again, more sternly this time. Pointing my finger toward the brick wall.

In the meantime, Adam had jumped down off the wall. Then, Sasha licked my finger and wagged her tail.

"It will be harder with the two of them, but you can do it. Start with her first, then."

Eddie had taken a seat on the grass and was laughing at me. But, I gave him a dirty look and continued adamantly with the training.

"Adam, heal," I said. "Sit."

Adam came to my side and sat obediently.

"Stay, Adam."

"Sasha, up," I said again. Then, I gave her fluffy body a shove towards the fence.

"No, don't shove her. She'll do it."

Sasha was panting and her open mouth looked like the joker grinning from ear to ear.

"Sasha! Up!"

Smith led Abby back around and up the short fence again.

"See!" I said. "Like that. Sasha, up!"

She looked at me blankly for a few moments and then exhaled all her happiness and slowly climbed up on the fence, one lazy paw at a time.

I motioned to Adam with my hand to stay and started walking beside her.

"Good, girl!"

At some point she looked like she would stumble, but she never fell. We circled around to Adam and then I told both of them the command.

Sasha looked at me as if to say, "Again?" Then she jumped up onto the wall with Adam behind her and they both walked down the long path.

"The next is the hoops," Smith said, letting Abby off her leash.

"Jump," he commanded.

Abby jumped through each of the five hoops with the grace of a racing horse. Her coat was sleek and shiny. That of the best breed. And she looked magnificent jumping through the hoops.

"That's neat," I said. "Okay guys, did you see that? Jump!"

They both looked at me vacantly.

I couldn't help but laugh with Eddie, who was rolling on the grass now. Then I held my smile back and yelled, "Jump!"

Adam set his right paw on the metal loop and then hesitated and came back to my side.

"It's okay, boy."

Sasha walked straight passed it, unsure why she had to pass through the hoop at all when she could just walk around. Then she sat down, a giant pile of fur, with her long nose pointed at me, stubbornly.

"Let's lower the hoops," Smith said and began lowering each by loosening a small screw at the stem of the three legs. It looked to me like the hoop stands were made from old camera tripods. Smith lowered them all the way to the ground.

"Jump," Smith said and led Abby back through the hoops.

"Jump," I commanded.

This time the wolves followed my command and Abby's example and walked slowly through each hoop.

We did it a few more times.

"Should we give them a treat?" I asked.

"No" Smith said. "We don't give working dogs treats. We give them toys."

"My curiosity is sparked," I replied.

Smith and Eddie raised the hoops a few inches off the ground and we repeated the exercise. The wolves understood what to do and were very obedient, always following my command and sitting back down at my side to be praised.

In no time, we had them going down the brick fence and jumping through the hoops at about three feet off the ground. But Smith didn't start the wall training yet. He waited till the wolves were responding perfectly to my every command. After several hours, we took a lunch break, and then were back at it again.

This time. Smith raised the hoops four feet high. Abby jumped effortlessly through them and the wolves followed, but Adam knocked one hoop down sending Sasha into disarray.

"It's okay," I said, petting them. "Try again. Heal."

Eddie hopped to Smith's side to help prop up the hoops again while I walked the wolves through the brick fence yelling "Jump" as we approached the hoops.

One at a time, Sasha and Adam leapt into the air and went through each hoop.

"Good!" I shouted.

"Now they are ready for the wall," Smith instructed. We walked over to the wall and he climbed a set of stairs, taking a place on the platform behind the top. The wall was about six feet tall. On the other side was a wooden platform with a set of wooden stairs that allowed the trainer to stand on the other side and the dog to land safely after his jump. Smith took out an old torn white towel and Abby's eyes lit up and her tail whipped back and forth vehemently.

"Jump," he commanded.

Suddenly, Abby leapt into the air, grabbing the top of the wall with her front paws and pushing herself up over the wall. Smith pet her and gave her the towel, which she began gnawing on without delay.

I giggled.

"Cute!"

Smith climbed down the stairs and walked Abby towards us. She brought her toy in her mouth and laid it down on the grass to continue gnawing on it.

"I have some for you. They can't have any scent on it. Hold on and I'll get them."

Smith disappeared and Eddie and I fell to the grass, sighing.

"Training is exhausting!" I complained.

"I had no idea we'd be working this long."

"Of course. It's Smith. We should have known."

We both smiled. I gave Eddie a kiss, only to be separated by the wolves, who always vied for our attention.

After a few minutes, Smith came back with two white towels and handed me one of them.

"Now, start with Sasha and play Tug-of-war with her. Get her to really love and see this towel as her toy."

I took the towel from Smith and showed Sasha her new toy. At first she didn't care, but as soon as I started jumping around with it, she realized it was playtime and jumped up for it. Smith let us play for a long time. Then, he had Eddie grab an arm protector from the shed. I strapped it on and wrapped the towel over it, then repeated the play so she'd bite at my arm.

"Now tell her to stop. Tell her *calm*."

"Calm," I said, halting my play and turning my back to her.

She stopped because she had already seen me as the alpha and didn't want to hurt me. She hadn't associated the word yet, but my body posture told her how to act.

After repeating that kind of play for a really long time, I tried it with Adam. His slick grey body was larger and stronger, making it extremely difficult to keep the towel away from him. He got it a few times and trotted away from me victoriously with it, only to bring it back and tease me to play again. I made him drop it and then pet him on his head and we started over with the game of Tug-of-war. But when I put the suit on, he refused to bite my arm. He just pawed at it and then slouched down in front of me.

"Don't worry," Smith said. "There are other things he can do. Like sniff out explosives! Let's finish for today. Good work."

"How do you know all this?" I asked.

"Abby's father was an old New York police dog. My dad was in the K-9 unit of the police force before he did all that top secret stuff with the military. And the New York City Police department only get their dogs from the best breeders up in Germany. Abby's dad was internationally certified. The police station paid about $20,000 for him at the time, which was big money. They purchased him with seized drug money."

"That's a lot of cash for a dog!" Eddie exclaimed.

"But they do a lot of training beforehand with them. My dad kept Abby when I was just a teenager from one of the litters with her mate and he trained her just as well. We kept some of the German commands. You know, for the good stuff."

"German commands?"

"Yeah," Smith said as we walked back to the others, who were already eating dinner in the living room. "Like the command for 'attack.'"

"What's the German word for attack?" I asked, sitting down at the table.

Smith leaned into my ear and whispered it.

"Angriff."

Later that night, Henry called us all into a meeting. Our main computer was the heart of the entire compound and rested in a medium sized room with grey carpet and off-white walls. Three rows of desks organized like a schoolroom were lined up in the middle of the room in front of a glass wall overlooking the biomes. Each row held about five computers on them. I imagined the place would have been quite busy in its time. But now only Henry sat there as we all piled into the room.

Henry swiveled around in his black office chair rolling towards us on plastic wheels.

"I've brought you here because I've found them."

"You did!" Reggie gasped in delight.

"Found what?" I asked.

"The pods, of course!" Henry smiled.

He rolled his chair back around and typed into the keyboard of his computer. A hologram of a world map appeared on the wall in front of us as he typed.

"How many did you say there should be?" Henry asked Reggie.

"About five, we think."

Henry brought up a series of locations on the map as red dots.

"Try thirty-two!" he said as they all loaded up and displayed themselves.

"Wow!" Ellen sighed, walking up to the hologram. She lift her hand to touch one of the locations and it flickered away for a moment before reappearing.

There were as many as ten locations in America alone, another ten spread over Europe, and the rest scattered around the planet in all of the world's most powerful countries.

"What's the plan?" asked Alexis.

"We can't get to all those locations," Alice said.

"No," Reggie replied. "But we can make public all of the locations. I'm going to break into the satellite network and send a worldwide message after our mission is complete."

Michael ran into the room and stood next to Henry, happily.

"Michael, leave Mr. Henry alone. He's working," Alice instructed.

"That's okay," Henry said, patting Michael on the arm so he'd stay put. "He's my man. I've been teaching him everything I know. He's a smart guy."

I had been so busy getting ready for the mission that Henry had taken over some of the course work with the children.

I hadn't realized how close the two were becoming. Michael sat right beside him and started doodling on a tablet that was laying on the desk.

"Stephanie," Reggie started. "How are you doing with your training?"

"We're almost ready. I can get up more easily now."

"And the wolves?"

"Sasha is learning how to attack and Adam found his first explosive last week. We'll need more time with them, though."

"You have one month. We'll go in July. I've organized a place to stay where we can be close enough to observe and provide backup support.

"Did you ever find out where we're going?" Eddie asked.

"Used to be Forte Meade, Maryland." John interjected. "Now all that's underwater."

"Now they moved to the good old state of Kentucky," Smith said.

"I like Kentucky!" Alice burst.

"I didn't say anything bad about Kentucky!"

"Who would have known Kentucky would one day be beach front property?" John laughed.

"It's not beach front property. There's still a little bit of the Virginian states," said Eddie.

"Anyway!" Alexis cried.

"Lighten up," said Alice, laughing.

"Okay, y'all!" Reggie motioned us to stop. "Let's get back on track."

Alexis crossed her arms and let out a smug grunt.

"The short of the plan is to set up camp somewhere close to Forte Meade. We'll set up our computers to be able to link into their security system. We'll do some practice runs of getting you onto the base before you ever attempt the actual infiltration. Got you set up as a new hire already. Everything has to be perfect."

Alice stayed home with her kids. Our mission was going to take awhile. Possibly even months. Dj was the only other to stay. We even took the wolves, figuring they should remain with me now that they were trained. And it was going to be a long journey. Anyway, the wolves were part of our family.

As we drove away from the compound, I recalled the look on Alice's face when she said good-bye to us. It was one of those sad smiles. Overcome by her apprehension, shining conspicuously through wet blue eyes. John hugged her one last time, then grabbed her hand hard and tucked it into his chest.

"We'll be home soon," he told her. "I promise."

Those words shot into her smile like a missile fired directly onto a dam. Her grin cracked momentarily, sending a stray tear streaming down her face. But she didn't let her tears burst out just yet. She'd most likely wait till the moment we closed the hatch behind us, then fall to her knees crying.

"Watch over the place," he told Dj as he joined us and climbed up the ladder to the exit.

I had been feeling a little nauseated during our hike to the car and somewhat colder than usual. And now that we all sat in the van as it swayed through the mountains of New York, I began to feel an uncontrollable urge to vomit.

"Are you okay?" Eddie asked.

"No," I replied, holding my mouth. "I think I need you to stop the van."

Orenda Dances at Night

I began to dry heave, but shut my lips tightly together.

"Hey!" Alexis hollered. "Stop the van!"

Throwing up in the van would have most definitely made for an uncomfortable trip the rest of the way to Kentucky. Everyone had drawn the same conclusion at the very same moment and began waving their arms frantically at Reggie, hollering for him to stop at the top of their lungs.

Reggie pulled over fast. I opened the side door before the van could roll to a stop completely. Jumped out, body folding over into the tall grass. My breakfast exploded from my stomach.

Eddie toppled out and put his hand on my back as I vomited. I couldn't stop throwing up and when there was nothing left, I began to cry as acid came up and my throat strained harder, breaking tiny blood vessels that stained the yellow bile with red streaks of blood. When finally I stopped, everyone was silent except for Reggie who was speaking softly to Henry in the cab of the van.

"Change of plan, guys," Henry hollered.

I lay on the ground, my body trembling from both exhaustion and my rising fever. Eddie sat down beside the road, so I curled my body up into his lap while he pet my hair.

"You don't look very good," he said.

The wolves jumped out of the van and came to my side. They sniffed my face and laid down besides us, also. Then, Reggie hopped out and came over, kneeling down next to me. For a moment I tried to look at him, but then thought it too much work to open my eyes, so I buried my face in Eddie's lap.

"Can you make it for a few more miles?"

"Yes," I mumbled.

"I know a woman who will help you. She's Iroquoian."

We had to stop several more times before we finally made it so I could vomit more stomach acid out onto the side of the road. Then, finally we entered a small village of log cabins surrounded by a tall log fence boarder.

"Where are we?" asked Ellen.

"This is the home of one of the wisest ladies I know."

"I thought I was the wisest lady you knew," Ellen joked.

Reggie let out a hoarse guilty chuckle.

"Well, her name is Orenda Dances at Night, and she's a Seneca medicine woman. She's one of the last of her kind to maintain the customs of her tribe. They've rebuilt their population back up to fifty. Fifty souls live here like their ancestors once lived. This is a sacred place for sure."

A group of Iroquoian Natives came out of their houses to see who had come through the gate unannounced. The buildings were long wooden structures reminiscent of cabins, but that were semi-circle and cylindrical in shape. The main longhouse must have been over a hundred feet long, and some six other buildings stood at least twenty feet long.

Everyone got out of the van before me and walked over to the Natives. I sat at the door, watching them motion towards me in the distance, as if they were explaining why we were here.

"Come on," Eddie said, helping me down from the van.

Adam and Sasha had been watching the Iroquois silently from the van. When I got out, they jumped out behind me as well. The Iroquois gasped and lurched backward at seeing the wolves. For a moment they were frozen. Then spoke to each other about the wolves in their native tongue. Just then, an old woman, whose wrinkles were like the ripples of a sandy beach, walked steadily towards the wolves.

Her long white braids flowed down over her chest. She wore a long leather dress with beautiful necklaces draped over her bosom. Her brown leather moccasins were beaded along the ankle and there was something that looked like a rattle in her hand, made from a turtle shell. The wolves lowered themselves into a menacing posture, threatened by this elder who showed no fear of them. The fur between their shoulders raised up in long course spikes and their teeth showed as they snarled a warning.

Before I could give them a command to calm, the woman spoke a few words to them in her native language, raising her rattle into the sky.

Then suddenly, the wolves lay down on the ground and began panting comfortably like they were back at the compound.

"What did she say?" John asked.

Reggie laughed hard.

"She just introduced herself to them and told them they were welcome here."

The woman turned her old gaze towards me. Her face was like the bark of an elm. She put her nose right up into my face. I could smell the smoke in her hair now, she was so close. Her eyes were hazed over with cataracts, transfiguring the deep brown of her pupils into a strange blue grey. She squeezed her small lips together and the wrinkles above her upper lip showed like a mustache.

"Come," she announced, finally. "I will heal you."

She waved her right hand to the others and then they all departed. But several, whom we learned later were her grand-children and children came to our side.

A young teenage girl who was quite pretty had skipped up to Ellen. Youth had gifted her cheeks with a soft rosiness and her lips with a bright sensual pink. She came so close that Ellen might have tripped over her moccasins. But Ellen didn't seem to mind and smiled back tranquilly at the girl.

"Please," she said, taking Ellen by the hand. "Please stay with us. I have corn cakes inside. Please come."

Ellen followed her and we all entered into the largest of the longhouses through a doorway made of hung animal skins. There was a fire inside the longhouse and an opening in the roof that allowed the smoke to drift up and out of their shelter.

Orenda motioned for me to lay on one of the beds lining the middle of the longhouse. It was closest to the fire. She tossed a woven blanket over me and I fell right asleep beside the heat of the flames.

When I awoke, many hours had passed and no one was around but the old woman and the wolves. She saw I had opened my eyes and handed me something warm to drink in a small ceramic mug. I took a sip and concluded it must have been made from some of the local vegetation. It had a dull tea like taste and leafy aroma, and seemed to be sweetened with maple.

"I've been talking to your wolves," Orenda said in a raspy alto voice.

The inside of the longhouse was dark. I could hear kids playing outside. And as I searched for them through the entrance, I could only see a very bright light shining through the doorway. It must have been midday. Resolved with my inability to do anything else, I collapsed my head back down onto the bed.

"I'm reminded of a story," she began, putting a large pot over the fire.

I tucked my arms into the blanket, shivering. Sasha got up and lay on top of my legs and Adam sat up next to me and begged for a kiss.

"I'm okay, Adam. It's just the flu."

"There once was a camp of Minnekoju who lived near the Crow Indian. One winter, their people were raided by the Crow and a young girl was taken by them for their bride. She was not happy with the Crow and wanted badly to escape, so the Crow women gave her a blanket and some food and told her to hide beside the creek. As the Crow men chased after her, a blizzard hid her and she escaped."

Orenda sat her old body down in a rickety wooden chair beside the fire. The chair creaked under her weight. She waited, as if she were reliving the story in her mind. Letting it play out in front of her eyes like a movie and catch up with her. Then, she let out a long sigh and continued.

"As she wandered in the blizzard, she became lost and a pack of wolves found her. They drug her away and brought her to their den. The young girl thought they were going to eat her, but instead the wolves brought her a newly killed deer. Then, the girl and the wolves lived together for a very long time. She began to smell like them and she learned the language of them. She took their food and prepared dried meat for her to eat in the winter. But still, the girl thought of her family."

Her voice filled the air like the deep tones of a water drum. Each word that bellowed out of her lungs, trembled like a dancing spirit in the smoke of the fire.

"Years later, some hunter wolves spotted the young girl's mother beside their den, so they came back and told her. The girl decided to go back and see if her tribe would take her back, even though she smelt like the wolves. The wolves told her to wave her blanket twice if she wanted to stay and once if she wanted the wolves to take her back with them. When she returned to her family, her family was very happy to see her because they had thought she was dead. So, the young girl waved her blanket twice and the wolves returned to their den without her. Her people then called her Iguga Oti Win, Woman who lived in the rock."

"Iguga Oti Win," I repeated, finishing the concoction she gave me.

"But I shall call you Tha:yo:nih No'yeh."

"What does that mean?" I asked.

"It means Wolf Mother," she smiled, and her bare gums glistened in the firelight. "That is the language of my tribe, the Seneca."

"Thank you," I said. "Please say it one more time for me."

"Tha:yo:nih No'yeh."

"Tha:yo:nih No'yeh," I repeated, weakly.

"Sleep now, my child," Orenda said. "There is still a sickness inside of you."

I awoke the next day, feeling much better. I was able to eat some breakfast with everybody and spent the morning lounging in the courtyard while the village children played.

"Orenda," Reggie said. "Thank you for everything. I think we'll be leaving this afternoon."

"It is better to stay, my friend," announced Orenda.

"But I feel better," I said, coughing.

"The sickness is still inside."

"Sickness?" Reggie asked.

Orenda stood up from her chair and walked over to me.

"In three days she will fall ill again," Orenda said, touching my chest. "She has... What do they call it in your language? Pneumonia?"

"Well," Reggie said. "If Miss Orenda says she has pneumonia than we should trust her. Do you all mind staying?"

"No," John replied, tossing a ball to one of the children.

"It's kind of cool here," Alexis said.

"We should probably get going as soon as possible," Smith interjected. "But if Steph gets sick, there's no use going anyway, so what the heck."

"Well," said Ellen. "There you have it. It's unanimous."

As the day wore on, I didn't feel particularly bad. I just had a slight cough and was terribly congested. But on the third day, just as Orenda had foretold, a fever started and I began coughing uncontrollably. Orenda decided it was time to perform the healing on me.

I lay on the bed with my persistent cough. The coughing attacks were suffocating me. I could barely get a breath in-between the coughing fits. My whole "family" sat next to me the entire day and into the evening. Sometimes I listened to their light conversation, and at other times I'd fall asleep, only to be awakened again by the rhythmic coughing.

When the sun set, Orenda entered with her family members. Only this time their faces were hidden by heavy hand-carved wooden masks. Some masks were red and others, black, with noses painted twisted and contorted and eyes frozen in terror. The Iroquois inched closer to me in the firelight, coming at me with a certain primitiveness. Knees bent. Shoulders slouched.

"The spirit medicine man was a great healer. He had a love for all living things," Orenda said.

Her voice was muffled through the twisted mouth of the mask.

"He met a stranger and they held a contest. Their contest was to move a mountain. The stranger made the mountain shake, so the medicine man said, 'You do have skill as a medicine man, but you cannot move the mountain.' Then he moved the mountain so quickly that the stranger broke his nose on it. After that, the medicine man showed him everything he knew. This stranger became a famous healer named Old Broken Nose."

She took up her turtle shell rattle in her hand, raising it high above her head.

"This is why we wear the masks. They are the masks of Old Broken Nose and they are sacred to us. They are alive with his spirit."

Orenda's son lit a pipe and began spreading it to everyone in the room. Orenda spoke in her native tongue, shaking her rattle like a maraca. Sasha and Adam stood up and began pacing the room and then Sasha gave out a long howl.

I felt an energy in the room with us, lurking in the heavy air. I tried to get up to see who was there and thought I saw someone standing in front of me in the smoke, but the figure was illusive and my eyelids grew too tired to keep open.

A deep sleep overtook me. I found myself walking with the wolves in the hills beside the compound. But these hills spiraled up and down like the tracks of a roller coaster. And the greens of the grass were blurred into a fog so it seemed like I wasn't walking at all, but floating along like a ghost.

I caught a glimpse of some people in a deep valley beyond the hillside and motioned to Adam and Sasha to come with me and see. As we floated closer, I became as wide and light as the sky and the wolves became two large fluffy clouds beneath me. We gazed down at the people in the valley together. As I looked at the people below, I realized I was viewing my own self tied to a chair.

"Get up!" I shouted to myself from the sky.

As I uttered the words, my voice roared like thunder and my anger became two lightening bolts crashing to the ground.

My own self was soaking wet, and the boys around her were dancing in the rain. Their laughter was out of control, like the giddiness of an insane clan of youth overcome by a spell of intense mania. They stomped their feet in the mud and it splashed up onto their pants and on their faces, causing them to laugh even harder.

"Get up!" I shouted again.

The sky darkened, but my own self still sat in the chair in the rain, crying as my voice became a rumble of thunder rolling through the sky.

Suddenly, a brilliant light cut through the clouds. And in that small beam of light, a small pocket knife floated down to me.

"Put it in your sleeve," whispered the light.

My sky self tossed the small knife down to my own self, tied to the chair.

"Get up!" I roared one last time.

Then, I saw the wolves, and their mouths were full of blood, and the blood dripped down their fur, staining the fur deep red. They stared at me emotionless. The yellow of their eyes was like a yellow ocean, and the ocean grew bigger as I looked closely at them. I was able to see the world swimming in their eyes.

Suddenly, I found myself walking through Times Square in New York. And beneath my feet were the corpses of all ages of people. Even a young girl in an Easter dress lay lifeless on the ground. I cried at seeing her, because I knew it was my fault these people were dead. It had been my storm that killed them.

I looked up at the famous Times Square billboard sign and the lights of the sign flickered and formed the shape of a man. The man was speaking to all the dead people, and he told them he was a king, but I knew he was only an impostor. I could see in his eyes the blackness of greed. And the bodies laying on the ground mounted up into piles and burst into flames.

I pinched my nose closed as the stench of burning flesh permeated the air. Suddenly, large white wings grew on my back. I could hear the heavy wings beating behind me, taking me up into the sky. There, I sat with my wolves a long time, looking down remorsefully at the devastated earth until the light poked again through the black clouds. I lift my hands up to capture some of the light in my palms. Took the light and flew through the grey sky with the wolves who swirled at each of my sides like clouds gliding along the wind. And I spread out the light over the entire land.

In a single moment, I was back at the compound with Adam and Sasha walking beside me. They began digging in the dirt of the hillside, so I looked into the hole to see what they were showing me. A small pink flower was growing out of the earth, but the flower was not full grown. It was a tiny sprout that had budded and barely opened. So, I sat with the flower and began praying on its behalf and my prayers floated away in the wind.

Orenda was muttering quietly in Seneca when I opened my eyes. The smoke of burning herbs had mingled with the fire and was swirling up out of the hole in the roof of the longhouse.

I felt something come up from my lungs and coughed a very hard wet cough, spitting up a glob of mucus onto the floor.

"Thank you," I said to Orenda the next day as we walked towards the van.

"You are welcome anytime!" Orenda said, giving me a loving hug.

She pet the wolves, muttering some words in her language to them. We were climbing into the van, but she stopped me.

"Adam doesn't want to mate with his sister. Do not be afraid when he leaves."

New Kentucky

When at last we came to New Kentucky, we found the base of Fort Meade just outside of Lexington. Lexington was a vast city with giant skyscrapers surrounded by beautiful landscapes of free grazing horses wandering lackadaisically along the hillside. The ocean came almost all the way up to the tall barbed wire fence surrounding Fort Meade, which was actually on part of old Virginia. But so much of the Virginias and North Carolina had been overtaken by water they combined what was left of Virginia with the state of Kentucky and formed New Kentucky. And unlike other bases, where a flurry of houses made the base look like an inviting and well maintained suburban town, this military base was surrounded by a fence with motion detectors and high voltage electricity. Even the unlucky deer who found itself lost along the boundary's edge met an ill fate.

It was obvious by the security this base had something valuable inside. There were two security gates along the fence manned with armed guards who checked everyone's top secret clearance before entering post. Some of the guards were soldiers, but others were hired private top secret security.

And from what one could see at a distance, there were several buildings on post. One in particular was a long black structure with walls composed of black glass windows and a white roof with a helicopter pad. There was very little green surrounding this large building, because the cars in the parking lot spanned wide and far. And every one of those cars got checked before entering through the gate each morning. And every one of the employees possessed a top level security clearance.

People talk about Area 51, and I'm sure Area 51 has its secrets, but Fort Meade had become the technological center for the United States. If ever there was a reason to protect a base, this base would be at the top of the list, purely for its knowledge. While other bases were able to strike down a country with their nuclear weapons, Fort Meade could strike down a country's economy with one push of a button.

Fort Meade may have been well known for its security, but it kept its physical forces small and the base itself modest in size. That was no threat to the U.S. though, with Fort Knox standing just over a hundred miles away, known as an army training center, but revered by the army as a military manpower.

"We had to be somewhere within ten miles of the base in order to tap into their security system," Henry said as we drove up a long gravel driveway.

"Unfortunately, they do surveillance of anybody living within fifty miles of here, so it was tough finding a place. But this farmer's family has been here for a few hundred years. They have family members who have passed due to the Cancer era, and they say the base disturbs their farm. So, they're ready to help."

Everyone came forward to the cab of the van to get a better look at the house. It was a brick house surrounded by a white wooden fence. Horses were sleeping and grazing along the fence as content as a postcard. The lawns were beautifully mani-cured and there was a sense of tradition about the place and a tranquil energy. A wooden bench swing was hanging from the front porch and a few pots full of summer flowers lined the edges of the steps leading to the driveway.

The front door was open, but the screen door was fixed shut, and I could see a figure standing behind the screen, although I couldn't make out their details.

When we parked the van, the screen creaked opened and an old couple stepped onto the porch hollering.

"Hello. Welcome!"

"We're so excited to have you. Please come inside," said the man. "Park the van in the barn. Will ya?"

He peered into the passenger side window and added in a whisper tone, "Are the wolves in there?"

"Yes, sir," Reggie replied.

"Will they hurt us?" asked the woman, coming to his side.

"No," Smith said. "They're trained like a regular dog."

"We have a dog, but we put him away. Didn't want no harm to come to him."

"That's okay," I said. "We can introduce them and they'll be great friends, I'm sure."

My voice was still quite raspy from the pneumonia. The old couple gave a nod and we slid open the van door. Everyone got out and the wolves jumped out behind me. The July sun was bright in the sky and the air was humid and sticky. I put my hand over my forehead to shield the brightness of the afternoon.

Adam and Sasha looked very out of place on the farm. They were large and menacing, with the majesty of lions, and seemed to be characters out of the wrong story.

"We live with our son and his two children. They're some seventeen and nineteen years-old now. Wife died of cancer back in 2065," said the man, looking apprehensively down at Adam who sniffed his calloused hand.

"They'll be back around suppertime," the woman added. "They work in the fields. Putting up a fence now. But they'll be back and you can meet 'em then."

"And your names are?" Ellen asked, putting out her hand to shake the woman's.

"My name is Janet and this is Clark."

"Hello," Ellen said, shaking her hand with a huge welcoming smile. "My name is Ellen. You've spoken to Henry and Reggie. This is Stephanie, Eddie, Smith, Alexis, and John."

"And the pup's names are?" Clark asked.

"The grey one is Adam and the one with the black is Sasha."

"Well, pleased to meet y'all. Will the wolves be needing to stay in the house, cause we prefer to put 'em out back?"

"Do you have an old barn?" Reggie asked.

"Well, we don't want those wolves scaring the livestock, but we got a shed out back. It'll fit the all of you's if you wanted. We don't use it much anymore."

"Thanks very much!" Reggie said, shaking Clark's hand.

"Well, bring out your things and get washed up," Janet instructed. "I'll start making supper."

When supper was ready, Janet brought in more chairs for all of us to sit at the dining room table. Then, she served a huge feast for us, saying grace politely before we all started eating.

"This is delicious!" John said, scooping a fork full of hot buttery mash potatoes into his mouth.

"Glad you like it," said Clark.

"So, Thomas, was it?" Smith turned to the man next to him. "Do you hunt?"

"Sometimes we get some elk around these parts. Mostly wild turkey now that the whole Global Warming thing happened."

Thomas had angled himself towards Smith and rested his right arm on the table, curling his hand into a tense fist. He shook it around, like he was shaking off his nerves. He was sunburned from working outside all day. The sunburn went through his thin dirty blonde hair, causing a little bit of flakiness from the dead peeling skin. But the anxiety from being spoken to had changed the pink of Thomas' sunburn to a bashful red that spread down his neck like a rash.

"I'm a hunter myself," Smith said. "What do you use?"

"Winchester 94," replied the young boy. "And sometimes we get a wild hog with it!"

"You don't say?"

Hunting was definitely not my kind of conversation, so I started another one.

"So, ma'am. Can I trouble you for some raw meat for the wolves?"

"Go right ahead," Janet said. "Anything in the freezer is fair game, except the turkey."

"We'll be paying you for the inconvenience of course," Ellen added.

"The kitchen freezer?" I asked, getting up from the table.

"Naw," the young girl said. "We got one out back in the barn used for keeping the slaughtered meat."

"Oh," I said. "Thank you."

"I'll show you where it is, ma'am," she said. "I haven't got a good look at your wolves yet and I'd like to see 'em."

She got up excitedly from the table, tossing down her napkin over her plate.

"What's your name again?" I asked.

"Linnea."

"Okay, Linnea. Come with me."

We walked outside to the shed. It was as large as a single story house. The wolves were upset they had been left alone. When they heard us coming, they sprang to the door and started whimpering.

"Okay!" I said, opening up the heavy shed doors. "Mommy's here!"

Linnea giggled.

She recoiled when she caught her first glimpse of them as the door swung open.

"Will... they hurt me?" she asked nervously.

Linnea's blonde hair was pulled back in a sloppy pony-tail and she had on tight jeans and a little flowery blouse which was fashionable yet durable for working outside. She was a pe-tite girl. Too young to have grown any womanly curves yet. She was one of those girls that was probably a size zero or some-thing. All the way around, she was very pretty. But beyond her body, was this youthful spirit. Out of all of them, she looked like she was the most intelligent. She was the one who might go to college. She was the one who may have looked at the army base with dreamy eyes, wondering what was inside the gate.

"No," I said, petting Sasha. "They won't hurt you."

Linnea came slowly towards Adam with her hand lightly closed, protecting her fingers from his sharp teeth. Adam and Sasha sniffed at it and then opened up her hand with their snouts so she could pet them.

"They're like dogs!"

"Wolves are very different from dogs. Don't be fooled just because they're with me and are trained."

"I'll show you where the meat is."

"I think I'm going to stay here with them tonight."

We walked back outside and found the barn. Then, Linnea opened up the freezer and came back dragging the carcass of a skinned pig behind her.

"Is this enough?" she asked, dropping it on the ground.

"Yes, thank you," I laughed.

We carried the heavy carcass back to the shed together and dropped it down onto the hay by the door.

The wolves looked at me for permission to eat.

"Go eat," I commanded.

"That's so cool!"

I giggled with her.

"I guess it *is* kind of cool."

Linnea took an innocent step towards the wolves, but they both turned towards her and growled.

"Don't get too close when they're eating," I said, stopping her. "They are very aggressive about their food."

"I'll bring you out some blankets and a blowup mattress," she said, backing away.

She ran off and I sat on a small bale of hay and watched over the wolves while they ate. When they were done, they came to my side and curled up at my feet. I combed my fingers through their long coats while they slept beside me contentedly.

Before long, Linnea had come back with Janet and Ellen. They asked me again if I was sure I wanted to stay in the shed, but I couldn't bare to leave Adam and Sasha. The place was too new for them. So, I reassured them I would be okay and they gave me my blankets and a guest cot to lay on.

We sat in the shed, talking and laughing about light-hearted things and then they went off to bed themselves. And as the night grew colder, the wolves cuddled themselves closer to me. It was very late when Eddie joined me in the shed. His breath smelt like beer. He gave me a drunken kiss, then put his arms around me as he fell into a deep sleep.

Jennifer Gonzales

"This is your military identification card," Alexis said, handing me a laminated card with my photo on it.

"And this is your permit to enter the premises. Don't lose this, whatever you do."

"Okay," I said, taking the certificate from her.

"A car is coming this afternoon. You will use it to travel to and from the base. Do not come here immediately after work. Go to the store or something. If they ask you where you are staying, tell them you are staying in a hotel while you find a rental. This is the address and the name of the hotel. Memorize it. The hotel is already reserved in your name. I suggest you go get the key and act like you stay there. All you have to do is go there after work. Let them see your car in the parking lot."

"Okay," I said, taking the eReader with the information on it.

We were sitting in the living room of the house on a 1800s antique American settee. Just one of the subtle signs these farmers were making a hidden fortune off their livestock. Although these were beautiful deep blue sofas, they were somewhat uncomfortable to sit on, so I shifted myself into the corner to gain a little more back support, but ended up buckling away from the wooden frame and repositioning myself at the edge of the cushion.

"Your name is Jennifer Gonzales," Reggie said. "Your birthday is April 15th, 2052. Memorize it. That's all your personal information and your basic history. Memorize everything and then delete the file plus all backups stored on the eReader."

Alexis took a sip of her tea and set it back down on the table gently. The minty warm scent lingered over the coffee table.

"Wow," I mumbled. My entire biography was on it, including fake parents and place of birth. My elementary school was listed as being located in New Florida. Even my fictitious first boyfriend was named.

"You okay?" Reggie asked.

"Yes, sir," I said.

"I know it's a lot of information, but they will check up on you."

"You have a masters degree in politics," Alexis said. "You are coming in as an entry level political analyst. Your job description is to review information coming in from the main computer and sort through the important things with a team of people who then analyze the information and pass it on to the proper government entities."

"Pretty much, they get all the personal information they can. The computer system sorts out all the financial information and then flags certain trends. Your job is to find those trends and take them to your upper management. Then, they use the information to dominate things, like political issues, the stock market. You'd be surprised what they can do. Imagine playing a card game with someone and you always knew their hand. You'd be able to get away with anything then, right?"

"Okay. And thank you for not giving me a computer degree, by the way," I said, sarcastically. "I was really scared I'd have to do something high tech."

"Oh no!" Alexis said. "We wouldn't want to blow your cover. This position is like working in the mailroom. You're basically an intern. You will do the grunt work and then report it to

your supervisor. The supervisor makes all the important deci-
sions."

Alexis finished up her tea. We walked out to the shed
where the others were helping Henry set up a surveillance system. They had turned the shed into a complete workspace now.
Henry was sitting at his computer just the same as he always did
at home, and Ellen was helping Eddie set something up at his
desk.

"What are you guys doing?" I asked as we joined them.

"Hold on," Eddie said, his feet sticking out from under
the computer desk.

"I think I see it now," Henry told Eddie. "Try tightening
the green cord a bit more."

"Hey, can you shine the flashlight a little more to the
left?" Eddie asked Ellen.

"Sure thing," she said, moving the flashlight. "We're
having trouble breaking into the video system on base."

"Wait a minute... There! I got something."

Eddie rolled himself out from under the desk and
brushed off the hay from his jeans.

"Hey, babe," he said, giving me a kiss.

"Those guys are tricky, but I got them. They can detect
anyone who taps into their security system within three minutes
of the breech. When there's a detection, it sets off the entire security system and there's a lockdown at the base. So, I set up
multiple programs that change up every two minutes and fifty-
nine seconds. I'm using one hundred interchanging programs, so
you can see how it would get messy. But now I have it."

He brought up the holographic screen and the security
camera video footage appeared in the middle of the barn.

Adam leapt to his feet and started barking fiercely at it.

"It's okay, boy." I assured him. "Calm."

"Where's the audio?" Ellen asked.

"We're not going to have audio. The walls of the building are coated with a special material that breaks up electronic signal. So, there's no cell phone coverage at all. There's no exchange from the outside once you go in."

"Look," Reggie turned to me. "Go to the hotel and check in. Then spend the rest of the day learning all the info we discussed. You start tomorrow."

"Are you ready?" Eddie asked, rubbing my shoulders.

"I hope so."

I noticed his gun right away as I pulled to a stop and rolled down the car window. My eyes followed his black uniform upward towards his face, but the sunrise was shining directly in my eyes, and he stood so close, the doorframe cut him off at the chest. I focused my eyes on the name tag on his vest and a few buttons on his uniform, blindly smiling at the mysterious figure.

"Welcome to Fort Meade, Fort Meade pride. ID, security clearance, and vehicle registration, ma'am."

I had my identification ready, lying in a mess on the passenger seat. I grabbed it quickly and passed everything to him. He in turn, glanced at it and then peered into the vehicle as I squinted back at him.

"Is this your first time here, ma'am?"

"Yes, sir."

"Step out of the car, ma'am."

He waved his hand and a second security guard stationed in his police car at the curb of the entrance got out quickly with a large leashed German Shepherd. I stumbled out of my car and stood beside the first guard, who I could see now was an amicable looking man with a dark complexion who carried his years around his belly. He may have been retired military. He had that indescribable personality trait most soldiers carry after basic, but it was softened by about forty years of life and possibly a wife who fed him well.

The other guard was dressed in the United States Army uniform. He still had that undeniable characteristic of a soldier, but he was in his early twenties and performed his job somewhat apathetically. He rounded the car hastily, letting the Shepherd sniff the seats and around the tires. The Shepherd didn't find anything alarming and came dutifully back to his side.

"She's okay," the second guard said, walking back to his car.

I drove slowly to the parking lot of the main building. When I finally parked, I felt like I was about a mile out from the entrance. Other suited civilians were walking from their cars towards the building as well. And there were a lot of soldiers. The difference between these soldiers and other soldiers I had seen before was that these soldiers were all armed. It was as if the base was always on high alert. When I arrived at the entrance of the building there were two more armed soldiers standing at each side of the door and my ID and security clearance was checked again.

There was a long desk in the lobby with about four soldiers sitting in chairs behind it and a directory posted on the wall. I was skimming through all the levels to find my location when I was interrupted by a tenor voice.

"Can I help you, ma'am?"

I turned around and scanned the soldier behind the desk. He didn't seem tough, like your stereotypical soldier. He had been stationed here awhile and was relaxing back comfortably in his chair. Then he sat up smiling, eager to be of some service to me.

"I'm trying to find Mrs. Hudson's office."

"Mrs. Hudson's?"

They turned to each other and shared a confused look. Then another soldier popped up from his chair.

"Remember the briefing?" he reminded his comrades. "There's someone new today. Just check her security clearance and ID."

The first soldier walked toward me.

"Do you have your security clearance, ma'am?"

"Yes, sir."

It seemed impolite to respond with anything less than sir or ma'am, but it felt awkward to say.

He read over my certification attentively and checked my ID.

"I'll show you up there, ma'am," he offered, handing them back to me. "Follow me, ma'am."

Then, he turned towards his squad and said, "I'll be back," as he led me to the elevator.

They didn't seem to care and went back to resting back in their chairs again and staring at their computer screens.

"How are you today?" I asked.

"I'm good," he said, pressing the number four as the elevator doors closed.

He was a natural redhead, but his hair had almost turned a red brown. Or maybe he had tried to dye his hair with a cheap dye, because he didn't like his natural red hair color. That didn't matter so much, because it was cut so short only the first eighth of an inch stuck out from his scalp. But what gave away his red headedness was the red tint in his skin most redheads have, his red eyebrows, and his Irish freckles which spotted his cheeks.

"My daughter took her first steps yesterday," he said proudly, after some silent contemplation.

"That's great! How many kids do you have?"

"She's my first," he said, leaning against the elevator wall briefly and then standing back up at attention when he realized he was getting too comfortable. "I'd show you a picture but we aren't allowed to have electronics here."

"That's okay. Maybe one day."

The elevator opened and I followed him into a grey hallway with glass doors on each side. We went some ways down and stopped at a door, but he didn't open it. Instead he pressed a button on an intercom and it beeped loudly back at him.

"Can I help you?"

"I have the new hire, Miss Gonzales."

The door buzzed again, this time unlocking from the inside.

We entered through the doorway and waited at a small desk another armed security guard was sitting behind. This guy was private security. You could tell by the black uniform instead of the green camouflage.

"I need to see your clearance before you can meet Mrs. Hudson, ma'am."

"Wow. That's the third time I think," I said, handing him my ID and certificate with a smile.

"Better safe than sorry," he said.

"Are you going to be okay now, ma'am?"

"Yes, thank you."

I glanced at the name tag on his uniform and read it out loud.

"Conner."

"Okay then," he said, smiling, and then took his leave from me.

"By the way, good luck with the baby!" I hollered to him as he went through the door.

"Thanks," he replied.

"That's a nice guy," I commented.

"You won't see many of those on this level," the security guard said, disgruntled. "Mrs. Hudson keeps everyone on their toes too much to have any personality."

"That's funny."

"You'll see. You're working for Mrs. Hudson, right?"

"Yes."

"Say good-bye to the outside world. This is your new home now. Say good-bye to the sun and anything relatively human. She'll get you looking at numbers on a screen until you're grey and ugly. But, congratulations on the new job anyway!"

"Well," I said, searching for something positive to say. "I like numbers!"

Immediately I felt the silliness of the statement, but it had already spun out of my mouth before I could catch it and dispose of the entire embarrassing thought.

"Do you now?"

He took the phone and put it to his ear, laughing at me as he dialed her extension.

"Mrs. Hudson. I have the new recruit for you."

I only had to wait a few minutes before Mrs. Hudson crashed through the door. She was not pleased to meet me. She was already disturbed by my tardiness and made a point of it as we walked down the hall.

"You must be here by 6:30 sharp. Not in the parking lot. Not at the gate. Not even in the elevator. You must be sitting at your desk by precisely 0630," Mrs. Hudson said, leading me briskly to my work space.

"That is because you will be relieving the night shift. Your tardiness is someone else's overtime pay. And if I see overtime pay, I will punish both the employee who took the overtime and the tardy. The only acceptable overtime is my approved overtime. And you will be here when I say, until I say. Is that clear?"

"Yes, Mrs. Hudson."

"Tonight in fact, you will stay until 1700. And I will need you everyday this week until 1700 and on Saturday for six hours as well."

She was walking fast down the hallway. I had a hard time keeping up with her, and every so often as someone would pass us, I'd fall severely behind, stretching my neck towards her with attentive ears, and then running back into place beside her.

She was in her fifties. Her hair had gone grey, but she dyed the white faithfully, so her hair stayed a deep brown. She had tied it into a bun, a favorable style for the office, which also lent itself to the bland atmosphere she was trying to maintain. There were no earrings in her ears, but a modestly thin gold necklace showed beneath the crisp collar of her white dress shirt and a large diamond ring on her ring finger signified a marriage. Her dress suit was a dark grey and her heels were simple, comfortable leather and raised only a conservative inch off the ground. I found in her a meticulous prudence. And although time had worn at the edges of her eyes, her character was so resilient as to even force the wrinkles away with her shear resolve to not lay down to her age.

Mrs. Hudson brought me into a dark room where several computers were part of a long console facing a large window that opened up to an amazing sight. What seemed like the entire fourth floor was a labyrinth of circuitry. Tall stacks of circuit boards with different colored lights flashed in continuous motion like Christmas Tree lights set on that annoying flashing setting.

"Welcome to the Key to the World," she said, pausing to look at the sight she most inevitably and so often overlooked.

She brought out one of the empty chairs from the computer console.

"This is your place. You will be taking over for Mr. Jackson's night shift."

Mr. Jackson had already leapt out of his seat upon seeing us and grabbed his bag. He was just waiting for the cue to leave and this seemed like the exact moment.

"Well, good night Mrs. Hudson," he said as he opened back up the door to exit.

"Good morning," she corrected.

"Right," he said.

But of course he would be going to sleep immediately after his shift, so it was easy to understand what he had meant. There was one other person in the room. There would be two workers at a time. She was a Philippine woman in her early forties, with a long black ponytail, flowing down the back of her black pant suit.

"Hi," she said, shaking my hand. "I'm Janice."

"I *am* late, aren't I?" I said, shaking her hand.

Janice giggled, but hushed herself nervously before it could be fully heard by Mrs. Hudson. She stole a quick frightened glance at her to see if Mrs. Hudson had noticed she was happy, but Mrs. Hudson hadn't. She was already sorting through the files that had been collected during the nightshift.

"Mr. Jackson did not see this here!" she exclaimed. "You must notify me if you see any trend over 30%. Even 30.001%."

She showed the files to Janice who tightened up.

"Mrs. Rodriquez, please train Mrs. Gonzales to do her job correctly!"

Then she stormed off, leaving Janice and I together in awkward silence.

"Don't worry about her," she said, finally. "She can be a bit of a micromanager, but for the most part, we are by ourselves all day. Nice to meet you!"

"Nice to meet you," I said, as we shook hands. "So, what do we do here?"

"We take the data sent to us from the supercomputer and analyze it for trends. A specific trend is 30%. Even 30.001%," she said, mimicking Mrs. Hudson.

"After we compile the trends, we send them downstairs. They take the data and use it for things like, directing the President on what to say during his speeches, Republican and Democratic economic agendas, future policies, influencing the world market and Wall Street. It basically allows the government to stay on top of the banks and its people and get the edge over the world so we can stay a world power. When the dollar slips, we take control and the dollar value rises."

"I thought this computer had census information."

"Oh, it does. But we couldn't waste something like this only on social security numbers. It's keeping all of the financial records for all the major lenders, as a sort of check and balance system for the banks. And when the internet became the world's main information network and terrorism became a threat, this computer was reprogrammed to not only catalog financial and personal information, but is linked to a sister supercomputer as well. If this goes down the other one stores the data as a backup. And we have another supercomputer to sift through web searches, emails, and cell phone texts for national security."

"Where are the other computers?"

"No one knows. It's top secret. We can't even see the information we are seeing. It comes up in code that is broken down on another floor."

"Who reprogrammed the computer?"

"Uh, I think it was a guy named Hue Bernstein or something."

I tried to hide my look of surprise from her, all the while wondering why Henry hadn't mentioned to us the computer had been reprogrammed by him. A family secret was more like a family career passed down from generation to generation. No wonder why he was so heavily guarded. I didn't know if this would change our plans to deactivate the software. Why would he omit that kind of information? Suddenly, I felt like this was all for naught.

"Are you okay? Don't worry, it's an easy job really. You'll do fine...Oh, that reminds me," she said handing me a tablet with an electronic pen connected to it. "Now that you know too much, you have to fill out these documents saying you are aware you are in a top secret security clearance position and vow to never tell anyone outside of this office what you really do or have learned at work, bla, bla, bla..."

"Look whose back?" Alexis said, legs propped up on the living room coffee table as I blasted through the front door. "Long time no see."

"Have you seen Eddie?"

"Naw. Might be out in the shed."

"Thanks," I said, rushing back out of the house, screen door creaking shut behind me.

The shed was empty, except for the wolves whom I gave a swift pat on the head to before leaving them in the cool shade. I did a sweep of the old farm house one more time, eventually finding most of everybody, before veering off onto the back porch of the house for one final search.

I decided Eddie was probably not here at all, but maybe in town buying something, so I slowed down as I rounded the side of the house to go back out to the shed. That's when I caught glimpse of two figures standing together in the distance.

"Eddie?"

I could see Eddie and Linnea strolling along the riding ring where the horses were meandering. Somehow I hesitated before running towards them. They seemed different. Their bodies were somewhat closer in proximity than friends. And before I could process what I was seeing, Linnea turned to Eddie and grabbed him by the hands. They faced each other intimately, fingers tangling for a long moment as my heart suffered with little knife stabs of pain. Then, Linnea began walking along the fence again, sliding her hand off his hand gently while he trailed after her with focused attention.

Trust

I lost my breath. Turned back around the corner of the old house and slid down the edge of the wall into the dirt. My heart pounded and all the adrenaline in my body spilled over me in an insatiable wave. I didn't cry. I was more mad than anything. And I gave myself hope by telling myself that maybe I had misunderstood what I had seen. Maybe there was still a chance Eddie loved me.

As I caught my breath, I kicked myself back up from the ground and jogged off to the shed where I knew the wolves were waiting with loving loyalty. And when I finally found myself back in the cool shed, I settled into a pile of hay and found consolation from threading my fingers through their thick coats.

I was able to get passed the first pangs of betrayal and sink into a deep fantasy about the millions of ways I would confront him with his cheating. Maybe I would run straight back to them and tell them I knew what they were up to and had caught them redhanded. Or I'd weave a trap and catch them naked in the heat of their passion. Maybe I would refuse to speak to him ever again, leaving him wondering why the sudden break up. I'd make him just as sick with longing. I'd make him feel this intense pain I was discovering.

"Hello Miss Stephanie," said Reggie, coming through the open door, light spilling around him.

I had been sitting in the dark. He turned on the barn lights and sauntered up to me with a mild smile and easy gate. He came right up to me and sat himself down slowly in the hay. Sitting in a low spot like that wasn't easy for him. He gave out a long sigh as his joints popped and suddenly bent under the weight of his body. Then he propped his back up with his right hand in the hay.

As he sat there, somewhat comfortably now, he had a chance to look at me and see I had been crying.

"Are you okay?" he asked, concerned.

"Yes," I lied, brushing the hair out of my red eyes.

"Work is hard I suppose," he said. "What's been happening over there?"

"We know very little. What comes out on the computer is just code that is sent to another floor. The boss is a difficult person and the hours are long."

"Do you think you can get the job done? Have you seen the room yet?"

"I haven't been in there yet. Security is really tight. But I did find out some information."

Reggie's brow wrinkled up.

"Henry had reprogrammed the computer and never told us. And there is more than one supercomputer. There are many, linked to each other, that have different jobs."

"I kind of figured that about the computers. But we'll talk to Henry before anything."

He paused and gave me a friendly look.

"You should always give someone the benefit of the doubt."

Then, he pushed himself back up out of the hay, wiping the loose straw from his pants.

"We had dinner, but we saved you some. Why don't you come in and get yourself some now?"

I worked at Fort Meade for months. And now it was early October and the days were getting shorter. I wouldn't know it though. As I was working from the dark of early morning until after sunset, and then I'd come straight to the hotel in order to avoid Eddie. I hadn't confronted him. I had taken one look at his beady hazel eyes and lost my nerve. But now as I nuzzled my face into my pillow, I heard something alarming from outside. It was the faint sound of the wolves' long howls piercing through miles of sky.

I quickly got up and put my pants and shoes on. The sound of the wolves was even more distinct from outside the hotel, causing an instinctive panic to sweep over my body. I rushed to the car and wrestled the keys into the ignition, pressing my foot quickly on the gas pedal and skidding out of the wet parking lot. I drove with urgency. My only desire, to hush their imploring cries. All the while, hiding my panic by obeying the speed limits and stop lights as my heart beat madly in my chest.

I knew they were calling for me. I could feel Adam and Sasha in my veins. When I got to the farm, Adam and Sasha rushed towards me, barking, and I fell to my knees giving them both a great big hug and pressing my face into their long, coarse coats. They smelled like the hay in the barn, which was not the most pleasant odor. Rather it smelled a little like horse manure. But, it didn't matter to me. The warmth of their bodies smelly or not, made my eyes wet with that loving urge to cry.

"I'm so sorry, Adam. I'm sorry, Sasha. I still love you and I haven't forgotten about you!"

Eddie was watching silently from the barn. He leaned his back up against the barn door and crossed his right boot over the other.

"Why didn't you quiet them?" I complained. "I could hear them from downtown!"

"I tried!"

He started towards me.

"I couldn't get them to stay quiet. They need to be with you. We should have released them to the wild long ago. They shouldn't even be here."

"Stephanie!" Reggie said, walking towards us from the house. "Have you found the door yet?"

"No," I replied.

"You have to hurry," he said, petting Sasha.

Sasha lay on her back, so he could pet her stomach, letting her tongue spill out of her mouth in ecstasy.

"Wolves are not local to this area. Every day we stay here, we're putting ourselves in greater danger of being found."

"Yes, sir. I'll sleep here tonight. Tomorrow, I'll find the key. It won't be long. I think I know where it is. I just don't have permission to get in there yet."

"I wish we could give you all the time you needed, Stephanie, but you'll have to find a way fast."

Henry had come up to the door.

"You!" I yelled. "Have you asked him yet, Reggie?"

"Well, yes..."

"How come you didn't tell us about reprogramming the computers, Henry!" I said, pointing my finger as I walked up to him.

"It wasn't important," he said. "Or I would have told you. You'll still be fine."

"I think it is important! What if he changed the programming?" I exclaimed to Eddie and Reggie. "Maybe he's trying to trap us!"

Eddie grabbed me by the shirt, pulling me back from Henry.

"You're really stressed out, Steph," Eddie said, calmly. "Why don't you get some rest? We all know Henry is a good guy."

I looked at all of them. I was shaking with anger. Suddenly, I was embarrassed for being so angry. But, I couldn't do anything and it was late, so I just walked away.

"You're new security clearance has been approved for the computer center."

"Good," I said, taking the new clearance from Janice's hands. "That's great news!"

"I'll give you the tour now and we can go over your new responsibilities!"

"Sounds fun," I said, following her.

We wandered through a few hallways to a locked door. She swiped her card in a slotted card scanner mounted at the right side of the thick metal door. Then, the door unlocked and she pushed it open.

"Don't follow me through. You have to swipe your own card," she warned.

She closed the door and I took out my ID and swiped my card, also. The door opened again with a high pitched beep and a flash of a green light. From the window where we worked the computers seemed huge. But standing with them in the room now, the computers were overwhelming. Long isles of control panels and circuitry were built from the ground up to the ceiling. We found ourselves lost in a labyrinth of machines.

"You're new job is to come here every morning and get the reports. They're this way. Don't get lost, but its down, then a left, and two rights. I'll show you now."

We wandered down the long isles. Janice was already desensitized to the greatness of it. I felt like I was exploring another solar system. I kept my eyes meandering upwards towards the ceiling, searching for that hidden door, but I could see nothing remarkable about any of the white tiles.

We found the place where the report was kept, strangely printed out on a long roll of paper with perforations at every page and folded onto itself in a brown plastic tray. I found it odd something so valuable would be left so naked. But with all the security checks, to me it was like a gem waiting for the player of a video game, glowing as it hovered in the air, to be taken now that we had worked for it and had finally earned it.

It was only on our way back when I thought I saw something different about part of the ceiling. But I couldn't be sure. One square looked like it was a little misplaced from the others and there was a chip on the edge, almost like it was purposefully placed there as a handle. I didn't have enough time to get a good look, because Janice had glanced back at me as she rambled on about being annoyed about her mother-in-law staying at her house with her for the holidays.

I couldn't wait to get back to the farm to tell the others, but I had to wait my entire shift and then go straight to the hotel first. I bought a soda from the charging station next door to the hotel and then got back in my car to head for the farm.

When I arrived, most everyone was in the dining room eating. I got myself a plate of food and sat in an empty seat between Smith and Janet.

"How's everything going with Mrs. "Hell"-son?" Smith asked.

"She's still the same spunky lady we all love to work for," I said sarcastically and then took a bite of my food. "But I got my security clearance today."

Suddenly, everyone's conversation stopped and their eyes focused on me.

"I may have found something. Where's Henry? I need to ask him what I should be looking for. So far, all the tiles on the ceiling look the same."

Thomas' boy put his fork down on the table and stared up at me slowly. I hadn't thought much about talking about things over dinner, because everyone was obviously in on what we were planning. But this little kid gave me the creeps. I was sure his freckled adolescent face was hiding something. He had a devious look in his eyes that I didn't like and a slight smirk on his lips. My instincts suddenly told me to stop talking.

"But, maybe it was nothing," I added.

I looked softly back at him and he swept his eyes back down to his plate, jerking his knees up under the table, shaking the plates with a clank as he stood up.

"Papa, I'm going to do my chores now. May I be excused?"

"Didn't you get all your chores done before supper?" Thomas questioned.

"Naw," he said, digging his hands into his pockets. "I forgot to put the slop out for the pigs. Just remembered."

"Alright then, you're excused."

The young boy ran out of the house, and I put my napkin to my mouth and wiped off some gravy from my lips.

"I've never seen a boy more eager to go feed the swine," John laughed.

"That's because he knows he's going to get a beating if he doesn't," Smith grinned, leaning his seat back on the back legs.

"Smith," I said. "Can you help me with something?"

"What?"

"It's in the car."

"I haven't finished eating."

"Please," I whined, widening my eyes at him so he'd get a hint. "Now!"

Smith stood up from his plate.

"I didn't know it was my birthday," he joked.

Once we got outside to the porch, Smith stopped at the steps and lit up a cigarette.

"Now, what is it you really want?" Smith asked, taking a long puff and flicking the cigarette ashes off the porch.

"That boy gave me a weird look."

"He's seventeen. They tend to do that."

"Could you follow him for me?" I asked, pulling on Smith's coat. "There's something about him I don't trust."

"You have my word."

Smith sucked in another large breath of smoke and then tossed his cigarette butt to the ground and stomped on it with his large boot.

"I love being out here. I can get myself back into old habits."

"Smoking is gross," I said, standing far away from him like he had a disease. "No one smokes anymore."

"This house is filled with wonderful goodies. What's going on with you lately, Steph?"

He stepped towards me.

"You seem to be stressed out. I mean, it's natural with what you're doing, but is everything okay?"

"Well…"

I didn't know if I should tell him about Eddie.

"It's just hard to know who to trust anymore."

"Well, you can always trust me, Steph. Consider me a big brother. I'll be there for you kiddo, you understand?"

"Thanks, Smith," I said, wrapping my arms around his large body.

For a moment his figure enveloped me. Then we stepped back from each other, and he gave me a friendly pat on the shoulder.

"Hey! What are you doing with my woman?" Eddie joked, opening up the screen door. "Just kidding. I heard you guys being sappy."

I put my arms around Eddie mechanically, to let Eddie know I was still his girlfriend and everything was okay.

"Hey," Smith said. "I'll get on the thing you wanted me to do right now."

"Thanks."

When Smith left, Eddie kissed me. I still wasn't ready to forget what he had done. I felt sickened by the falseness in his lips, so I pushed him away.

"What's wrong?"

"I saw you, Eddie."

"What do you mean?"

"I saw you and Linnea at the horse ring. She was holding your hand."

"What?"

He backed away from me.

"Are you in love with her?"

"No," he said, angrily. "I can't believe you, Steph. What are you talking about?"

"I saw you! I saw you a couple months ago at the horse ring with Linnea. You looked like you were being really intimate. You held her hand!"

"Oh! Really," Eddie smiled. "Linnea was just confiding in me that day. She wants to leave the farm and come with us. That's all."

"You shouldn't be holding any girl's hand."

"You just hugged Smith! Isn't this a little one sided?"

"I don't care!" I yelled. "What I did with Smith was in friendship and what you did with Linnea was not right. There are boundaries!"

"I can't believe this!" Eddie exclaimed, walking down the porch steps and kicking his shoes into the dirt. Then he turned back to me.

"You go ask Reggie! She's been talking to us about coming, but doesn't want her father to know. That's all! I thought you'd trust me more than this!"

Eddie disappeared into the darkness and I sat myself on the porch steps, crying.

A few minutes later, Ellen came outside.

"Is everything alright?" Ellen asked, sitting next to me on the steps.

"Everything's fine," I said, coldly, wiping tears off my face.

Eddie's figure had disappeared completely in the shadows now. I searched the front yard for him, but everything was still, except for a lone cat jumping down from the hood of Clark's old truck.

"Tomorrow I'm going to bring the suit to work with me. I think I've found the Key and I'm going for it."

A Rat in the Maze

"Once you're inside Fort Meade, you will have no direct communication with us. The building is impenetrable by audio signal. But we *will* have visual communication from the moment you step into the building via their visual surveillance monitors. So, you will need to signal to the camera once you've come into contact with the correct tile."

"What should I signal?"

"Just look up at a camera and touch your nose like this."

Henry brought his hand up to the bridge of his nose like he had a headache.

I played his words over and over in my mind as I walked down the hallway to my desk. Once I arrived, Mr. Jackson leapt up from his seat as usual.

Janice gave me a once up and down with her eyes.

"Love the pants suit," she smiled.

I had to change up my attire a bit in order to conceal the suit underneath my clothing. My choice ended up being a brown suit with black one inch heals. Of course I wouldn't even try to wear the boots in the office. Anyway, they were too bulky for the climb into the little computer room and would give everything away. Not like the suit wouldn't. But by the time I put the suit on, I'd be risking death anyway so what the hell.

I sat down at the desk and we started working, but a few minutes later Mrs. Hudson came in.

"Jennifer!" she said, bursting into the office. "You received your security clearance for the computer center yesterday."

She said it as if it were news to me.

"Yes, ma'am."

"I need you to bring up the new files."

"Yes, ma'am."

"Have you found a place to live yet?" she asked.

She hadn't asked me out of concern. It was probably something she needed to check off some list she had in her office: Make sure new recruit has a place to live.

"No, ma'am," I said. "I haven't really had time to look for one yet, ma'am."

"I see," she replied.

She puckered up her red lips and ground her teeth tight, then stared her mean eyes at mine like she did it just so I'd shutter away from her. But I kept my composure instead just because I hated her, and stared back at her. So, she turned away and started opening up the office door. She didn't turn to look at me, but stopped in the doorway.

"You should try looking in the suburbs. They have a lot of large farms that may have a room available."

"I can't believe she was so nice to you!" Janice commented after Mrs. Hudson left.

She had been a little too nice. If I waited any longer, I think I might be too nervous to do what I needed to do.

"I guess I'll go get the files now."

The Ranch

"Henry!" Smith hollered.

Henry was busy monitoring the holographic screen of the video surveillance cameras at Fort Meade for Stephanie's signal.

"Yep," he said without looking at Smith.

"We have a problem."

Henry glanced at Smith and then went back to his screens.

"What's the problem?"

"You know Thomas' boy, Johnny?"

Smith came right up to Henry, but Henry was only consumed with his task at hand. So, Alexis spoke for Henry's lack of interest.

"What's wrong?" she asked.

"I followed him the other day. He's definitely talking to the people at Fort Meade."

"Does he know you followed him?"

"No. He didn't see a thing. I didn't let on anything."

"We have to warn Stephanie. She's already in there."

"We can't," Henry said.

He stole a quick earnest look at the two and then focused his eyes back on the screens obsessively.

"Why's that?" Smith asked.

"Because we have no audio," he reminded them. "We have no way to speak with her at all. She can only give us her signal. Then, we have to be ready."

"Damn it," Smith cussed. "She's walking right into a trap!"

Fort Meade

"You know where you're going?" asked the guard.

"No, sir. The usual guy got sick, so I'm filling in for him. I normally stay at the office."

"Well then," the guard pointed his thick finger towards the side of the building. "Go to Building 8057 there. Beside the big black one. It's on the right side. You'll see it as plain as day."

"Thank you, sir."

Eddie drove the borrowed electric company van through the gate and parked near the right side of the building.

"You can't park here. You have to park over there in the space for visitors," shouted an MP from his station.

"Oh, thanks," Eddie said. "I'm new here."

"Can I see your ID please?" he said, walking up to Eddie's van and peeking into it through the window.

"Sure," Eddie handed the soldier his ID. "Sorry about that."

"No problem," the soldier said as he gave him back his ID.

That made Eddie slightly late and he knew it, because he was already late picking up the van. But he couldn't quicken his pace to the building. He had to act casual. He took his toolbox out of the back of the van and walked up to the side of the building to take the reading on the electricity. If he was late, it was going to be bad. If he was early, then he'd have to find a way to stall. When Eddie was sure no one was around, he whispered to Henry in his headphone set.

"Do you see her yet?"

"Nope. Be sure to hit the power button when I say. Did you set up the device?"

"No, not yet."

"Not yet! You better do it. She's going to need that fast."

"Security took longer than I thought. I'm doing it now."

Eddie pulled out the gauge reader from his toolbox and also took out a small device he clamped onto one of the metal pipes.

"Oh shit!" Henry said over the headphone set.

"What's wrong?"

"Uh, nothing. Just wait for my signal. I'll be right back."

The Station

"Don't be worried, Ellen, but I brought a gun."

"That doesn't worry me."

Ellen was being sarcastic.

"Just thought you should know."

"I know."

"Are you ready?"

"Not yet."

Ellen took Reggie's hand. They were both sitting in the car, so she had to turn at an angle to face him and it was a little cumbersome.

"We didn't get a lot of time together," she concluded.

"This won't be the end," Reggie reassured her, taking her hand with both of his hands.

"My husband was a good guy. I never thought there'd be any other love in my life. And after all these years, you come along."

There was a short silence. Reggie was surprised she was confessing this much. He wanted to kiss her, but felt like it was perhaps too early. Then suddenly, he felt the words exploding from him, nervously.

"I love you too, Ellen."

It was the first time he had told her, but he wanted to tell her before they went in. He had been searching for the right time. Now there could be no other time. He leaned into her and they caught each others lips. Then, they both rested their heads on one another.

"This won't be the end. Two old souls in a world like this got to be living for a reason. No, don't you worry, Ellen. This will be over and then I'm really gonna hold you. Okay?"

They both rested with each other for a long while, memorizing how it felt to finally be close to one another. Memorizing the smell of his musky oiled hair mingled with the scent of her coconut shampoo. Memorizing the feel of her moist cocoa butter wrinkles against his rough leather palms. And breathing in the warmth of their breath for the first time and possibly the last.

They waited awhile with each other and then finally Reggie spoke.

"Ready?" he asked.

"Yes."

Stephanie

I walked slowly through the hallway, scrutinizing each tile. When I came to the one I thought it was, I stopped. But now that I had a chance to look at it more closely, it didn't look to me like the right one. It was just worn and cracked along the edges and seemed to need replacing. So, I started winding through the maze of computers, becoming more and more desperate to find it.

I had no choice but to grab the files and start walking back when I didn't see anything of value. I decided to take a detour. I could always say I had gotten lost. After all, it was my first time alone in the computer center. So, I zigzagged through the hallways, so panicked I felt like I was going to pass out.

"Hi," a voice said from behind me.

I turned around to find a soldier nearing me.

"Do you need help, ma'am?"

"Uh," I stuttered. "This is my first time here and I'm a little lost."

The soldier grinned.

"Everyone gets lost. Where are you going?"

"Back to Mrs. Hudson's floor."

"Follow me."

I was worried he'd take me all the way back, and I tried to think of an excuse for him to lead me back into the center but couldn't think of anything.

I glanced upwards in a final attempt to find the tile and suddenly, there it was. I could almost laugh, it was so obvious. Painted into the tile was an off-white key. It was unnoticeable, unless you were looking for it, and then it was as plain as day.

But the soldier walked fast and with intention, and led me all the way to the door where I first entered.

"Here you go, ma'am," he said, opening the door for me. "Let me know if you need anything else."

"Thanks," I said, giving him a big smile and waiting by the door just encase he'd leave.

But he didn't. He waited until I was cleared back through the door and the door was locked again behind me. I pretended to be walking back to my office and then waited in the hallway, counting the moments until I thought he'd be out of sight. Then, I returned to the door and swiped my card again. The door beeped and flashed the green light as it did before, but this time I rushed straight back to the tile.

I gave the video camera our signal, placing my hand on the bridge of my nose like I had a headache.

"Come on," I muttered under my breath.

I was sure I had caught someone's attention on the surveillance monitors by now.

Fort Meade

"She's giving the signal!" Henry said over the headset.

Eddie pushed the button to activate the device that cut power to the building.

"How long do we have?" Eddie said, walking briskly to the van.

"A delay of sixty-seconds before the power goes off and about three minutes before news gets to the gate to close down post."

Eddie opened the driver's seat door and tossed his tool-box into the passenger side. He struggled with the ignition, but got the van to start, and then rolled slowly out of the parking lot counting the seconds in his mind. His adrenaline was pumping. If he was caught, it would be the end for him, but still, he couldn't leave Stephanie in danger.

He almost didn't go out the gate. Then decided it was time to trust in her and that he needed to stick to the plan for everyone's safety. He rolled down his window so he could hear the gate personnel as he passed. Someone had just gotten a call as he drove out of the entrance and he could hear them uttering the words to each other.

"FPCON Delta. Yes, sir," the guard said into the receiver of the gate phone.

That was Eddie's cue. It was time to take off. He was already out the gate, driving down the road. But he stopped just passed the turn, contemplating going back in his head. Eddie looked back at the post. He could almost see the gate from where he was. The booth was hidden passed the turn, but the soldiers putting out the cones weren't.

That meant the base was closed to the public now. Eddie's heart sank. It was like he was drowning in fear as he sat there waiting for her. Knowing he should move forward to the spot where they had previously agreed to meet, but feeling like it would take every muscle in his body to move against his instincts to protect her.

He put the van into drive.

"Be careful, Steph."

Stephanie

I kicked off my heels and tore off my clothes, tossing them between the computers. The lights had gone completely out, leaving only the faint glow of computer lights flickering throughout the passages. This was going to be more difficult than I first thought. One, there was no chair. Two, after the lights went off I wasn't even sure I remembered which tile it was. I backed myself up and took off running as fast as I could towards the tile in the dark, then kicked off the wall of computers and leapt up into the air, pressing hard against the ceiling, forcing a tile to pop out, before slamming hard onto the ground with both feet.

I searched again in the half light for the ceiling. In the dim light, it looked as if I had chosen the right one, but I couldn't be sure. This time I would leap into the room. I backed up again and took off running a second time, pushing myself off the wall of computers, and springing towards the ceiling. I grabbed at the edge of the opening with my fingers and pulled myself up in a pull up, squeezing my arms to my sides and engaging all my abdominal muscles to lift myself into the room.

I gave myself only a moment to breathe once my entire body was safely inside. My heart was pounding. I could hear the sound of soldiers running around beneath me in an attempt to secure the building and turn the lights back on. The room was about eight feet cubed. Up against the wall was a computer built into one side and an old wooden chair that had collected decades of dust.

I sat down in the chair and stared at the console.

"This is it," I whispered.

It didn't look like much. There was a small display screen built into the computer desk. I wiped the dust off the display. It read only the name "Bernstein" in cursive. There were a few buttons and lights and a computer keyboard just below that. And up on the wall was a myriad of tiny switches that resembled an early 2000 jet interior.

I took out the key I had hidden on a chain around my neck and searched the console for the keyhole. On the left part of the wall was a small hole resembling a keyhole. I tried to put the key into it, but it didn't fit. Then, I saw it. Down at the right side of the keyboard was a small brass circle and a keyhole at its center. I was sure this was the place. I steadied my shaking hand, pressed the key into the hole, and turned it firmly.

Suddenly, the display screen changed from the word Bernstein to a welcome message. It flashed fast, so I almost missed the very first part of the message and had to read fast to catch up with the scrolling words.

Caution: Any further action will result in the termination of the following key operating systems and their files.

Avisa Financial Integration Operating System
Zion Debt Records Operating System
Babble Credit Union application
Federal Reserve Operating System
Federal Reserve Backup Driver
Information Sensory Processor
CIA Integrated Technology System
FBI Integrated Technology System
United States Department of Defense Budgetary Files

United States Treasury Department Operation System Management Software

Avisa Population and Statistics Records

Avisa DTO driver

Federal Personnel applications

Babble Communications Net software

European Union Financial Integration Operating Systems in accordance with 2052 Peace Sanctions

Asian United Financial Operating Systems in accordance with 2064 Peace Sanctions

African Union Finance Operating Systems in accordance with 2038 Peace Sanctions

Russia Financial Operating Systems in accordance with 2038 Peace Sanctions

South America Union Financial Operating Systems in Accordance with 2063 Peace Sanctions

To continue press ENTER.

I took a deep measured breath. Soldiers voices gathering louder and louder and then fading away in the distance as they moved through the building. Then, I pressed my finger gently on the enter key.

The screen flashed a red square with the words "DELETING FILES" and a bar indicating the completion of the task at 30, 50, 80, 100%.

"FILES DELETED"

My head spun as I realized what I had done and that I would still have to leave the building undetected. I poked my head down out of the hole in the ceiling. It was dark, but not for much longer. I had to get myself back down and put my suit on before the lights turned on. I jumped down from the ceiling and fumbled in the dark for my clothes.

My mind was focused, but my body was running away from me. I felt like I would get a terrible migraine from clinching my jaw so tightly. And my heart beat so out of control that I feared I would faint while leaning over to put my pant legs on. I buttoned up my blouse, grabbed the files off the floor, and ran back towards the exit.

Suddenly, the lights flickered on.

"Are you okay, ma'am?"

A group of soldiers came jogging down the hall towards me.

"Yes," I said, breathlessly. "The lights went out and I got lost."

"Please return to your office, ma'am. We have to search the perimeter."

"Yes."

Janice was sitting in the office like always when I returned.

"What happened? Did you get lost? Did you see the power go out?" she said.

"I was in the computer room. Yeah, I got lost."

I tried to steady my voice.

"This is the most fun I've had in thirteen years!" Janice smiled. "Did you get the files?"

"Yeah," I said, handing them to her.

"I almost feel like there's too much going on to actually work today. This is great! Did you see the soldiers with their guns?"

I flashed her a smile of recognition which settled her into looking over the files. She divided them up for the both of us.

"But Mrs. Hudson will know if we don't work," I reminded her. "Hey, I have to go to the bathroom. Can I take a break?"

"Sure," she smiled.

I turned to the door and paused to looked back at her.

"It's really nice working with you," I said as she started inputting the records.

She looked softly up at me.

"Thanks," she said. "Same here."

When the Blind Can See

The Station

"I found it!" Ellen called out as she turned the doorknob.

Reggie came up behind her.

"Great work," he said, flashing a flashlight into the vacant room.

They had found the TV station news room.

"Now you just have to make sure nobody comes through that door," he said, flicking the lights on.

The studio was massive. At least three professional news cameras surrounded a staging area where a large prop desk normally housed the news cast. And there were other stages on the same set for the weather report and other such shots. After Reggie switched on the studio lights, he started turning on all the stage lighting as well. They were huge hot lights on tripods that shown brightly down upon the stage.

It was easy getting through the building. When you're an old couple, no one really cares about your presence. They think it's cute you're old and that you are probably the grandparents of somebody working at the station. But once Reggie started turning on cameras and lights, someone could get the idea they were up to something and try to stop them.

"What should I do?" Ellen asked.

"First, watch the door. I'm going to need you to press record on the camera in just a minute. Other than that, guard that door!"

The Ranch

The wolves started pacing at the barn door and whining to themselves. They were suddenly restless after having watched Stephanie contentedly on the hologram for hours.

"What's wrong, guys?" asked John.

Then, Linnea ran into the barn.

"There's a bunch of government vehicles coming up the street! What should we do?"

"It was Thomas' boy, Johnny!" Alexis said. "Where is he?"

"He's in the house with Grandma and Grandpa. Is everything okay?"

"We have to get out of here as fast as we can," Smith said. "Henry, break that computer down, quickly. Linnea, help. Alexis and John come with me."

Smith and John grabbed a 240-Bravo off the wall of the barn and Alexis chose a 249-SAW and grabbed some drums of ammunition, following behind them. As they opened the door, the wolves ran outside and started snarling at the black vehicles making their way up the road.

Janet and Clark came to the porch door.

"What's happening?" asked Clark.

"Johnny's been talking to the government. Haven't you?" Alexis said, glaring at him.

Johnny was hiding behind Janet. They turned towards him, scowling.

"Is that right, boy?" Clark asked.

"I told them you didn't know nothing. So, we're all safe!"

Johnny knew he was about to face their wrath. Janet got right up in his face and slapped him across the cheek.

"You're too young and you don't know anything!"

"Get out of this house, boy," demanded Clark. "Go to the feds for protection. You're not welcome under this roof."

Johnny was hurt, but he didn't understand how the world worked yet. His face had turned red like his Daddy's and his eyes got all glassy, but he stopped them from crying by biting his lip. The first set of cars was stopped beyond the white fence. Alexis, John, and Smith were standing out front with the wolves and their guns. Johnny passed through the door out of the house and stepped into the bright light of the porch. He was shaking and his body was leaned over awkwardly. He turned around to leave his last words with them.

"You're all gonna die!" he said, deceitfully.

Then, he turned towards the cars and vans, holding his hands up.

"Don't shoot!" he begged as he walked towards the government officials.

"Sorry about this," Clark said to Smith, referring to Johnny's behavior.

Clark pulled out an old rifle and charged it. It was clear what side he'd taken.

There were at least fifteen federal agents with loaded weapons taking shelter behind their vehicles now. One of them was talking to Johnny inaudibly in the distance. Then Johnny climbed into one of the black cars and the fed turned towards the house shouting.

"Come out with your hands up!"

They all took shelter behind the porch, but the wolves stayed right there in the middle of the field, fur spiked up on their backs, growling deep horrifying warnings.

"Sasha! Adam!" yelled John, rushing outside from the house.

The wolves didn't retreat.

"Get them to come back!" Alexis shouted to Smith.

"They don't belong to us," Smith said.

The fed motioned to one of the soldiers in a van who opened up the back and let loose a set of Shepherds. On the keeper's command, the dogs attacked. But when they reached Adam and Sasha, they realized they were facing a wild animal and stopped. Snarling. Poised low.

They were foaming at the mouth. Displaying their canines. Waiting for the right moment to attack. Then, Adam leapt on the German Shepherd in front of him, biting him lethally at the throat. And all the dogs attacked each other, rolling on the ground, kicking up the dirt so much it was hard to see who was the victor.

In all the commotion, Smith took it upon himself to start firing at the vehicles. The feds retreated, crying out in pain as the rounds ricocheted off their car. Hitting some of them. They shot back at the house with M-4s. The rounds punched holes in the wooden wall of the porch and took chunks out of the cement foundation.

Smith, John, and Alexis had a weaponry advantage over the feds, but the feds had the American government on their side. After half of them were lying dead behind the cars, the main agent radioed in for backup.

Adam and Sasha limped back to Smith. Sasha was badly hurt, but Adam had killed his opponent in one swift move, ripping out his juggler. Both the German Shepherds lay dead in pools of blood in the field. Janet ran into the house and pulled out her medical kit and a bunch of towels. She wrapped Sasha's bloody body in the towels and tried stopping the blood with her hands.

Henry and Linnea packed the equipment in the van and drove up to the side of the porch fast, hollering.

"Get in!"

Sasha snarled at them when Henry approached. But, there was no time to coax her. They had to get her in the van fast. As Henry and Janet reached for her, she whipped her head towards Henry and bit him in the arm, causing blood to drip down his sleeve. Henry forced her muzzle closed and trapped her head under his arm as they carried her, finally resting her wounded body in the back of the van.

"Where's Thomas?"

"He's out tending to the livestock."

"Leave him," shouted Alexis.

Janet jumped out of the van.

"This is my house," she said. "I live here and I'll die here."

Clark's eyes were sad, but he knew as well as her their place was on the ranch. He climbed back out of the van and took her hand. Then, he lift his rifle and began shooting at the agents himself.

The others took this as their opportunity to go, so Henry floored the gas pedal and the van skid out, tearing through the white fence surrounding the farm. The agents separated into teams. Some raced off in pursuit of the van and some stayed behind to capture Janet and Clark. But the main agent had already called for backup. He smiled when he heard the beating of helicopter blades above him.

The gunman in the helicopter took aim first at Clark. He was a soldier and his aim was 98%. He calmly shot a bullet into Clark's head. Janet shrieked and fell over his cold body, crying. The gunman reloaded his weapon and took aim again. This time his mark was Janet. He didn't say a word. He tried not to think about the morality of these things. You couldn't do that in his business. He didn't want to know the story behind them either. He just did what his command told him and all in the name of America.

He shot Janet in the back of the head and she collapsed on Clark's lifeless corpse.

Stephanie

I was pressing the elevator call button and waiting anxiously for it to make its way up to our floor when I heard a cold voice behind me.

"Jennifer Gonzales."

I swung around to see Mrs. Hudson with two soldiers perched at her sides.

"Where may I ask are you going?"

"I'm on a break," I said, nervously.

"Oh," Mrs. Hudson touched the collar of my shirt, swiping the tips of her fingers over the fabric of my bullet proof suit. "But you just went on duty."

She looked at me straight in the eyes. I'm sure my eyes were huge and frightened.

"May I have a word with you?" she said, cooly.

The soldiers had their rifles with them and were holding them at the trigger.

I knew if I ran I'd be shot at, so I went with them compliantly. I followed her into a vacant office with the soldiers and she sat me down at the desk.

"We've been having trouble with the computers today," Mrs. Hudson began.

"What kind of trouble?" I said, innocently.

Mrs. Hudson snapped at me.

"Don't you know?"

She leaned her body over me, hands stretched out on either side of the desk.

"Don't be coy," she smiled. "You were the only one in the computer center when the lights went off and you went back twice. What were you searching for?"

She sat herself on top of the desk.

"You know, I always wondered about you. There was something off about your history. Something that didn't sit right. Now cooperate with us."

The soldiers grabbed me by the arms and tied them behind my back with a thick rope.

"What do you want?" I exclaimed.

"Tell us how to fix the computers! Tell us what you did!"

"I can't."

"Make her talk," Mrs. Hudson commanded her soldiers and stormed off.

"You don't have to do this," I pleaded. "Please help me!"

They didn't say a word though. They just smiled at me which caused me to remember my dream. I had brought my pocket knife for luck. If only I could reach it in my back suit pocket. I might be able to tear free from the ropes.

The Van

"Where are we going?" Smith asked.

"Gotta get rid of that helicopter, then get the others. That is, if they're still alive."

"Sasha's lost a lot of blood," Alexis said, pressing the blood soaked towel against her.

"What do we have here to stop it?" Smith asked.

"Janet left her medical kit in the van."

"Okay," Smith said. "Then, look in the kit and see what you can find."

Alexis fumbled through the kit while the van was bombarded by gunshots from the helicopter.

"I think I found something!" she said, lifting an old tube to her eyes to read the small print. "It's glue for large cuts."

"Okay then."

Sasha turned towards Alexis suddenly and snarled at her.

"I don't think I can do it," she said, handing Smith the tube. "Can you?"

Smith took the top off the tube of glue and leaned over Sasha carefully. He sifted his fingers through her fur to find the exact spot of the cut. It was long and went from her back around her side to the stomach, but it wasn't bad.

"I found where she's bleeding. She'll be okay."

Then, he started smearing the glue on the cut to seal up the long wound.

"Was it deep?" Linnea asked.

"It's a bit deep, but it doesn't go to any organs or anything. She just got scratched up is all."

That didn't stop the pain though. Adam put his nose on Sasha's face and whimpered.

"She'll be alright," Smith said. "She'll be alright."

The Station

"You're on, live in 3...2...1." Ellen told Reggie, who was fidgeting nervously with the tablet in his hands.

"Hello," Reggie stuttered. "My name is Reggie Codwell. Today, I am speaking to every corner of the world."

The camera lights had made him sweaty. He wiped his forehead quickly and took a deep breath to calm himself.

"I am speaking to rich men and to poor. I am speaking to young and to old. I am speaking regardless of race, gender, or religion. I am speaking directly to you."

An employee passed by the door and saw Reggie reporting. Reggie's words could be heard all over the station from small television displays mounted to the ceiling of the hallways. The man tried the door handle, but Ellen had locked it.

"We have been blinded. Some of us have become blind by the black tar of greed which swept over this world and consumed us. In our own lust for gold we forgot our humanity. We forgot to respect and nurture one another.

"Some have become blind in our struggle for survival. We forgot how to fight for change. Or how to be bright beacons standing against injustice. How many men, women, and children are taken by population control everyday while others turn their guilty eyes away? While these atrocities are committed, we resume our mindless lives of work. But we are only slaves in this bottom heavy society."

Ellen came up to the door.

"Open the door!" the man shouted through the small window, but his voice was muffled.

Ellen motioned that she couldn't open it and smiled. It was a pretty thick door. There was no way he was getting through it.

"But today I say to you that we are a better world. We are a better nation. And we are a better society. We must stand together to turn down those who wield their bitter whips against us. And today, we have a chance to be the human beings we were created to be. We have a chance to reinvent our constitutions and our global laws so peace may prevail against greed at last.

"The clock has been reset and there is no John Doe. There is no rich man nor poor standing beside you. There is only a soul with the same chance to enjoy life, liberty, and the pursuit of happiness as our forefathers had intended. Today, my brothers and sisters, we are all equal."

The man brought over a security guard from the building and a group of curious witnesses surrounded the window in the hallway as they listened to Reggie's unprecedented speech. The security guard took out his baton and banged it on the window, but the glass was too thick and it didn't break.

"I beg you to look deeply in your hearts as we set this grand clock again. Do not hate your brother, but be kind. Do not grab up gold, but love. Rewrite our laws to truly stand for our rights and happiness. Let us move forward under the grace of God, whosoever God that may be, and pen now our futures.

"My friends and I erased all financial data from the face of the earth. The slate is clean. The choice is yours. We must again weave the threads of this great world in the image of peace. How did we find ourselves in another Holocaust when we swore to never commit such a crime? But then again, we witnessed the horror of ISIS as they demolished entire populations under the pretense of religion. And now, the taste of death is again upon our lips. And we cannot turn our heads from the crimes of the one percent. We must stand against them as citizens of the world. We must demand a resolution and fair income for our endeavors."

The crowd in the hallway stood dumbfounded. Even the guard almost dropped his baton.

"Do not be complacent. Take courage, dear citizens, and claim honesty as your shield, lean on love for your strength, and put peace in your mind. Work together as citizens of earth for a better world. Collect yourselves up in homes to discuss new politics. For it is your world and your legacy. Let not the evil apples of this barrel corrupt the bounty of our crop. Smother evil from every corner with the light of our spirits standing together uniformly.

"Today, I will be giving you the locations of every cancer treatment facility. Yes, ladies and gentlemen, the cure for cancer has been kept secret from you as their ultimate weapon of control. The locations are as follows…"

Stephanie

"Come look at this!" a soldier rushed into the room.

"We have orders not to leave."

"You don't work for anyone anymore," he said. "Look on TV!"

The soldiers ran out of the room.

I had found my pocket knife and took the opportunity to start chiseling away at the wide rope. After a few minutes of sawing, the rope finally began unraveling and I was able to twist my wrists out. I ran out the door and down the stairwell.

In the lobby, the guards were all listening to Reggie's speech. The news media had gotten hold of it and was replaying the speech as the number one news breaking story of the century. No one spoke a word and no one took their eyes off the television screen. I walked out the front door of the building without being noticed. I was thinking I might make it. I may have gotten lucky. But someone stopped me in the parking lot.

"Conner?" I exclaimed, confused.

"You can't leave. You're to be taken under custody now."

"Conner," I said. "Don't you understand?"

Conner grabbed my hand and started leading me back, but I pushed myself away.

"Why'd you do it?" he yelled. "Are you some kind of terrorist?"

"No, Conner."

I brushed the hair away from my eyes.

"You work for this country, but you also work for your child. I believe in the constitution just like any American. But I believe we need to change. Don't worry. The government isn't all bad. But, the rules have been cheated for way too long and you know it. Let me go, please! Go back to your daughter and your wife and start building this country again."

"I don't understand."

"We are all pioneers now. Adventurers. Go back and lead people to be better. What are you?"

I pointed to his rank.

"First sergeant."

"Lead them. Keep the foundation, but tear down the walls. It's your chance."

I took his hand.

"So, your daughter won't have to worry about cancer. So, she'll never be a slave for the rich."

Conner grabbed me by the arm and shoved me into his police vehicle.

I had said all I could. I lay my head in the backseat as he drove us up to the gate.

"Post is closed," said the gate guard.

"I have a prisoner. I'm taking her up to the federal prison for interrogation."

The gate guard looked through the back window at me.

"I didn't hear about any prisoner."

"Mrs. Hudson is moving her secretly."

He eyed him for a moment and then moved the cones.

Conner rolled the car out the gate and down the road. Then he looked at me through the rear view mirror, moving it just slightly so he'd capture me fully in the reflection.

"Where are we going?" he asked.

I smiled at him.

"To an abandoned overpass just outside of town. Thank you!"

The smoke billowing out of the factories downtown all stopped spilling out of the chimneys that day. One by one, workers laid down their smocks and walked out the doors. They stepped into a late-afternoon sky they had not witnessed for years. The sun was blazing down on them.

As Connor and I drove to meet the others, we saw them flood the streets by the hundreds. All were in a daze, looking out at the horizon and softly at each other. A question could be read on their faces. Their eyes were flickering with light. As if they were struggling to wake up from a deep sleep. What was next? Now that the burden of debt had been lifted off their shoulders.

A small girl raced away from her nanny's arms and towards her mother's embrace. The mother reached down for her toddler in the street and picked her up, holding her tightly while rocking her from side to side.

The first deep breath spread over the earth, hushing every town in unanimous astonishment. As people realized they were free from debt, they celebrated. As they realized they didn't know what was next, they stood in an overwhelming daze. Because this was not the world they knew, but a new one. This was not the mold, but the clay.

I lift my head to glimpse the abandoned overpass in the distance. There, I observed a small group of silhouettes emerging in the light of the setting sun and the majestic form of two grey wolves.

Part Three:
King of the Mountain

Games

Mr. Copperfield

"Mr. Copperfield! Mr. Copperfield!"

The man knocked hard on the door, suit jacket drifting up below his buttons in the breeze.

"Mr. Copperfield!" he proclaimed, collapsing his hand down to his side as Mr. Copperfield emerged at the glass in front of him. "Thank God you're here! Open the door. I've come for my money."

The man spoke with assurance he'd be given his entitlement, but Mr. Copperfield kept the door locked, only drawing himself closer to the glass until his suit brushed up against the spotless pane.

"Money?" he asked, raising his voice at the end as to notate dramatic confusion.

"Mr. Copperfield."

The man stood tall with his Italian leather shoes brought firmly together, hands balled up in fists at his sides. His face reddened as he inhaled to begin speaking.

"I have billions in this bank and you know it. I demand!"

"I no longer know your name. I have no records of any money nor whom it belongs to. What was held electronically has forever been lost in an abyss somewhere."

"Mr. Copperfield!"

The man's glassy eyes oozed with hatred and his cheeks throbbed as his whole body painfully stayed standing in disbelief.

Five men appeared with guns behind Mr. Copperfield. They flashed their long black rifles as a warning, but did not lift them to aim at the man on the street as there was no danger yet.

"But the money in the safe?" the man pleaded. "I hold several safety deposit boxes at this branch."

Mr. Copperfield shook his head and a sinister smile spread across his cheeks.

"I'm sorry, sir. Due to the lack of information, we can no longer function as a bank. Therefore, the money in the safe..."

"Mr. Copperfield! I swear I will return with lawyers if I have to!"

"Like I said..."

He stepped away only slightly from the window, as if he were finished speaking with the man.

"There is no evidence of your existence nor of mine. The money in the safe belongs to me now. Good day."

Mr. Copperfield disappeared into the building as the guards grouped together in quiet discussion.

The man sat on the curb just outside the entrance of Copperfield Bank. Disparaged, he took a shiny silver Glock out of his inner coat pocket. He held it in his hands for a few moments, toying with the heaviness of the gun and crying a little as he thought about his family and his mansion in France. Then, he brought the Glock to his mouth.

The pop was heard by the guards from inside the building, but they didn't run outside to find the dead body. Instead, they quietly walked up behind Mr. Copperfield, who was too busy counting gold bars in the main safe to care about security.

"Not now," he said, brushing them away as he piled as many bars as he could onto a metal cart.

The men looked at each other once more for affirmation.

"Even, right?" one clarified.

Then, they all lift their rifles at once and pointed to Mr. Copperfield. Mr. Copperfield turned towards the men dropping one of the gold bars to the ground in a desperate attempt to put his hands up in surrender. He was about to say he would share with the men if they spared his life. He would have offered them huge sums of money for seeing to his departure somewhere safe. But the guards hadn't given him a chance. They thought about their families struggling and sick at home and recognized their unique opportunity. So, there wasn't much hesitation when they shot Mr. Copperfield down.

Rebecca

Rebecca pressed her naked body against the porcelain of the tub until her breasts were fully submerged under the warm bath. She dipped her head back, moistening her cropped grey hair and then pulled herself up again so she wouldn't drown. But drowning herself was a thought she had contemplated repetitively as she clinched her wrinkled hand at the tub edge.

A thin stream of salty tears flowed down her cheeks. She pinched her eyes shut. Guilt had festered in the form of thousands of tiny pangs of pain jolting through her entire body like electricity. She dipped herself again into the water, this time letting her entire face disappear beneath the surface. Water seeped into her nostrils and ran down her throat. She sprung up, instinctively coughing out the harsh liquid. Now her face was red from crying, but she silenced herself as she habitually did.

There was a knock at the door. Despite being lost in overwhelming grief and culpability she composed herself and hollered, "Coming!"

Rebecca washed her hair quickly and then dried and dressed herself in her usual way, only pausing a moment in the mirror to assure herself her reddened face and puffy eyes were not noticeable.

"What is it?" she asked a man who was holding a large electronic file.

"There has been a major occurrence, President Kampf."

The man stuttered at this point. He wasn't even sure if he should have addressed her then as the President, but decided it was better to continue as usual. After all, this was the United

States of America. His eyes stole a quick glance at the guards and then rest again upon President Kampf's eager face.

"I'm afraid we must speak in private Mrs. President. May we venture towards the Oval Office?"

"Yes," Rebecca replied.

This time she followed him more carefully. What had happened that couldn't be discussed in front of her security at the White House Residence? She grew more anxious with each passing step. And when finally they arrived in the Oval Office, she was met by her full committee of advisors. They turned to her in unison as the man closed the door behind them. All staring at her with the same look of horror in their eyes.

A Sweet Homecoming

Stephanie

"Welcome Home!"

Alice threw her arms around me as we entered the compound.

"I missed you so much!" I said, squeezing her. "How are the kids?"

"They were a handful, but luckily DJ helped a lot."

"That's good."

Suddenly, Alice caught sight of the wolves coming in as John and Smith carried Sasha to the couch.

"What happened?" she exclaimed.

"A truly long story," Reggie interjected. "But the mission has been accomplished. Hopefully, we've made some sort of difference."

I knelt at Sasha's side. She gave out a long high pitched cry.

"It's okay, Sasha."

I calmed her, running my fingers through the long strands of black fur around her face.

"I'm so sorry! But, I heard you helped save the day. You did a good job!"

Sasha tried to lick me on the face, but I didn't let her. Instead, I put my arms around her, gently hugging her so I didn't bother the long scratch.

"The feds showed up at the farm," John explained, drawing Alice closer to him with his strong hands and finally kissing her.

Henry sat down next to Sasha on the couch and pet her lower back.

"The people helping us, Janet and Clark, died. Sasha and Adam were fighting these other two dogs. Good thing Smith, John, and Alexis were there. I've never seen anybody go up against anyone like that."

"Wow!" Alice said, stunned. "I'm so glad everyone is okay."

Just then, I saw Eddie. Right away, he began walking up to me and the others, but I stood up to leave. His hazel eyes were penetrating. I wanted nothing more to believe he had been loyal to me. As I looked at him, my heart felt like a ship caught in a storm, the waves of my own emotions lapping fiercely against reason as I tried to hold myself back from falling into his arms. His arms had been the only anchor in my life that brought me any pleasure and peace. He was a pillar of strength I danced around. And just by grazing his being, even with my fingertips as I tumbled and turned in my life, I could feel a sense of belonging to something stable and was given purpose by him.

And yet something held me back. The same thing that led me to him repelled me. I hated and mistrusted him and had very little reason to do either. The same passion I felt in lust for him fueled my anger and made me sick with longing. I was left numb, standing there looking into his eyes and feeling nothing; The result of me feeling so much I couldn't understand and was afraid to succumb to.

"Stephanie," he said, taking my hands. "Please. I'd like to speak to you."

He glanced around the room, catching several spying eyes and added, "In private."

We walked to our bedroom where I collapsed on the bed in total fatigue. He sat beside me and then leaned over to kiss my face. His lips stirred my feelings as if Poseidon himself were raking his trident over the sea. But I turned away from him and propped myself up on the pillows.

"I need some time, Eddie."

"I didn't do anything. She's a friend who I helped. That's all. She means nothing to me."

"If that's true, you'll give me some time to sort every-thing out."

"What needs sorting? I love you. You love me. Don't you?"

I rolled my eyes at him and turned towards the wall. It was more than that. Love is complicated. Love takes a commit-ment to cultivate. It's actually an art unto itself. And just as a surfer learns to first stand on their board and then week by week, hour by hour, to grow more comfortable with the waves, until finally they can time it so perfectly that as they ride through the barrel it looks effortless to the people standing on the shore. Just as those few moments are the culmination of years of practice, love is also a process. Because without thought, it dries up from millions of tiny offenses until not even a drop is left.

"I love you, Eddie," I said. "Just give me some time."

There was a knock on the door. Then Henry poked his head in.

"Can I talk to you guys?"

"Sure," Eddie said. "What's up?"

"Well, I wanted you to be the first to know."

Henry sat down at the desk and leaned close to us, resting his elbows against his knees.

"I just went into the computer room and was listening to some of the news. It's not looking very good out there. People are rioting and shooting each other. Do you think we made a mistake?"

"No," I said. "It's just new. Let them adjust."

"We didn't really leave them any plan," Eddie said.

"Reggie told them to start new," I said.

"That peace and love stuff doesn't work in the real world," Eddie insisted.

I stood up. Maybe he was right.

"Let's go talk to Reggie."

Total anarchy was my deepest fear. But I had figured the good would eventually outweigh the bad. As we searched the compound for Reggie I could barely breathe. The guilt of what I had done weighed too heavily on my chest.

We found Reggie in the kitchen making a sandwich with Ellen.

"Reggie!"

He turned to me concerned.

"What's wrong?" he said, putting down his sandwich and examining our worried faces.

"There are riots on the outside. People are dying," Eddie explained.

Reggie sighed.

"That's what I thought would happen."

"So," I said. "What are we going to do?"

Reggie looked at me sadly with his dark brown eyes.

"We have to wait it out."

"Don't you think we should be leading them?" Henry asked.

"In time we will. But first we must wait."

I clasped my hands over my face and stretched my neck back in frustration.

"We did this," I said. "It's our responsibility to fix it. We have to see it through. We can't wait."

"Yes," he said, calmly. "But tonight, it is better to get some rest, regardless."

Ellen didn't say anything to him. We all left the room to tell the others, but in the end everyone was tired and agreed to go to sleep and make a better plan in the morning. And so I lay in bed, tossing and turning as I imagined all the struggles of the world.

A week had gone by, and I suffered with every moment as I waited for Reggie to give us his command to intervene. Yet everyday he gave us the same answer. That it was still not time to go out. The government had called a state of national emergency and declared martial law. But still people roamed the streets, stealing and killing when they could, some in order to survive and others to accumulate commodity before new trade regulations were established. A desperate search was led by the CIA, FBI, and high military officials to find the extremist group who did this and to retrieve the coveted lost files. But as much as they tried, they could not recover the lost information.

Identity records were reverted back to paper files and a call was made for every citizen to report to their city office to fill out by hand a paper form declaring their name, social security number, and place and date of birth. The city officials knew full well this was only to regain a small hold on the people. Anyone at this point could change their name, social security number, and place of birth to whatever they wanted. Some people took full advantage, giving themselves the name they had always desired. Illegal aliens were finally able to claim the United States as their country without the fear of being kicked out. And people who wanted to hide their criminal past took their opportunity to write down a different social security number and name and create a new and spotless identity.

Thus was the trend for the entire world. Like a ripple traveling across the ocean from an earthquake on one side of the planet that finally reaches the other continent as a Tsunami, our actions created a mass world-wide hysteria accompanied by a great burden lifted off of millions of impoverished as they had the lucky chance to start again.

But as I sat in my room with Adam and Sasha lying at my feet, I wrestled with the philosophical aspect. Was all of this worth it when so much violence and devastation ensued? The chaos of the world settled heavily on my shoulders. Crippling me as it smashed down on my body with the guilty, bloody death of thousands. That ugly scar of hate on the earth was etched into my heart as I writhed in agonizing helplessness.

Adam stretched himself out and opened his jaw into a wide yawn. Then he sat with his long nose resting in my lap. I looked into the black irises of his mysterious yellow eyes.

"What do you think I should do?"

I don't know if animals really understand us, but there were times in which I was certain Adam and Sasha knew exactly what I was saying. Times when I thought they didn't only listen to my commands as the harsh sounds of consonants ricocheting off vowels, but that they knew the definitions of entire sentences which were spoken in passing. Sometimes I thought Adam and

Sasha could smell more than my physical body, but sensed my feelings as well, and that maybe things were clearer for them.

Now Adam's eyes looked straight into my soul. His steady gaze stirred me, and I shuttered a little in surprise. What golden sea of pain flowed from his iris? The pain of all humanity glowed like raging flames. But in the black of his pupil, I saw the clear reflection of my spirit, my courage, and my will to press on. His focus penetrated my heart like the sharp tip of a sword. There would only be strength if all else was gone.

"It's time to go, isn't it?" I confirmed to him, petting him behind his long soft ears.

I pulled on my black suit while Eddie sunk into a deep sleep on the bed. Then I snuck into the kitchen and pulled out as much food as I could, packing it into a black backpacking pack. I took one last look at the community room before loading the wolves onto the shoot. I took in the soft smell of the wood table Eddie had made and the slightly mildewed morning air of an underground compound that had not been aired out all night. This was home to me. Sage and Michael's toys were scattered around the carpet. Everything was still and pleasant.

But I had pushed the button to delete the files and I couldn't stand waiting as thousands died. I knew in my heart we must take control now, before some other unrelenting evil did. We had to direct them. We couldn't just hide because we were wanted. And so I pulled on the long rope and the pulley slowly spun around, creaking and moaning as the wolves were lift up.

The Swamps

Stephanie

The sun had no recollection of the things happening in the world news. It rose up boldly, orange light suffusing the round globe, competing with the night like a sibling pushing her brother further from their coveted mother. But, Mother Earth divided light from darkness equally, and as fierce as her children were, her spherical shape was stronger and her love more consistent. She separated night from day with endless patience as the sun spread over the earth with all her mighty force, only to be invariably repressed by the deriding night.

I reached the border town of Easton, which stood on the Pennsylvania-New York line and decided to park the car in the bushes. I put on my backpacking backpack. There was no way to drive to New York from Pennsylvania directly. Only one highway had been rebuilt after the first polar ice cap melted. That road made its way from north Maine all the way south to New York City and then turned back towards Philadelphia before becoming another highway. It was rather like what the highways used to be along the Golf of Mexico before the land completely disappeared. It was built on huge cement pillars that lifted wide cement slabs out of the water.

Easton, Pennsylvania had been decimated by climate change. Its vast population of twenty-thousand was cut back to a mere seven hundred fifty by the dogs and then whittled to an unremarkable fifty-four people when the Delaware River overflowed. Leaving it a barren wasteland of abandoned brick buildings wading in shallow watery graves.

The trees stretched long lifeless branches up into the sky as their thick trunks drowned in a sludge of muddy swampland. The entire valley twinkled in the crisp morning air as huge shallow pools of water reflected up the morning light. And what was left above sea level was a deserted grassland where only the toughest and most stubborn inhabitants remained.

I glanced wearily down at Sasha. She seemed to be doing better and was able to walk as long as she didn't do anything too strenuous. I figured we could take our time winding towards New York and get there by dark. I hadn't wanted to travel with the wolves in any populated area during the day. They got out of the car and ran off in search of breakfast. After some time of walking, they appeared again in the distance. Adam was carrying the carcass of a wild rabbit in his mouth. I didn't worry very much about them. They were always more self-sufficient as they were still half wild.

I figured Adam was right and that it was time for breakfast. I sat myself on the old porch of an abandoned house which had been reduced over the years to a pile of bricks with a rooftop collapsed in on itself, and pulled out a sandwich from my pack. Adam and Sasha returned to my feet and Adam dropped the bloody rabbit down in front of me, panting happily.

"That's okay, Adam."

I was resisting the urge to vomit.

"Go ahead and eat it yourself."

Adam tore a bite out of the rabbit's flesh and went off a few feet to finish eating it. Sasha had been sitting patiently in the distance. She knew Adam would have to eat first or there'd be a fight. But once he had left the carcass lying on the road, it was her turn to finish. She was hungrier than Adam had been. I presumed he had eaten a few rodents along his way back to me. So, she devoured what was left of the rabbit contentedly. After they were done, they both wandered back to me. Adam lay down to take a quick nap as I finished my sandwich, but Sasha sat with her bloody mouth, looking lovingly into my eyes.

"No, you will not finish my sandwich. And stay back. You're stinky!"

I shoved her smelly snout away from my food, but she returned just as charmingly.

"Go lay down, Sasha!"

With that, she retreated to a nice spot in the grass and commenced to licking her face clean.

Hours of hiking left my boots muddy and wet as I trudged through the marshlands of outer New York. Still, we made our way through the desolate landscape, wandering down lonely streets that had once been busy downtowns and upscale suburban neighborhoods. The potent smell of mold permeated the air like the putrid corpse of a ghost town. And the old houses were whispering as the angry wind blew through broken windows.

Adam and Sasha perked up their ears. I searched the distance for what had caught their attention. A house was propped up on a hill and a woman was standing on the porch. She had pulled out her rifle and was shouting at two vagrants who were trespassing on her property. She was hollering at them to get out, balancing her rifle on her right shoulder, aiming the long barrel at the two men.

I motioned to Adam and Sasha to come to my side. They sat down beside me growling at the intruders from a distance. We hid behind an abandoned car half submerged in murky water and overtaken by years of weeds.

"Don't you know?" one of the men started. "Every one of us is free now. And all your stuff is free, too!"

"You better get out of here or I'm going to put a cap in you!"

The men laughed and began walking fearlessly towards her anyway.

Sasha looked at me inquisitively.

"I'm not going over there," I answered, peering out at them from behind the car. "It looks like she can handle things better than us."

Adam inched his body towards them on the ground, snarling, long canines showing. Sasha pressed her nose into my leg and then glanced back towards them.

"Nope. I'm not going. I'm perfectly content right here. I've changed my mind about saving the world."

A gunshot rang through the lonely landscape. The two men had grabbed the rifle and it went off in the air. I was suddenly fearful of someone getting murdered right in front of us. The only moral thing to do would be to try and help the poor lady, although I suspect she was quite capable of handling herself in this case. But still, if the men made off with her stuff and hurt her in the process, I'd be partially to blame. Wouldn't my standing by become some form of tacit approval?

"Okay, then. I guess you better hurry. Angriff!"

I walked towards the house as the two wolves ran up the hill and tackled the men. Sasha grabbed the man with the rifle in his hands by the arm before he even knew they were there. He screamed out in pain as she drug him down to the wet ground, tail wagging violently.

They were both standing there with the men in their mouths when I caught up to the house.

"Hi. Did you need some help?" I asked, rhetorically.

"Thank you!" The woman exclaimed in shock.

From this close, I could see her age. She was in her early forties. She had the beginning lines of crows feet sketched at the edges of her eyes and her hair had thick streaks of white in it.

She took back the rifle from the men and stood in front of them with the long barrel pressed up against one of the men's cheeks.

"When we let you go, you better get the hell out of here! Understand?"

"Yes, ma'am," they whimpered.

I gave the wolves my hand signal and they let the men go and the two ran off, stumbling as they went.

We both laughed, the woman staring at Adam and Sasha.

"Do you want to stay for some coffee?"

"No, thank you. I should be going."

"Where are you going with those two wolves?"

"New York City. It seems we have a lot of work to do there."

"Work?"

I didn't want to explain myself any further. I was embarrassed to tell her I was the one who deleted the files. She realized I wasn't going to stay and started walking back to her door.

"Well, take care," she said. "Be careful."

"Thanks."

The wolves were happy to continue our journey and we didn't meet any other person along the road until we came to the New York Wall. From afar, I could make out my target right away. The One World Trade Center had been a symbol of American resilience for decades. Rebuilt after the 9/11 terrorist attacks, it stood 1,776-feet tall, the same number as the date of the Declaration of Independence signing. But what was the most precious of its commodities wasn't the wealthy companies who had become its pricey tenants. Rather, it was the 758-ton spire that served as the largest broadcast antenna for the area of New York City and was linked with satellites broadcasting around the world.

At first, the home to several broadcast companies. The property at One World Trade Center had recently been overtaken by WBN, World Broadcasting Network. This private company had monopolized the broadcasting industry by taking over the main satellites through a dirty NASA deal. Since NASA was a US government agency, government corruption had even penetrated NASA's projects, interfering with space exploration and causing profit for private business to become a major priority in all things space and science. Greed overshadowed the judicial and honest nature of what science once was. Huge loop holes in regulations gave birth to this dirty giant. WBN was now a government puppet, making it easier to spill out propaganda from the tall tower, with no private business as powerful to compete. WBN became an unstoppable force in media. A force that could tell any lie it felt was necessary to keep the population in check.

I walked with the wolves passed the long line of vehicles waiting in traffic to get through the wall. As the pedestrians who were walking on the sidewalk caught notice of the wolves, they gasped in horror. Some ran away. Others stepped back to let us through with a look of shock on their pale faces. Thus, the way to the One World Trade Center was cleared for us as we made our trek towards the city center.

Even the front entrance of the One World Trade Center was remarkable to look at. Besides the glass revolving doors and large frosted awning with the words ONE WORLD OBSERVA-TORY, a glass window reached even higher creating a majestic display of historical architecture.

"It's alright," I comforted the wolves. "Come in."

Adam and Sasha hesitated as the doors turned round and then scurried to my side. I guided them through the revolving doors to the lobby. A large mural stretching the full length of the long lobby was the most striking of the decor. The rest of the architecture was sleek, with tall marble walls and vaulted ceilings and a quality resembling early 2000 modernism. But as I looked around the lobby, I realized it was vacant. There was no guard nor desk concierge and the entire place felt abandoned and cold. For a moment, I was confused. I had half expected the guard to detain us. But, no one was in sight.

So, we walked to the elevators and pressed the correct button for WBN. Then, were lifted up through the lower levels up towards the sky. As the elevator doors opened, I glimpsed a man sitting back in his chair at the front desk. He had been drinking his coffee complacently until he saw the wolves. The fear and shock of seeing two animals come out of the elevator, let alone anyone on this level made him almost topple over in his seat and his coffee spill onto his desk.

He stood up and backed up against the wall of the office.

"Please don't hurt me!" he begged.

"Sit," I commanded the wolves.

Adam and Sasha sat, and the man, believing I was speaking to him, sat as well.

He was in his early twenties, had short African hair and smooth dark skin, was clean shaven, and wore the latest office fashion.

"Is there anyone else here?" I asked.

"No," he stuttered.

"Then why are you here?"

"Because," he sat up in his chair and fixed his suit. "When everything gets set right. And it *will* get set right. I will be here to become CEO. I worked through college. I kissed a lot of ass and I never got anywhere. But now, I will be in charge. If someone else comes. They'll start all over again. They'll hire people. No. I will be the one hiring this time. I'm sitting here until everything gets set right."

"What happened to the real CEO?"

I thought he may have killed him. I wanted to make sure he wasn't some sort of nut.

"He disappeared with his family. Now, he's just as poor as any, so why waste time. He went off to claim one of his mansions. Everyone is putting their stake on what they want. And I want to be CEO of WBN!"

"Oh no."

"What?"

"I did this. I deleted the files."

"Then, I should thank you."

"You shouldn't thank me! I didn't want this to happen. I guess I just didn't think about it that far. I have to use the satellites to send a message. Can you help me?"

"Sure, you're like a hero to me. I wouldn't have been anything without you."

He walked me down the hall to one of the broadcasting rooms and started unlocking the door.

"You were always someone," I told him. "What's your name?"

"Josh."

He opened up the door and the scent of fresh cool air wafted out.

"Josh, it doesn't matter if you are a CEO or not. You shouldn't judge your self worth by a job. What makes you who you are is your good character."

He looked at me only for a few seconds. He may have understood me on some level, but this wasn't his day for revelations. He just changed the subject, because he wanted what he wanted and he wanted to hang onto societies ideals. He flipped on the light switch and started up all the video cameras from the director's console, gazing fearfully at the wolves as he did.

"Are those two dangerous?"

"Yes, but as long as you do what I say, they won't hurt you," I said, jokingly.

He didn't laugh at my joke.

"Go stand over there."

I stood on the stage and he pinned a mic to my shirt. Then he went back to the console.

"Say something," he directed.

"Hello."

"Hey, can you call them over to you?"

"Sure, come."

Adam and Sasha laid down at my side.

"Good. I have a great shot of you altogether. Everything will be rolling when you see the light. Got it?"

"Yes."

I suddenly felt nauseated staring at the green light, but I took a deep breath and gathered up my nerves. Then, the light flashed to red. I gazed into my reflection on the camera.

"Hello. My name is Tha:yo:nih No'yeh, Mother of the Wolves, and I am the one who deleted the files along with my companions. We did it because we hoped to give the world a fresh start, but it was only the first step in a great journey to re-build our civilization. I'm here to tell you to stop vandalizing and go back to your jobs. We need goods, and you as citizens only hurt your community by stealing or refusing to work reasonable hours. President Kampf, we request a meeting with you and de-mand a revised constitution. We demand a document amending the electoral voting process for the President of the United States and which forbids the manipulation or bribery of our executive, legislative, and judicial branches with a modern working check and balance system. Our democracy has slowly eroded. And what is democracy when it doesn't work any longer? It is as use-less as a clock that has forgotten to be wound. Without limita-tion, the one percent has become a dictatorship, causing forward motion of our ever evolving civilization to stall. We must save ourselves by discarding the parts of our old system which have become irrelevant and by creating something new and beneficial to us in our own age. For instance, most jobs require an educa-tion, relevant job experience, and a thorough background check before employment. Why is the position of the most important job, the President of the United States of America, based on wealth and popularity? It's time we change things. I urge all the citizens of this world to build relationships with one another. Be-gin trading goods and creating bonds. Now that the constraints of economic prejudice have been lifted, set yourselves right again by offering up your talents for the good of all as free beings.

Let's come together as a nation to rebuild our broken system. I look forward to hearing from you Mrs. President. Thank you."

The red light turned green again and Josh jumped out from behind the console.

"That was great! I'm going to have so many employees now!"

I shook my head at him.

"Let's go," I told the wolves.

I was about to press the button for the elevator, but Josh stopped me.

"You better take the stairs. They'll be after you."

"Thanks."

He was right. As I left the tower, I could already see five soldiers with rifles marching up the street towards me. Their heavy boots thudded on the pavement with unsettling urgency. Rifles were clenched to their chests, barrels flat across their left shoulders.

The Executive Branch

Rebecca

I quietly observed the long table of advisors, military officers, and such. There was a short silence before a young man, who was a representative of the FBI, stood up with his tablet in hand.

"Her name is Stephanie Elliot. She worked briefly at Fort Meade under the alias Jennifer Gonzales. We believe she has co-conspirators. Two names have been revealed as Reggie Codwell, a longtime radical who has been wanted for investigation of sundry crimes against the US and treason. And Edward Levine, who is thought to be her lover and was noted as having run away with her in late 2075."

"Do we know where they're hiding?"

"It's unclear at this time. We believe they may have a home base somewhere in New England. The destination is still unknown."

An unfamiliar redhead suddenly caught my attention. He was seated next to the Sergeant Major of the army.

"Who is this?"

The Sergeant Major stood up with hands locked at his sides.

"This is First Sergeant Conner. He can ID Miss Elliot. We feel he has first hand knowledge of her intentions."

I walked up to Conner who began blushing, but he arose like a good soldier, saluted me, and stood at attention.

New meat for the slaughter. Young little prick.

"Mrs. President, at your service Mrs. President!"

"At ease. Please tell me what you think. Is this Stephanie Elliot dangerous? Do you believe she wants what she says she does?"

"No, I do not believe she is dangerous, Mrs. President. But she is smart. She was able to infiltrate Fort Meade and escape from me as my prisoner."

I took a moment to survey his muscular body. Then, looking deeply into his blue eyes, leaned into his ear.

"You don't look like you could be beaten by her."

At this Conner shuttered. We both knew he had let her go. He pretended I hadn't discovered by my female intuition what the FBI had ruled out was a possibility from hours of interrogation.

"I'll tell you what," I said, strolling back to my seat. "Set up a meeting with Miss Elliot and Mr. Codwell."

"Excuse me, Mrs. President," said the Sergeant Major of the Army. "Under our very own law, they are wanted for treason and should be prosecuted."

"If we prosecute them now, there will only be more chaos. They've become a symbol for the American people. A symbol of equal rights. She's like some sort of modern day Robin Hood now. No, no! Have we thought about amending the constitution?"

The room rumbled with a large ruckus of people whispering to each other.

"Mr. Johnson, do you know the last time the US Constitution was revised?"

A man named Mr. Johnson stirred at his desk.

"Isn't it always being revised?"

"2021. And do you know how many times it's been revised since its creation?

"No, Mrs. President."

"Twenty-nine times since its creation out of over fifteen-thousand attempts."

Everyone was silent.

"It's time to revise the constitution. It's the only thing that will restore order. And unless you want this world power to fall just as the Romans, I suggest you give me my meeting with them."

The Alley

Stephanie

When we left the One World Trade Center it was that time of night when the last bit of sun has barely sunk behind the horizon, leaving the air suddenly filled with shadows melting into darker and darker hues. I ran with the wolves into an alley, listening to the marching of soldiers behind us. It was almost curfew and New York was filled with the sound of shouting soldiers ushering civilians inside their homes.

Fresh raindrops trickled down the storm drains to Street Level. I peered down through the net of square metal holes on the panel I was standing on, but couldn't discern anything in the darkness below. So, I settled on listening to the rushing water flowing interminably through the gutters.

I passed through the depressed city streets. As the night thickened, the busy New York landscape became eerily abandoned. Street lamps illuminated scattered remnants of trash with a foggy white light. Trash drifted and rumbled through the wet streets in the mild autumn breeze, and distant houselights of hundreds of bustling apartments emanated out of rectangular windows, guiding our slow way home.

The wolves had trouble walking along the road and often entangled their claws in the large paneling of Level One. I urged them to walk in the gutters, but they still tried to go where they couldn't and I'd have to stop to help their stuck paws. I was relieved when we finally made our way out of the maze of alleyways.

But then we began our eery descent into the black stretch that lay beyond the city. The massive New York Wall towering in front of us. The black night enveloping us so we could not even see our feet touching the ground as we walked. It was as if we were swimming towards the wall in a black dream. When we reached the wall edge, light from the top of the wall showered down on us.

Adam and Sasha turned back towards the darkness and growled.

"What is it?"

My eyes searched the tarry night without luck for the stranger whom they smelled in the shadows.

"Come on. Let's go."

A beer can toppled over and clanked loudly on the cement.

I froze and the wolves raced into the darkness.

"Heal!"

Sasha and Adam turned reluctantly back towards me. They cowered at my feet.

"I mean you no harm! Please!" begged a man's voice.

"Sit," I commanded the wolves.

The man threw up his arms and inched himself into the light.

"Who are you?"

"I saw you from the TV. Please. I have a proposition for you."

The wolves didn't like him. I stepped back from him, instinctively.

"We're not interested."

"But, I can help you."

The Noose

Rebecca

I fashioned it out of a thick garden rope. The one left over from when we built the tire swing a few summers back. We had cut some rope to fit the sprawling willow and then left the rest in the shed. Mold had eaten at the strong white strands in the fall months, and in the winter it became a hardened mass. Alone, it lived in the dark cold shed. And then, in the spring, spiders wound their sticky webs around the thick neglected coils, finding solace in the mildewy smells emanating from its tight braids.

I fashioned the noose out of the thick garden rope and kept its image locked inside my mind. I coveted the day I might bring the rope out of its silent grave. I saw myself draping the noose over the same limb of the apple tree in the backyard where the kids used to play. Their ghostly voices singing merrily as they skipped around the tree while I admired them from our desert porch. That could be my auspicious home as well. And out of all the scenarios running through my mind. All were hell, except for that one peaceful day. That day my lifeless body hung silently from the branches of the old apple tree. Swaying and spinning solemnly. Hopeful my soul could soon join them.

"Mommy," she would say as she took my hand in her little hand. "Can we have special time together?"

"Yes, baby. Yes," I would say with a smile. "Let's play."

The Man

Stephanie

The man stepped into the lamplight. His face was rough as sandpaper with cheeks that bore more craters and divots than the moon. His thick antique leather jacket was worn and stained. He stood illuminated in the lamplight, gazing back at me confidently.

"How'd you get that jacket?"

A real leather jacket was a rarity in this day and age. Only a few were left, and normally they were too expensive for the average person to wear. Although he looked like he came from working on a barge ship, the leather was a sure give away he was part of the one percent. And what was more mysterious or rather unnerving was that he would wear it while strolling down a vacant New York alley in the middle of the night during curfew.

"It's one of the only things I have left. That's all. It fits me well, doesn't it?"

"Who are you?" I asked, suspiciously.

"I'm an ex-politician. Name is Steve. Steve Bachman. I was laid off last year. But I think I can help you. See, I was working in the White House."

"Why were you laid off?"

I didn't move any closer to him, but I leaned my ear into the darkness, curiously.

"Let's just say I didn't like what was going on. Anyway, I can get you in touch with the President. I still know a person or two."

My nature was to invite him in and trust his every word, but life had taught me to be cautious. I didn't want him following me, but if he was telling the truth, then I might need him. I looked him over as well as I could. Adam and Sasha still looked upset. I decided not to trust him, but I couldn't let him know.

"I'll be making a trip to DC soon. Let your contacts know we'll be coming. We want a meeting with President Kampf."

"Don't you want my number?"

"Steve Bachman?"

He nodded his head.

"We'll get in touch."

I turned from him and the wolves started walking along the road with me. He stayed in the alley, watching us go. I could tell he was staying put, because the wolves had relaxed. But I couldn't leave New York just yet. The New York Wall was always guarded and now more than ever. It was better to leave after the curfew had expired. So, I spent the rest of the night huddled up on the porch of an abandoned barber shop near the wall. Icy waves lapping relentlessly against the cement; the slow heartbeat of a dying city.

Threats

Rebecca

"A man from Babble is here to see you."

"I'll meet with him later."

"I think it's pertinent, Mrs. President."

I cocked my head up from my reading.

"His name is Frederick Rodham. He's the President of Babble itself."

"Very well then. Send him in."

I placed my eReader on the lamp stand and stared into the flames of the fireplace. It was a large room, and drafty even during warm weather. But I was used to the isolation and the quiet, quiet room. The flickering flames seemed intrusively loud in this grand and silent place. As I sat waiting for Mr. Rodham, even my breath seemed reticent to escape from its humid chamber into the vast place.

It made me think of Sammy and Jacob. They always knew how to fill a room. They for sure would be rolling on the ground. Kicking each other. Laughing. Crying. Something. I was never the one to be able to control their crazy theatrics. David would've put them to bed. He would have been there to round them up at this time of night. He would have scooped Sammy up in his arms and hauled her off to her room. Little did he know I'd be the President of the United States one day. This big hall wouldn't have phased him though. He would've carried her anyway, with Jacob tugging joyfully on his pant leg.

"Me, Daddy! My turn!" Jacob would've said.

But Jacob was too big to be carried. He'd start to cry. His tears made my heart hurt. I'd hope David would break down and carry him, also. That hallway was too long, but it wouldn't stop David. David would roar ferociously and scoop up Jacob in his other arm, thrusting him over his shoulder, with Sammy dangling and spurting deep laughter from her ribs.

I could hear their happiness flowing down the hall and I could even hear them in this ugly vacant room, laughing joyously as they were carried off to bed. Laughing and screaming ear piercing shrieks.

"Excuse me, Mrs. President."

"Oh," I stood up and shook his hand. "Please have a seat."

"I hope I'm not disturbing you, Mrs. President."

"Not at all. How may I help you?"

"Well, I normally don't go intruding on the President of the United States at this time of night, but I felt it was necessary to make haste. I've spoken with the Vice President and have been informed you intend to revise the constitution."

Frederick had turned away as he was speaking with me. I considered this odd. Most people being granted private office with the President would at least look me in the eye. It was a respect thing. I watched him examine an antique statue in his hands and then cast it back onto the table.

"It's rather late. I'd hoped you'd get to the point."

"Yes, Mrs. President. The point being that we at Babble Credit Union and Avisa Financial Enterprises have great interest in the US Constitution and an invested interest in the Executive branch. Some might say a proposition like this one could lead to impeachment."

"Some could say you are trying to blackmail me, sir. Would I be correct in presuming?"

"Presumptuousness has led to the fall of many leaders."

He finally looked me in the eyes. His face was a sickly grey tinged with a jaundiced yellow. And his eyes had a distant quality, as if he were peering beyond me. I had taken on many more powerful than he in a fight. I wasn't nominated for President because of my good looks. I knew how to play a room, and I knew how to win a debate. But when he looked at me at that moment, I sensed evil in him. I realized just then he was no ordinary CEO or politician. He faced off with me with the detachment of a sociopath and I was actually worried for my life. But, over thirty years of being a politician had taught me how to wipe all emotion off my face. I smiled at him with that same smile that had twice won me the election.

"You do understand that under Article V of the constitution the President does not have the power to amend the constitution, but that that power lies with the Congress," he said. "It would be a great undertaking for someone even of your caliber to initiate a request of this magnitude. And last I heard, the Congress was elected by the one percent."

"Babble and Avisa may have once held a majority of power in the Legislative branch, but things have changed Mr. Rodham. Last I knew, I still hold the power to sign off on legislation and last I heard, I command the US military. In fact, I have great power Mr. Rodham. You underestimate the power the people place in me. Thank you and I hope you have a wonderful night."

I walked him to the door and opened it, giving my private guards the nod to escort him out. Frederick turned his lanky body towards me once again before he made his way passed the guards.

"Goodnight, Mrs. President."

I shut the door on him and my smile melted off my face.

I had painted a target on my head. A very big target. There was only one option for me and I had to act quickly. During no point in history had a National Constitutional Convention been successfully held. It called for two-thirds of the states to apply to congress. But if I could succeed in getting them to apply, congress would have no jurisdiction. I pressed the on button on my phone ear piece.

"Dial Patricia... Hello? Sorry to wake you. I need you to send a message to every state governor and their state legislatures... No it can't wait."

When You Don't Come Home

Stephanie

I had come to know those red maple trees as my home. And when I saw the fallen birch that had been so lackadaisically strewn beside our entrance amongst the forest of thick maples, I felt a great ease sweep over me. All I'd have to do is open the hatch and I'd be safe again. Sheltered from the madness of the real world and the hatred which burned like a raging wild fire above. If I could just lower myself down into that deep hole, my underground family would take me back with a tenderness characteristic of all good homes. They'd give me a great big hug and everything would go back to normal again.

But as I reached for the hidden latch, I discovered something.

"Adam?"

My voice sank like an iron weight in the silent forest. Sasha rolled over onto her back in the damp leaves, stretching her paws up into the air. I pet the long grey fur on her stomach.

"Where's Adam?" I asked, confused.

I sat myself beside her and looked out into the trees, my heart beginning to crumble into a million hurt pieces.

"Adam?"

I wanted to shout it louder, but I was too close to the entrance of the compound. I knew Adam would know where to find us, so I waited. Waited until the leaves began to cast cold shadows over the earth. Waited until Sasha let out a high-pitched moan and balled herself up on my lap. Then, I knew.

A Lifetime to Love

Stephanie

"It's dinnertime."

I didn't say anything.

"Orenda said he might do this."

Eddie sat himself on the bed next to me. I couldn't speak. Every word was choked by my tears. I had let Sasha up on the bed and pressed her head into my stomach, combing my fingers through the long fur of her neck.

"Everyone is glad you're home, Steph. Why don't you come out and join us?"

I tried to say, "I can't."

Eddie lay next to me. His body was partially hanging over the edge of the bed, so he scooped me up in his arms, pulling me tightly towards him.

"Adam will never leave you. I know this for a fact."

I looked up at him teary eyed.

"Are you sure?"

"Yes. I'll tell you what. Why don't you come down for dinner and after we will take a little walk above ground? Maybe he'll be there waiting for you."

I gave Eddie a kiss.

"Okay," I cried, smiling through my tears now. "That sounds like a good idea."

Eddie led me into the dining room. My friends could see right off I had been crying. I sat at the table awkwardly. During dinner they made light conversation around me. I felt like a ghost in the room, but Eddie would touch my leg from time to time and sometimes he'd rub my back. I knew I should feel comforted by this, but it only made me feel uneasy. It only made me feel more distant, because even his touch was far away. It unsettled me that I was the only one who seemed to be affected by our actions of late. I wiped my hands and mouth off with my napkin.

"I went to WBN and gave a speech on air."

Reggie set down his fork.

"We know."

"Why didn't you say anything?"

"You didn't seem to be up for the talk."

"I met a man in New York. He says he can get us a meeting with the President."

"Do you trust him?"

"No."

"Why do you want to work with him then?"

"What choice do we have?"

I stood up.

"Let's get a small party together and go to DC," I said.

"That sounds pretty dangerous," Alexis interjected.

"Once again," I continued, rolling my eyes. "We have no choice. It's really our only card and I'm doing it with or without you."

I looked firmly at Reggie who knew I wasn't bluffing. He knew my mom would have gone.

Everyone waited silently, observing the both of us as we stared into each others eyes.

"Stephanie, I believe you are conquering more than just the monsters in *this* world. And I want you to know we will always stand by you. Let me think about how we should do this though. Give me a few weeks. Don't you go wandering off again. We got your back. Promise, Stephanie."

"I promise."

"Now come here and give this old man a hug."

"Yes, sir."

I walked over to him, hugging him like the family he had become.

"Ready to go for that walk, Steph?" Eddie asked.

"Okay."

The season had already turned, but the weather hadn't set the autumn leaves free just yet. And as the sun set, the yellows and oranges clung to the dry branches and that beautiful red of the maple trees speckled the thick forest like the whimsical fanned brush strokes of a painting. Eddie held my hand as we walked deeper into the woods, night slowly enveloping us with its misty sadness.

"Adam!" I hollered.

My eyes searched for him in the trees. Sasha had rushed off sometime before, and I could hear her howling in the far distance. I sat down on a fallen branch and tucked my head towards my boots.

"I don't think it's any use," I said.

Eddie knelt in front of me.

"But we'll try everyday."

He lifted my chin up to him and my eyes met his.

We were vanishing in the twilight.

"Stephanie."

He stuck his right hand in his jacket pocket and balanced himself with his other.

"When you left, I realized something."

"Eddie…"

"I can't be without you. And it may take a lifetime before you understand I'm going to be here no matter what. It may take a lifetime before you trust I really love you. But Stephanie, I want to be with you every day and prove my love to you."

He brought his hand out of his pocket and opened his balled up fist.

"This is your mother's ring. Reggie gave it to me when you left."

I was shocked.

"Will you marry me?"

I took the ring from him and turned it in my hands. It was a modest sized diamond with a yellow gold band, soldered together a long time ago. I could tell that Eddie had cleaned it carefully, but still the small thing carried the wear of time. I could feel my mother's energy in it. As I grew to know myself, I could more easily sense her spirit. I felt its details with my fingertips. Its color was disappearing in the twilight. My mother's ring became instantly precious to me.

In the same moment I felt flattered by his proposal, I felt as if I was standing on an iceberg in the middle of a lake. I could almost feel the warmth coming from the forest, but I was left immured on my lonely iceberg. Lost on a solitary prison. Perplexed by even the simplest of ideas; that I could swim to him. How could I possibly swim to him? He seemed to be so capable of love. What was wrong with me? Why was I the one stranded here with my heart?

"If you need time, I understand."

I wanted to hold him, but fear paralyzed me. I looked into his eyes. His face was overtaken by the shadows of the forest. I searched for him with my hands.

"Eddie…"

I could feel the hair that grew lightly on the back of his hand. I tangled my fingers in his. His palms were warm.

"I want to believe you, but it really may take a lifetime for me to learn how to trust. Are you sure?"

Eddie smiled. He pressed his lips against mine. His breath was warm, but the wetness of our kisses cooled fast in the crisp eventide.

"I'll love you forever," he promised.

He held me in his strong arms. He devoured me with kisses. He pressed his face against mine with the rapturous greed of a starving man. Thus I uttered my affirmation to him as the night enveloped us and he feasted on me with the ravenousness lust of a madman.

The Dry Well

Rebecca

"I just got off the phone with them."

"What did they say?"

"We have a date for the National Convention set for March 17th."

"That's actually pretty close."

Jack typed his notes quickly into his tablet. Then looked up at me.

"Are you going to get in touch with them?"

"I think they should be there," I said.

I had taken my morning tea on the White House balcony. I touched the hot liquid to my lips and then slowly brought it down to the table, watching the steam drift up into the brisk air.

"There's a man named Steve Bachman who says he can contact them."

"Oh Steve, I know him. Didn't he take a voluntary termination for something?"

"He was being investigated for alleged fraud."

"How do you know we can trust him then?"

"It's not a matter of trusting him. He's a weasel. He can weasel his way into anyone's circle. If he says he can find them, I think he can."

"Well, then. Set up a meeting between the two of them. Tell him to pass the message along that we got forty-two states to petition for a National Convention."

I looked out at the White House garden. It was December already and yet the grass was still charred brown in places by the incessant sun. The autumn leaves had turned but forgot to let go of the brittle limbs in which they clung to, and over time the evening frost had mildewed their beautiful yellows and reds and cracked their shriveled edges leaving behind the rotten corpses of an autumn left unheeded.

I still grappled with the dirty history of the past few administrations. In part of my soul, I was glad years of genocide had finally come to an end, but in another, I was horrified. There was an awful truth festering under the guise of politics.

The year Arizona became uninhabitable we knew the water was running out, but for some reason we had thought by being part of the one percent we would be helicoptered in supplies. The bottomline was we had let the water get too low.

"I thought there was another five gallons here."

"I told you we used that last night."

His salt and pepper hair came just passed his ears. He hadn't had time to shave. We had been awakened early by the governor's message that the last reservoir had run dry. He had declared a state of emergency at 3:25am. We thought we had another week. Then, we waited, thinking help would come.

How could they leave millions of people to die? And we were the one percent. We would certainly be saved.

By early afternoon we decided to pack the car and head east with everyone else who was evacuating. When we got on the highway, I had that first unpalatable feeling we may not make it. I remember looking back at the kids in the backseat. They weren't playing video games or fighting like they normally did. Their eyes were wide and their skin pale as they stared at the desert highway; an ant trail of thousands of cars lined up bumper to bumper.

"It'll be okay," I told them, smiling gently.

"There's water just up the street," Daddy said.

"Will there be enough for all of us?" asked Jacob, pressing his cheek against the window.

"Are we going to die?"

Sammy said it first. As if kids knew by instinct what adults were too afraid to say.

"No, Sammy," I said. "There's lot's of water. It's just a little ways a way."

"Why is everyone leaving, Mommy?"

"Everyone wants the water."

"I want to go home."

"Don't worry, baby. We are just going to get something to drink."

Hours later, we still found ourselves in the middle of the desert. Some people had tried to drive off the highway and got stalled when their tires all flattened from the thorns of the sharp cacti. We watched as families piled out of cars stranded in the middle of the desert and started hiking by foot. We passed the cars that had run out of electricity. We passed people alive who would soon be dead.

"We are running out of power."

"Should I try to get around these cars?"

"It's too dangerous. Look at all the people who got stranded. It's worse for them. No, we can't take the chance."

Suddenly, there was a thump. The kids gasped. It was a mother walking beside our vehicle. She was holding up her baby.

"Please, let me in! My baby and I are dying!"

Sammy started crying.

David rolled down his window. We saw she was with her husband. I nodded to him that we should let her in.

"We don't have room for the both of you. Only you and the baby."

She looked at her husband. She started crying.

"Okay," she said and gave him a salty kiss.

"I love you," he said as he embraced her.

"I love you."

He kissed his baby's forehead once more, and she climbed in our car between the kids with her baby held tightly to her breast.

"Thank you."

Her face was red and she had trouble speaking it.

The kids were still crying.

"Why do we have to leave him?" Jacob yelled.

"Because we can't fit him in the car. Don't worry. Someone else will pick him up."

I turned away from them. I couldn't take it. Our car slowly rolled on.

There was nothing beautiful about the White House garden. Every blade of grass that sucked life out of this dry planet was a bitter reminder of the millions of lives lost in the desert.

"Nice weather we're having," I said.

"Yes," Jack replied. "Very warm for this time of year."

Adara

Stephanie

"The National Convention is being held at the capitol," Alice said.

"Do you think it's a trap?"

John stepped forward.

"Bachman seemed to be okay. I don't think we should trust them though. Bring Sasha just in case and a lot of weapons."

"They'll never let you get in with weapons when there are so many politicians and the President is there," Alexis said, sarcastically.

"We won't come in. We'll wait outside and do the guarding."

"Send a message back to Bachman," I said. "Tell him we will only attend if we can help with security."

"Sounds like a good plan. Everyone is dismissed," Reggie said.

"It's March," I told Eddie, sadly.

"I know," Eddie kissed my cheek. "You want to go up and look again?"

"What's the point?"

"Never give up."

The months of Adam's absence had hardened me a little. I had let go of any hope of finding him again. A whole season had passed and I had kept walking. Every day, searching for him above ground. Then, something inside me decided it was over. But still my feet kept ceremoniously making the hike as if my body hadn't been told what my heart had decided when it broke.

"Let's just go for a walk. And if we see him, then we see him. If not, it won't be so disappointing."

We put our jackets on and climbed the ladder to the hatch. It had snowed the night before, but already the sun had come out and was melting the beautiful white powder that had settled everywhere.

"Wow!" Eddie exclaimed as he lift himself out of the hatch. "It's a beautiful day today. Look at that sun!"

"Where do you want to go?"

"Let's hike over to the ridge today."

We started trekking through the thick forest and up through the mountains. The trees felt alive this morning. As if they had awakened from their winter slumber. I felt like a tree absorbing all the light. I raised my arms up into the air.

"That sun feels so good!"

We hiked for hours until we found a nice place to sit along the rocky ridge overlooking the forest and the beautiful lake I had grown fond of. The white of the mountains was bright. Sasha sat beside my feet.

"You're a good girl, Sasha."

Eddie was still investigating the area. I watched him explore the rocks on the ridge.

Then, Sasha perked her ears up.

"What do you hear Sasha?"

There was a faint sound rising in the air.

Sasha sprung up suddenly, tail wagging and began to howl. Her long howl echoed through the valley like the silky alto melody of a clarinet.

Eddie looked at me.

"Do you think?"

"Let's not get too excited. But maybe…"

Sasha paced back and forth. Her tail was whipping violently behind her. Then, a long faint howl sounded in the forest and Sasha darted off.

I stood up.

"It's Adam! It's Adam!" I shouted, running towards the sound.

But Sasha had gone off so fast and the howling was so far in the distance, that I didn't know where to follow. We ran towards the lake and sat beside the edge.

"It's okay," Eddie said. "Let them come to us."

At first, I was excited. But an hour had gone by and our excitement was replaced by apprehension. I sat watching the lake surface ripple in the cool breeze. A few ducks were nestling their bills in their warm downy feathers as they floated along. I had been told at one time the birds were as sundry as many great cities and that they flew in flocks that sometimes numbered in the hundreds. It made me appreciate the few that were left who had survived by feasting on the algae when the fish populations dwindled.

At last, I saw him breaking through the forest.

"Oh my gosh!" I exclaimed.

Adam had broke through the tree line and was standing beside Sasha and his mate. But, the female at seeing us, began growling.

"Uh-oh," Eddie said, freezing in his tracks.

"Don't show her your fear!"

Adam ran up to us with a talkative bark and began licking my face happily.

"I love you!" I said, petting him.

I sunk my nose into his fur and kissed him.

"She's looking at you," Eddie said.

"It's okay."

I put out my closed fist to her, but she didn't come to us.

"Give her time," I said. "She's wild, remember."

"I don't know how this is going to work."

"Maybe she'll become part of our pack. You never know. Hey, look! She's pregnant!"

I could see from this distance she was very pregnant. Sasha nudged at the new wolf. She wanted to roll around in the snow, but the female just stared coldly at us with her deep yellow eyes as Adam looked back lovingly at his new family.

"Do you want to go home, Adam?"

But the question remained, where was his home?

"We have good news and bad news," I told everybody in the common area. "Adam came back."

"That's wonderful!" Reggie exclaimed.

"But he has a wild wolf with him and she's pregnant. She won't come down."

"That's going to be a problem," Reggie sighed.

"I know."

"You may have to let him go."

"I don't want to. Adam had to have come back for a reason. Maybe he still feels like a part of our pack."

"Okay," Reggie said. "Let's see what happens."

"Where exactly are they?" asked Smith.

"In a cave about a quarter mile from the compound entrance."

"All you can do is try to get her to like you. Go up again tomorrow."

"Yes, sir."

I hiked to the cave diligently every day for several weeks. Seven pups were born, but there was still no sign from the female she would trust me. I decided to name her Adara, because it meant "Fire" and she was for me like an untrusting flame that refused to be contained.

I approached Adara and she began growling and barking again. Adam came up to me with his tail wagging and barked loudly at her, as if to say everything was safe.

"Hey, girl," I said, sitting ankles crossed on the cold ground.

She came slightly out of her cave, pups slumbering behind her.

"That's it. It's okay. I'm okay."

Sasha went up to the her and sniffed her behind. Adara did the same and then they wagged tails. But Adara wouldn't play because I had seated myself too close to her den and she was being protective.

"You're going to have to get used to me. I'm family," I said, smugly.

I was a little scared of her to be honest. Adam and Sasha were pretty much domesticated, but this wolf was my first wild encounter and wolves are even more protective if they have young. I knew at any moment she could jump at me and bite my neck and that the only thing stopping her was Adam. Smith advised me to show my dominance without pushing her too much. So, I had taken this time to form a bond with her.

Sasha sat next to the pups and busied herself licking their ears. One of them woke up from its nap and started batting at her with his paw playfully while Adam lay next to me as he always did, looking lovingly in on his den.

I studied Adara's grey coat. She was not as black as Sasha, but had a fluffy coat like her. And she was not as long and sleek as Adam. She was something in between the two with only a touch of black on her face near her ear and undercoat. She was smaller than Sasha. I wasn't sure, but she looked like she may not even be a hundred pounds. Maybe it was because she hadn't been fed as well in the wild. But she was still a beautiful wolf. When she stood, she had an aura of elegance about her.

The rest of her pups awoke and I watched them suckle on her, blindly. Sasha and Adam started playing with the few pups who were finished, and Adam lay down on his back while one of the pups tried climbing on him. The tiny pup was chewing on Adam's stomach fur. I think he was looking for a nipple, but Adam gently batted him away.

Then the little pup waddled towards my scent. Adara got up on all fours and growled again. Adam took the pup up in his mouth. She thought he was going to carry the pup back to the den, but he came straight towards me. Adara came up behind him, growling menacingly, but Adam didn't mind and dropped the pup into my lap anyways. It was so young that it was still blind and deaf.

Adara had had enough. She growled viciously and sprang towards me.

The Floating Capitol

Stephanie

"I held my breath and squeezed my eyes shut. I know it probably wasn't the best thing to do, but sometimes our most basic survival instincts are to freeze. Luckily, Adam jumped on her and forced her to the ground. She submitted to him and cowered back to the den, this time watching me, sadly.

I felt only slightly at ease. I stared at the cute little pup in my lap for a few seconds, wondering if I should pick it up. Then, I decided to trust Adam and took the pup up into my arms, holding it up to my face. It was a girl.

This one looked like ashes to me. She looked like she had gotten caught in a fireplace. Her fur was all dusty and wispy looking.

"Hi, Ashes."

Ashes licked my face. I nestled her in my lap and stroked her soft baby coat. But soon Ashes jumped off of me and found her mother's scent again. She was very playful. She had more energy than any of the others in the litter.

Adam nudged me towards the den.

"No, Adam. I don't think so."

I stood up and watched Adara carefully. She seemed to have submitted for the moment, so I inched slowly and steadily closer until I was about five feet away from the den. Adara's fur stood straight up on her back. She raised her upper lip at me and hummed a soft growl. Then, looked up at Adam and her ears went back in submission.

"Adara, I'll stay right here tonight. Don't worry."

I stayed seated in front of the den opening until it was time for Sasha and Adam to go hunting for their dinner. When I stood up to leave them, Adam's eyes were sad. He started to come with me and then paused and glanced back at his pups.

"You don't have to go. I'll understand if you need to stay."

Sasha was waiting in the van with the others. I climbed in with Reggie, Alexis, John, Smith, and Eddie while Adam stared longingly at me.

"I'm not dragging you, Adam. You have to get in the van yourself. It's your decision."

I reached for the sliding door. Then, Adam put his large paws on the step and wagged his tail.

"Good boy, Adam. Come on!"

He leapt in, and I stroked his fur, lovingly burying my fingers in his long coarse coat as the van door slid tightly shut.

The National Convention was being held just a short distance from the White House in a new City Hall near the Potomac River. The Convention itself was not open to the public, but it was a televised and publicized event with the President and many other high political officials in attendance. Most streets were barricaded off, making traffic extremely difficult to maneuver. Not only did the police and FBI line the streets, but also ambulances and media trucks were parked along the road on both sides. It was a great public spectacle, which gave me a bad feeling.

We had to first drive to the White House and then be escorted to the City Hall by official police who were most assuredly secret service agents. The van rolled slowly through crowds of thousands of citizens who had gathered to voice their opinions with large signs and joined hands, chanting things like, "Fresh Start. Rip it Apart!" and "There's one solution. Toss the constitution!"

Eddie and I shared a quick worried look as the police pressed large shields against the masses who were edging angrily toward our van.

When we arrived, we were greeted by the head of security and a few of his guards.

"Only Stephanie and Reggie have clearance to participate in the meeting. You others must remain outside."

"We're part of security."

The man spoke quickly on his radio to verify.

"Keep the wolves in the van."

"Those wolves are better trained than your canine unit," Smith gloated.

"Can you guarantee they won't hurt these civilians?"

"I'll stay with them and do a parameter check," I said.

The man gave me a hard look.

"Very well."

"You can come with me," he instructed Reggie. "All others take direction under Captain Johnson."

The Captain nodded his head and we split up.

Captain Johnson handed us our passes and directed us to our duty stations. After meeting with the chief of the canine unit, I began my walk around the building with Sasha and Adam. I had been hoping I could be present during the meeting, but I knew Reggie would do well on his own.

The new City Hall was built as an Amphibious building that rested on a concrete dock and was attached by a steel guidance system at the sides which allowed the building vertical motion but restricted horizontal movement during flooding. When the water rose during a storm, the building floated up to three meters high and then settled back down as the water receded. It was a Dutch idea that finally caught on in mainstream America in about 2040.

When the government lost Miami, Florida, it drew a line across the American continent. There were those properties that would be completely buried beneath the sea, not worth saving, but worth evacuating. Then, there were the properties that could be renovated for the heavy flooding and storm surges. That's when flood barriers were made to protect certain historical cities and landmarks such as New York and Washington DC. There was a great boom in construction mid century as people worked to build these amphibious homes along the new continent edge, especially to relocate the millions of displaced citizens. But the City Hall was a recent innovation combining the ideas of old architecture giants with the brilliant mind of Nadia Vasiliev, who floated the large structure with a recycled plastic combined with other eco-friendly natural elements to form a buoyant new construction material. Washington DC was one of the new cities, a tribute to the "Floating Country" of the Netherlands. It had bestowed on it the nickname of "The Floating Capitol" because during the annual flooding season the entire city was lifted off the ground, leaving the walled White House surrounded by a moat of water, bedazzled by thousands of floating structures which emanated from its center.

"Hey, I got this part."

It was a secret service agent with a leashed German Shepherd. The wolves went up to sniff the dog and wagged their tails in greeting.

"Sure," I said, looking apprehensively at him.

I started walking in the other direction. It was odd he had taken over my part of the route. I wondered why I hadn't been told by command over the radio. And after I thought about it for a few seconds, I decided I better radio in to double check.

"Captain Johnson?"

"Roger, Miss Elliot."

"Have you changed my route?"

"Roger, Neg."

I looked down at Adam and Sasha.

"Something isn't right."

Cactus Pickles

Rebecca

"President Kampf. This is Reggie Codwell."

"Hello, Reggie. Please to meet you. Will you sit with me?"

He was a tall man with deep black skin. Yet, it was his eyes which were remarkable to me. For behind the smokiness of his cataracts I could clearly see his humility and wisdom.

"Yes, Mrs. President," he smiled.

He had a soft welcoming character. Freckles sprayed like stars across his old cheeks and teeth yellowed with age. I wrapped my arm around his and walked with him to the hall.

"This is a great moment in history, Reggie. But it will be a long week, if not month. Do you have any recommendations now, before the brawl breaks out?"

Reggie laughed as I led him to our seats.

"Well, religion wasn't supposed to be part of state politics. Let's keep it out of the agenda this time. I'm a Christian myself, but I don't want that pinning me to a party if you know what I mean?"

"Alright. We'll take a look at that. You be sure to speak up if there's anything else. These old suits get pretty stubborn at times, but it looks like you and I have about ten years on any of them."

"Yes, Mrs. President!" Reggie laughed.

"Attention!"

A man dressed in a black suit struck a gavel hard three times.

"My name is Judge Malone of the supreme court. I'm here to preside over this convention on behalf of the senate along with President Kampf and Vice President Howard. I'd like to thank our supporters, Jeffery Brown, governor of New York, Angelika Reyes, governor of California..."

The world has practically ended and they still have time for formalities, I thought.

He continued the tedious introductions.

"Mommy! Carry me!"

"You have to walk. Walk by yourself."

"Carry me!"

Sammy was dragging her doll on the ground and crying behind me. I was too tired to remind her to lift it up off the ground, and I was too tired to carry her any longer.

"Let's sit under that car," David suggested. "We'll dig a hole in the ground."

"We should have stayed at our car in the first place!"

"We would have burned up in that thing. We couldn't stay. It's even hotter inside the car and you know it!"

I stopped in my tracks, looked at our two kids and their red cheeks and sweaty foreheads, and glared back at him in the hot sun.

"What's then the difference between our car and that car, my dear? Besides it being a mile away from the road!"

"I want to stop," Jacob complained.

David sighed.

"That's a truck. It's higher off the ground. We can crawl under the truck bed and get protection from the sun. If we can dig a hole in the ground then maybe it will be cooler for the kids. Then, I'll go find a Hedgehog and we'll have something to drink. Okay?"

Tears soaked my eyes, but I hadn't given myself permission to cry. I was still mad at him, so I stomped off towards the truck. It seemed like a good plan, but I'd never tell him that.

"Come on kids," I hollered back, sulking. "Just walk to the truck."

The red dirt was hot underneath the truck bed. I nestled the children in my arms and wiped away the sweat from their faces. Sammy fell right to sleep. I worried she had fainted. Jacob just stared off into the desert, watching the string of cars stopped along the highway.

"What's going to happen to that Mommy?" he asked.

"I don't know."

"Will she die?"

"No."

"Will we die?"

"No."

"Where's Daddy?"

"He's getting some water. He'll be back, don't worry. Try to rest, honey."

"I'm scared Daddy's going to die."

"Daddy won't die."

"Promise?"

I looked out at the line of cars. I couldn't see the end. It disappeared over the horizon. I was afraid death was inevitable for all of us.

"I promise."

It was already dark when David brought back the cactus. He had stripped off its skin and cut it into pickle sized pieces with his pocket knife and had about five of them gathered up in his ball cap.

Jacob jumped happily into his Daddy's arms.

"Come on, Sammy."

I nudged her, wiping her brunette hair from her eyes.

"Sammy?"

I don't know how long I had been holding Sammy's limp body. The desert had kept her so warm I hadn't noticed when she passed. I held her to my breast as a deep overwhelming pain grew in the pit of my stomach. When I opened my mouth to cry, the pain was so unbearable it took my voice from me. So, I shut my eyes and screamed mute, crying without tears.

It was David who rushed to my side and took Sammy frantically up in his arms, wailing like a desert wolf as Jacob stood in the dark, squeezing the sticky cactus in his trembling hand.

City Hall

Stephanie

I stepped into the cool shadow of the City Hall. The man had gone, but where? I gave the hand signal for Adam and Sasha to work and they began sniffing the concrete at once. Adam sniffed his way over to a metal beam which lay inside a track alongside the wall of the building. He sniffed hard a few times and then let out a series of long deep barks.

"Good boy, Adam. Good, Adam!"

I spoke into my headset.

"We've found something on the South side of the building. I repeat, we've found something. Suspect is about five foot eight, with short brown hair and brown eyes, wearing a black rain jacket. I repeat, we've found something on the South side."

"Roger that, Miss Elliot. Sending in a squad now."

I knelt down and peered into the dark space between the metal beam and the concrete tub that housed the building, but couldn't make out anything abnormal. The building was cool and smelled of algae. The guy must have dropped something small into the crack and walked away.

Moments later, a squad came in and ushered me away from the scene. They confirmed there was something there with their bomb detection devices and began the process of dismantling the bomb.

As I walked away, I caught sight of the strange man walking in the distance.

"I am in pursuit of the suspect!"

I didn't really know how to say it on the radio, but I had seen it in the movies a long time ago and grabbed for the only phrase I knew. The Captain confirmed and the man saw me and took off running.

I chased after him. He was fast and had already crossed the bridge of the river and was heading South-East on the walking path. I caught up to him by jumping into the water and racing across the surface of the Potomac, leaving the wolves behind. He turned back to look at me again and when he saw I was gaining, veered off the path and into the street. I ran towards him on the grass but just then, a car sped up to him and opened up the passenger door. Then, the man climbed in and the car sped down the road.

"Darn it!" I said, turning back towards the City Hall.

When I walked back to the building, I saw the bomb squad was still working hard to dismantle the bomb. They were having trouble getting into the deep crack to access it.

Eddie was up ahead.

"Eddie!" I hollered, running towards him.

"Back up!"

The team started yelling, racing away from the wall. Someone hollered into their receiver while the others got behind protective shields. I only had time to look back at the building before the entire wall blew, blasting me several feet, debris flying around me and hitting me in the right shoulder and leg.

A long siren went off on the street. My body was shaking and clammy. My mind raced, but the adrenaline made me sit there paralyzed and confused as the wolves whimpered and raced away.

Eddie emerged from the cloud of smoke. He was running to me. I knelt on the ground in horror with my bloody knees and palms. He pulled me up shouting and waving his arms for me to follow him to safety. As we ran towards the street another blast went off, then a third. Sirens wailed and bloodied civilians were shouting. The serene day had transformed into a war zone.

I looked towards the building. The cloud of smoke was dissipating around it, revealing it had only partially fallen, but was badly damaged on three sides.

We weren't fast enough.

Captain Johnson radioed in.

"Team count off!"

"1."

"2."

"…"

"3, location. Kyi, count off…"

Another radioed, "Sir, he was inside."

"Count off."

"4…"

I stood solemnly with Eddie and the wolves.

"Is the President safe?" I asked on my headset.

"Her security are not answering. We're sending a rescue team now."

"Send me. My wolves can find them."

"Rodger that. But, my team will accompany you."

"I'm going, too," Eddie said.

I nodded to him and then gazed wearily at the City Hall.

"Come on Sasha and Adam. Come."

What Was Left in the Desert

Rebecca

I batted my eyes open, but the dust from the explosion had covered my face with a thin powder that had gotten into my eyelashes. I was buried underneath the desk and some of the wall that had fallen. I opened my mouth to spit out the blood that had pooled under my tongue from biting it.

"Are you alright?"

"I think so," I said in the dark.

I tried to open my eyes by first squeezing them shut and shaking my head and then peered into the darkness. A small fire was flickering in the distance. I managed to make out Mr. Codwell's shape in the light of the orange flames. He was sitting underneath a part of the desk, but the debris had blocked him in.

"Don't worry Mrs. President. Someone will help us."

"There's a piece of rubble across my chest, but it's balancing on the desk so I can breathe. I think I'm okay."

I couldn't see anyone else because of the dark. Someone's dead body was slumped over beside me. I couldn't make out the colors, but thought it might be Judge Malone because of the large form.

I closed my eyes and remembered listening to the steady pulse of a helicopter blade turning rhythmically in my ears. Remembered, trying to lick my cracked lips and then resting my face against the hot desert ground again, tasting red rocks. I was too weak to even attempt lifting my head up from the ground. I tried to open my eyes, but could only see light, so I closed them back up again and hoped for death to take me. My hunger was nauseating and swallowing just made me choke because my mouth was so dry my throat had started to stick closed.

I passed out and was suddenly jolted awake by the same sound. But this time it was louder and a male voice was calling out in the distance.

I felt someone standing close to me, yet I couldn't turn to look up at them.

"Check this one."

"They're dead."

There was a melancholy in their voices. In their voice was the sound of men who had walked across a desert filled with corpses. They were men who had witnessed an atrocity beyond any ever seen in history. Their tone conveyed the hopelessness of mankind. They had seen the fall of man.

"They're all gone."

I closed my eyes and gave my body permission to fade back into the desert clay. I felt like I was an apparition listening to them from the painful despair that had consumed me and become my living hell. But some greater being in this universe wouldn't take me. Not yet.

"Hey, she's breathing!"

I was flipped over. My half opened eyes glimpsed two men standing over me, now shading my face from the scorching desert sun. A man wet my lips with some water. The drops from his canister rolled passed my lips, moistening the bloody cracks and dripping over my dry tongue. It tasted sweet, sending a euphoric spike of adrenaline through my system that made me grab instinctively at the bottle and try to drink some more.

"Take it easy. Don't drink fast. Just a little now. There'll be more on the helicopter."

I was having trouble thinking. I couldn't remember all that had happened. They loaded me onto a stretcher. I searched my mind, knowing somehow I shouldn't leave.

"Wait," I said, weakly.

"I'm sorry," the man said. "Your family is gone."

They had already tied me to the stretcher. I looked frantically for them.

"Wait!" I shouted, lifting up my neck.

"Don't leave them! Leave me here! Leave me here!"

My salty tears washed some of the desert away from my eyes. The men carried me away. I could see Jacob's small body curled next to David's. I tried to break myself out from the stretcher, but I didn't have the strength. They lifted me up into the helicopter.

"No!" I sobbed. "Leave me here! I can't leave them! It's okay! Leave me here, please! Don't take me!"

Now I lay crushed by the large beam. God had spared me again. The miracle of my life was a painful curse. A burden branded on my chest, etched more deeply with each tantalizing breath God forced back into my lungs. Why did God keep me here? Why did God let me be survived by my own family in that desert? Was this justification God didn't exist? That we just live our lives with no significance or greater good? I used to believe I could make a difference. Then life stole away from me all who I had loved. Life carved a path for me I did not wish to step. And I became a rag doll lost on a barren road. Button eyes that don't see. Stitched ears that don't hear. My heart stuffed with the lost hopes of children crying from their graves, "Save me."

China

Stephanie

Adam and Sasha had helped us find twenty-one souls, but, Reggie and the President were still lost somewhere in the rubble.

"I think this is where the hall would've been," I said.

"Yeah, it looks like the door was here. This is the frame left over."

"Okay then, look over here."

"Adam, come."

Adam sniffed the fallen concrete slabs that lay crumbled at our feet. Then, he started wagging his tail again and let off a single bark.

"One here!" I hollered to the medic team.

"Is it Reggie yet?" asked Eddie.

A woman shifted her aching body under the debris.

"What's your name? Can you speak?" I asked.

"Amy," she said. "Thank you."

"You're going to be okay, Amy."

The medics rushed in and started freeing her from the rubble.

"Hello?" I hollered into the darkness.

"Stefanie!"

I recognized Reggie's voice calling out to me from the debris.

"Reggie!"

I made my way through the collapsed meeting hall. Adam and Sasha wagged their tails and started yelping short happy songs.

"We're going to get you out of here!" I said, excitedly.

"The President," Reggie said. "She's here. Get her first. I'm okay."

I looked over to where he had nodded into the darkness. A red flame was flickering, revealing an old familiar face.

"Mrs. President?"

The old woman smiled underneath the fallen beam.

"You're really lucky," I said, examining the beam which laid strewn across her. "This beam just missed your head."

The medics soon surrounded her and after much effort, her and Reggie were cut out of their concrete tombs. I scoured the rubble for many hours for other survivors and then went back outside to check on them. I found Reggie and the President sitting in an ambulance.

"Are you okay?"

The President was sipping some water as the paramedics looked her over.

"I'm fine. I'm pretty achy, but they say I'll be just fine."

"And what about you, Reggie?" I asked, giving him a big hug.

"Just fine," he smiled.

"How many survivors?"

"Forty-eight so far."

"We need to continue our work. I know exactly who did this and I've reported it. We need to take refuge at the White House. Tell every survivor who can walk to go there. We're going to finish our business."

"Mrs. President," said the paramedic. "You need to go to the hospital now."

"No, I'm going to the White House."

Old age had made President Kampf hardheaded. She put down her water and stood up.

"We don't have the security to get you safely to the White House right now, Mrs. President," the Lieutenant in charge added.

She still looked resolved to go.

"My people can take her," I offered as a solution. "It will be better anyway. No one will suspect her in our van and we'll have the wolves to help protect her."

The Lieutenant paused for a moment. He wasn't sure about it, but the circumstances were out of the ordinary. He knew they had been sabotaged from the inside. If the bombs came from Babble then most likely the CIA and FBI were compromised as well.

"Fine," he announced.

He handed her a brown blanket.

"Wrap yourself in this Mrs. President and go with them. But be careful."

Rebecca wrapped the large blanket over her head and let if fall around her body down to the ground. Her makeup had worn off in the explosion, so she looked like a regular senior citizen now. And with the bruises and cuts on her face, she may have looked even poor, that is, if you didn't look down at her leather shoes.

"I'm ready," she told me.

I led her to the van and we all piled in around her.

She was about the same age as Reggie, but she was far from being a frail old granny. She was thin and wrinkled, but had a strong youthful life force. I liked her immediately. There was something gentle and motherly in her face, yet she was confident, even in these dangerous times. She was charismatic and strong and looked like she was born to lead.

The van drove through the gates of the White House. She brought us through the kitchen and led us into the China Room, a large red room with a small circular shaped couch in the center whose walls were lined with wooden china cabinets. It was a good large place for the wolves to stay, but we found the decor to be somewhat outdated and cold, although it had obviously passed through many attempts at refurbishing it.

"Would you like something to eat?" President Kampf asked.

"Oh no, we'll be fine."

"I'm going to request something if you don't mind."

The President began to walk out, but we stopped her.

"Mrs. President," Reggie reminded. "We must stay with you at all times."

"I really can get a sandwich by myself," she said. "This is the White House after all."

The six of us were struck speechless. What could you say to her? She was old, which meant we should respect her, and she was also the President of the United States.

Rebecca marched passed us.

"Do you think we should follow her?" Alexis asked.

"I'll go with her," John said, getting up from the red couch.

He tried the door.

"Someone's locked the door."

The King

Rebecca

I searched the kitchen for Mr. Tiller, the head cook, and his employees with no luck. So, I popped into the refrigerator and pulled out a pre-made turkey sandwich myself and poured myself a tall glass of lemonade. It was when I made my way out to the dining room that I found Mr. Rodham standing near the dining room table, staring at me with his demented eyes. I feigned apathy and strolled leisurely towards him, placing my lunch casually on the dining table.

"Mr. Rodham, I didn't know you would be joining me for lunch. You must have been concerned for my safety, but I assure you there's no need to coddle me."

"Let's get to the point," he said, pulling out his gun. "'US President' has been nothing but a title for many years. I am the real king and the world is my kingdom. Understand?"

I shuttered at the sight of his black pistol and then gathered back my courage, steadying my old body with my hand on the chair.

"You have nothing, Mr. Rodham. While I do have my title. I am a symbol of leadership. I represent the strength of America."

"But look at you!" he yelled. "We all know how weak you are, taking depression medication, crying like a weakling. You are no leader of the free world. There's no use talking to you, old lady."

Mr. Rodham raised his gun to my face. It was a split second and it was an eternity. As the wolves stormed in and dragged him down to the ground, time froze for me. He made me realize I had been playing games with myself for all these years. I was no leader, although I acted the part, because I didn't believe it inside.

Stephanie grabbed me by the arm and made me run down the hallway while Reggie and his friends overtook Mr. Rodham. I heard some shots fired. I don't know what happened, nor did Stephanie, who only wished for my safety as she led me into the Queen's Sitting room and locked us inside. I think I was crying. She sat me on the couch and took me by the hand.

"It's okay Mrs. President. You're safe now."

"No, Stefanie."

A tear ran down my cheek. It was the first time I cried in front of someone in fifteen years.

"I'm the leader of the free world, but I am empty inside. Mr. Rodham is right. I shouldn't be President."

Stephanie's brown eyes searched my soul. She seemed to be looking passed all my wrinkles, through all the walls I had built up for decades. She seemed in that moment to be finding the deepest part of my being and speaking directly to it. My lips trembled.

"I see a leader," Stephanie said. "I see someone who understands the suffering of the people she leads. Someone who finds strength from her pain. Someone who can make something out of nothing. That is the person who should rebuild this world. That is the leader we need."

The Blank Screen

Stephanie

"This is the White House private bunker called the PEOC, President's Emergency Operations Center. It's the place I would be taken during a nuclear strike and it will serve us well today."

We entered a large room that had a long oak table with black leather chairs around it. The guards stayed outside in the hall to guard the entrance. The President turned to give one last order before they closed the door.

"Tell any survivors to come here."

"Yes, Mrs. President."

"Please, take a seat Mrs. President," Reggie said, holding out a chair for her.

"Wow, it's cold in here," she smiled, sitting down.

The room was quite plain. I looked around and saw the power switch for the computers, so I flipped it on, then sat next to the President while Adam and Sasha came to rest at our feet.

The circular table had built in computer screens with touch sensitive keyboards at each seat. I gazed down at the loading screen shining a green and beige light up at me.

"You know?" said the President, quietly to me.

I looked questioningly back at her.

"I always wondered why I was alive. My entire family died in the drought... Did you know the government had left us to die in the desert?"

We all stared at her as she spoke. Her eyes turned red as she remembered.

"They had blocked the roads off. That's why no one was getting through. They were afraid there would be too many people. We all would have starved anyway. There wasn't enough food. Remember that Mr. Codwell?"

"I was in Chicago at the time. I remember that. I thought they tried rescuing everyone out in the desert."

"No, they let us die," she said, calmly.

She was smiling.

"They sent a few choppers into the desert after they were sure everyone was dead. Just politics. Just to say they had tried. And I wasn't supposed to have survived. But, I was unbeatable. I was one of one hundred and fifty-nine survivors. One hundred and fifty-nine survivors out of four million."

"Mrs. President," I said, touching her hand. "You don't have to tell us."

She held my hand. Her wrinkled hands were warm.

"It's okay, dear," she smiled. "Let me tell you. There were food shortages everywhere. Refugees around the world desperately flooding into the very few habitable places left on earth. It seemed there wouldn't be any land left for life. So, the government started killing off people any way they could. Cancer was just a population control. It was an excuse. And when people tried to escape to safety, the government reported that it was the natural disaster that killed them every time. Because we knew. We knew there wasn't enough food or water for everybody. That total chaos would ensue unless we could somehow control the numbers."

The President looked straight at Reggie.

"I lost my entire family to global warming."

Reggie's eyes were wet. I knew he had lost many of his loved ones as well.

"I always wondered why out of all those people I had to survive. And time kept ticking for me. My body shriveled up, but I never died. I think now it's because of this. I have to write our new constitution. I have to lead us into the future."

She took her hand from mine and clicked open the word application. None of us said anything. The others sat down. We all stared at the blank document. Soon, a few surviving politicians entered. They took their seat quietly along side us. The room slowly filled and we all stared down at the blank document on the computers.

It seemed like hours had gone by although it could have merely been minutes. Lunch was brought in but no one ate. We all just stared at that screen, imagining the world we wanted. For a long while we sat like that. The room became musty with the smell of our bodies in the confined space as more and more people gathered around the table. It gave off that religious energy of a church. A contemplative quiet only interrupted by the occasional sound of achy limbs shifting uncomfortably as we thought solemnly about our country.

It was then I felt something in the air. A spirit of love came down upon the room, filling the air like a thick sweet perfume. We all seemed to smile at once, looking at one another's certain eyes.

"Let's begin," she said.

Endless Light

Stephanie

Adara appeared first through the trees. Her majestic grey form was followed by her pups, who had since grown lanky bodies in the months we had been away. They ran towards each other, first sniffing, before rolling excitedly on the ground. And I smiled happily at the sight of their reunited family.

The others went inside the compound, and I could hear Alice through the open hatch door greeting everyone. I could hear their laughter spilling out onto the forest. I could feel their love like I felt the sunlight on my shoulders. The world was a better place. Everyone was content. I sat crosslegged on the moist forest floor and gazed towards the wolf pack as the sun broke through the tall trees. Adam and Sasha came up to me and sniffed my face. Then, Adam licked my cheek and turned back towards his mate.

Adara stared coldly at me. She paced a few feet in both directions and then brought her sleek body to a stop about twenty feet in front of me. I looked into her yellow eyes. They were the eyes of a wild animal. It was then I knew she would never learn to trust me.

And I believe Adam knew as well. He lay his head in my lap. He licked my hands and I cried as he licked my cheeks. Then he joined his family, leaving Sasha and me staring at him disappearing into the thick maple forest. Sasha turned her head up towards the trees and howled. Her eyes were wet. I didn't know wolves could cry. I watched her, unsure if she would go with them. It was okay if she went. I would understand.

Sasha put her paws in my lap and wagged her tail. Then, she paced around me.

"I can't go," I said. "But, you can."

I pet her thick beautiful coat. I pressed my wet cheek against her and inhaled her freshly washed fur.

"I love you."

She opened her mouth and started panting. The black fur around her face was soft and full. For a second I thought she would stay, but then she turned her gaze towards the forest and ran off, and in a single moment she was gone. I touched my hands to the cool earth and imagined the wolves running through the hills together. I imagined their muscular bodies flexing and stretching as they traveled through miles of deep forest and mountainous terrain. I imagined their paws striking the same rich soil I was straining through my fingers as they ran towards their new home.

The old forest stood like a steady friend. The sun shined down through the trees like the constant love of God, illuminating deep reds and greens. I saw the continuation of life moving forward. It was beautiful and miraculous, with a delicate grace only matched by a relentless strength to survive. And we were not surviving for the sake of surviving. We were surviving for the sake of living.

Made in the USA
Columbia, SC
28 June 2023

19592517R00200